"Do you intend to ravish me?"

He reached over and drew her close to him was very strong and Meg was quite helpless in arms. His lips sought hers and he pressed close.

Startled though Meg was, she could not he admitting to herself that the sensation thus pro duced was pleasant—but the circumstances were decidedly unpleasant and she wanted none of it. She swung her hand up and slapped him smartly across his cheek.

"What the devil!" he cried.

"Why are you doing this? Do you intend to ravish me?"

"Good Lord! What do you take me for? I have no such intention. I have merely abducted you."

"Only villains abduct young females. Heroes elope with them! Are you, then, a villain, Mr. Roanceford? For you are certainly no hero!"

Meg Miller

Margaret SeBastian

A BERKLEY MEDALLION BOOK
published by
BERKLEY PUBLISHING CORPORATION

BERKLEY MEDALLION BOOKS are published by
Berkley Publishing Corporation
200 Madison Avenue
New York, N.Y. 10016

BERKLEY MEDALLION BOOK ® TM 757,375

Printed in the United States of America

Berkley Medallion Edition, AUGUST, 1976

Chapter One

"Mrs. Miller!" shouted Sir Samuel as he came storming into the sewing room, his normally ruddy complexion more inflamed than ever by anger. He planted himself on his stocky legs in front of his wife.

"Mrs. Miller, I demand that you speak to that scapegrace daughter o' yours! If she addresses one more word to me, but one more word, I tell you, I shan't be responsible! As old as she is, I'll— I'll—"

"Now, Samuel, please contain yourself," said Lady Miller calmly as she put down the embroidery she had been working at. She patted the cushion beside her. "Here, sit beside me, my dear, and tell me all about it. I am sure it is not as bad as you think."

Failing to elicit the faintest tremor of concern from his wife, a small brunette just past forty, Sir Samuel began to calm down remarkably quickly. He snorted a few times and made as though he would not do as she wished, but finally her small fine hand on his arm brought him to the seat as surely as though it had been a hand of iron.

"Honestly, Bess, Meg has gotten completely out o' hand and something must be done. She talks such complete nonsense that I'll be da—, er, blessed, if all the brass we laid out for governesses and that flash academy isn't like milk spilt upon the ground. What the girl needs—you know what that girl needs? A husband—that's what she needs! Aye, a husband with a good strong arm and the sense to use it on her where it'll do her the most good.

1

That's what she needs, I tell you!'' He peered and glared about the room, his jowls aquiver. He was a huge man, obviously of tremendous physical strength, for even as his anger shook him, so the couch he shared with Lady Miller trembled.

Elizabeth Miller had retrieved her hoops and was placidly resuming her stitching. She cocked an eye at her husband and with a slight smile asked, ''Have you finished, Sir Sammy?''

''No, by heaven, I have not! I—I— devil take it, Bess!'' He exclaimed as he turned to her with a grin. ''You don't play fair! Here I had me a right royal tantrum boiling up and you must go off with your 'Sir Sammy'!'' He chuckled as he disengaged her hand from her work and took it between his two great paws.

It was a big joke between them. Samuel Miller had received the accolade of knighthood at the hand of the Prince Regent in recognition of his highly effective application of Mr. Watt's hissing monsters to the milling trade. That Sir Samuel had become enormously wealthy as a result of his innovation had, no doubt, gone a great length with the government to convince them of his outstanding merit.

When, as quite a young man, Samuel Miller had inherited the huge family mill, with its great, groaning, creaking waterwheel, from his poppa, he had also become heir to all the secrets of the fine art of producing flour and meal from grain. For generations the Millers of Harlington, not three leagues west of London, had served the farmers of Middlesex and had established a reputation for honesty and quality of product. Young Sammy, with the build and stamina of a blacksmith, had not diminished that reputation in the least. By dint of hard work and good management beyond the capacity of his fellow millers in the neighbouring villages, he had amassed enough funds which, together with what he had received as his patrimony, enabled him in a matter of four or five years to

2

buy up any mills in the area which could not show a profit. Their failure, of course, was primarily due to his own inroads upon their custom. Before Sam had reached his thirtieth birthday, he was sufficiently affluent to look about him for a wife—and he would look higher than his own humble origin.

In the business of the heart, just as in his commercial enterprises, Sam's lucky star continued in the ascendant. For some years, at their annual meeting in December, the men who managed his mills were always surprised to learn that their employer had spent an inordinate amount of time visiting that mill which was located nearby the deFranche manor. That particular mill-operator had great cause for complaint and gave voice to his colleagues about his concern that he should be so closely monitored. He might well have rested easier had he known that it was not business which brought Sam to his bailiwick, but something quite precious belonging to the deFranches.

Lady Elizabeth deFranche, had she been wealthy, was pretty enough to have commanded the attention of many eligible noblemen; but the deFranche estate, which dated back to the Conquest, was impoverished. That circumstance was particularly fortunate for Sam. He had been aware of Lady Elizabeth; in fact, he had been quite smitten with her. He believed, nay, he dreamed, that she might someday be his, but beyond dreaming of that glorious prospect he did not hope. The difference in their social status could hardly have been greater, and he did not dare to try his luck even though year by year his wealth grew.

Sam, with his great breadth of frame and strong rugged features could never have gone unnoticed by the gentler sex no matter what his station in life was; and, as his circumstances improved, so did his appearance. In the well-tailored clothes from London's best clothiers, his appearance was not only commanding but attractive as well. Lady Elizabeth was given every opportunity to note this, and her interest appeared to have been captured—or

3

so Sam liked to assure himself. There were the glances, the turning away of eyes, the blushing—all those little signs that mean so much to lovers even though no word was spoken, no notes were exchanged.

Despite the obvious obstacles and the certain disfavor of society to such a union, when Sam was ready, he, though quite prepared for a rejection, sought out Lord deFranche. It was an unheard-of piece of behavior, but Sam knew that he must learn his fate anent the Lady Elizabeth or he could never rest easy again.

Lord deFranche could hardly look upon this suitor with any pleasure. Although he could not have wished for a more manly son-in-law—he was well aware of Sam Miller's developing affluence and his fine reputation—he could have wished him even wealthier and certainly of better blood and breeding. But his lordship was a realist and a true gentleman. It was just possible that the deFranche destiny hitched to the prospects of Samuel Miller might, at least, slow the rate at which the manorial assets were dwindling away. In any case, it was so unlikely that Lady Elizabeth would encourage the pretensions of so low-born a suitor, that deFranche, not knowing whether he could tolerate such a son-in-law or could be more easily resigned to the loss of such financial assistance as Sam might be able to afford him, threw the problem into the laps of the gods and gave his permission to Sam to speak with his daughter.

Two more bewildered men were not to be found in the kingdom when, after a fortnight of Sam's paying assiduous court to her, Lady Elizabeth accepted him—the one to discover his wildest dreams about to become a reality, the other to discover that he did not resent the unlooked-for outcome as much as he had thought he might.

Samuel Miller's fortunes continued to rise, but now the rate of increase to his wealth bordered on the fantastic— and it was because of his new lady. Lady Elizabeth Miller, née deFranche, after three months of wedded bliss, with

Meg already on her way, had the temerity to suggest to her lord and master that with all the great wonders the steam engine was performing, it certainly would be beyond strange if the invention, applied to the grain mills in lieu of waterwheel or wind fan, did not make the life of the miller infinitely easier.

Sam's first impulse was to gently assure his wife that there was no need for her to bother her pretty head about men's concerns; but, not being given over to hasty retorts, his second impulse quite caught up with his first and completely displaced it. The idea was remarkably to his liking and he showed his appreciation on the spot with such enthusiasm that it left the both of them breathless.

Sam was no great hand at inventiveness himself, but once put on the track of a promising idea, he became shrewd and clever beyond belief. It was not long before his mills begin to grind faster than anyone else's, and as his funds increased and he became fully acquainted with the advantages of steam-powered millstones, he began to build new mills and locate them where he thought best without having to be near swift watercourses. Now he could bring his milling operation closer to the farmer or to the marketplace—on the very outskirts of London, in fact, which was, obviously, his newest and largest market.

No small amount of his success was owing to the efforts of a young expert mechanic whom he garnered in later years. Colin MacTavish was a red-headed Scotsman who not only understood the devilish, steam-driven contrivance, but who also demonstrated an uncanny ability to handle men. All this, together with his native business acumen, soon brought him to a position of distinction in the affairs of Samuel Miller. By the time Meg, his firstborn, reached her twenties and still had not found one to capture her heart, Mr. Miller began to nurse hopes that Colin might well come to fill the shoes of a son; for Lady Miller had obliged him with three daughters but never a son to take over from him. His two younger girls had married well—their husbands were both prosperous merchants—and it disturbed him no end that Meg was still on the shelf as it were. If only she and Colin would make a match of it, he could ask for no more.

Alas, his accolade for revolutionizing the British milling industry had come, and the wonder of it no longer a matter for remark, and still Sir Samuel's eldest daughter was a worry on his mind. What was particularly troubling was that now the girl was pestering him with the most outrageous demands. No father would stand still for such nonsense and neither would he. That was why he came to his wife in such a fury for a solution to the problem.

"Whatever are we to do about Meg?" asked Sir Samuel of his wife.

"I do not see a crying need to do anything about Meg. She is quite old enough to know what she wants and I have little doubt that she will know how to go about getting it."

"Well, it will be over my dead body and longer still before she gets what she is asking for now!" exclaimed Sir Samuel wrathfully.

"Oh? And what has she asked for that has you so overset, my dear?" asked Lady Elizabeth. Now that her "Sammy" could append "Sir" to his name, she was very much at ease with the fact that she was now as much "Lady" by marriage as by birth. It had been a cause for great discomfort to her that she must bear a title while her husband had none and she had put up with it for the sake of his pride in it.

Sir Samuel sighed and shook his head slowly. "Not only is the idea complete nonsense, but she makes such a case of it, I can make no headway with her. If only she would apply herself as skillfully to getting a husband, we should all be happier"—he paused with a smile—"well, I would be happier but I doubt if her husband would, the poor soul."

6

Lady Elizabeth smiled at his little joke and resumed her embroidery.

"Meg would have it that as she is the eldest-born and knows so much about the milling trade, I should allow her to share it with me and—now, hark to this!—with a view to her succeeding me as proprietor. Did you ever in your life hear of such a thing? Please, Bess, have I not been a good father? Do I deserve to be served up such a mess of tomfoolery at this time of life? Why cannot she marry Colin? I know he would consider himself blessed to get her—the only fault I find in his otherwise superlative intellect—and I would take him in as partner on the instant."

"And let *him* fight this battle out with her, I do not doubt," interjected Lady Elizabeth with a twinkle in her eye.

"Aye!" agreed Sir Samuel. "And if he wins it, I will gladly admit he is a better man than I."

After a short pause, while he thought over the happy prospect with pleasure, the master miller continued. "Needless to say, I did not hesitate to point out the perfectly obvious fact that the trade was not for women and never had been. And my daughter, my own flesh and blood, had the temerity to demand what that had to say to anything; that she certainly had no objection to being the first." Sir Samuel threw up his hands in disgust. "I tell you, Bess, this girl has got to be married, so that she can devote herself to husband and family. Oh, why could she not have been a son to me?"

"There, there!" said Lady Elizabeth as she patted his hand soothingly. "There is no point in getting yourself so up in the trees about this. Meg is endowed with a deal of common sense. I am sure she was only teasing."

"Teasing! Teasing me, her father? What do you say, Bess? Am I some bull to be baited? I tell you, I shall not have it!"

7

"Oh dear, it is too much, I do admit; but the child is bored, Samuel. I have seen it coming on for some time. You forget how proud you were when you taught her how to keep the books and she learned so quickly—and, too, how you showed off her knowledge of the mills, and how they were run, before your colleagues and your customers. Well, Meg is an extremely bright little thing and she must put her mind to something. I daresay she *could* run the business almost as well as you, but, of course, that is not to be thought of."

"I should say not!" Sir Samuel exclaimed with indignation. "What say you to Colin MacTavish? He would make a fine son-in-law. He is industrious and smart. I should never fear for Meg's comfort, or for the business, with him as my successor."

"Yes, it would be ideal. But it will not do, my love. Meg has informed me that Colin is not the man to put 'stars in her eyes' as she put it."

"What flummery is that! 'Stars in her eyes,' indeed! How many times I warned you that allowing her to read those rubbishy novels would bring her to no good, I cannot count. But no! You would have it so—and, now what do we have? 'Stars in her eyes'? She is too old for such nonsense."

"Oh, do you think so! Ours was not so much of a courtship, yet I understand perfectly well what Meg meant. And if you will remember, my dear, a certain starry-eyed maiden, now married and grown old, you may yet discern stars in her eyes, I think," said Lady Elizabeth blushing prettily.

Sir Samuel looked long and hard at his still-pretty wife and a smile played about his lips. He chuckled. "Ah, well, I never was a match for you or Meg, and when you're both against me, I stand never a chance. But," he pleaded, "you will not encourage her in this lunacy of hers?"

"No, I shan't, but something must be done. We are too

8

isolated here. What Meg needs is a sojourn in town where she can meet people and give her thoughts a wider play. She has been to London on many occasions before and is quite young lady enough to behave fittingly. What say you to her visiting the Hobcourts? They will see to it that Meg does not lack for company nor for amusement.''

"Certainly, my dear. That would serve very well indeed, if only Meg will agree to it.''

In response to the summons from her mother, Meg came to the sewing room without delay. She entered with a warm smile of greeting on her small, dark-eyed countenance and walked over to her mother. She was of no great stature, yet there was an imposing air about her. She walked with grace, feminine but not coy. She did not glide across the room with the gait affected by so many ladies of all ages. It was as though her posture, her attitude, declared to the world that ''I am Meg Miller and will not be daunted.'' Such an imposing manner might have been more suited for a Junoesque matron, but on Meg it was as charming as it was unexpected. There was nothing bird-like about her; her manners showed not the slightest sign of the tiny twittering female.

"You wished to speak with me, Mamma?" she asked.

"Yes, my dearest. Please sit beside me so that we may have a comfortable chat.''

Meg did as she was bid.

"Darling, I have a bone or two to pick with you,'' began Lady Elizabeth. "I do not like to hear of you badgering your father. You know he is sincere in his desires for the best of everything for you, and it is not a nice thing in you to bedevil him so.''

"Oh, Mamma, he is a dear and you know I love him; but it is beyond me to refrain from picking at him when he is stuffy—and he can be so stuffy at times.''

"Yes, dear, I know. Still that is not excuse enough for such behaviour on your part.''

"Yes, Mamma. But it is not fair! Oh, I know that it is outrageous in me to wish to do something other than sit about reading all day or gossiping, but I get so horribly bored with it all. I am sure that I could be a great help to Pappa in the business. If I were a man, it would have been so. It is not fair!"

"It is not fair and I am quite in agreement with you, but it is fruitless to struggle against it. You are not a man, nor do I believe you are sincere in your wish to be one. I think perhaps that is a part of your trouble, Meg. You are too prone to say things you really do not mean."

Meg shrugged and grinned. "But it is so amusing to see the shock in people's faces."

"That is childish to an extreme. You are really quite clever and you should be wise enough to know that that is not how to get on."

Meg sighed. "I suppose I do. Very well, Mamma, I shall go to Pappa and apologise. I did not mean to upset him so."

"That will not be necessary. I have spoken to him and he is not so upset as you think. It was more frustration on his part. He would so like to see you settled in life, for he truly loves you and is concerned that you show not an inkling of a desire for marriage and children."

"Oh, Mamma, do not say that!" exclaimed Meg. There were tears in her eyes, but she did not weep. "I am your daughter and I want exactly what you have had—a husband I can love and respect. I envy you that! After so many years of married life, you two still bill and coo like any two turtle doves. I want my life to be that way—but it seems so difficult. I feel nothing for any of the gentlemen I have met."

"But what of Colin? I know we have spoken of him before. He quite adores you, you know. He is not of the gentility, but then neither was your father. Or is that so important to you?"

"Colin, always Colin!" exclaimed Meg with impatience. "Must we always come to Colin? I am sure he is a fine man—but for someone else! I like him well enough, but it is not in me to love him. In fact, were he the only man in the world, it could make no difference. I could not be happy with him and you do want me to be happy, don't you, Mamma?"

This time it was Lady Elizabeth's turn to sigh. "Oh, well, I did not think it would be otherwise; but you just cannot remain so shut away from all things. You are much too young for that and have need of society. Do you not think you might find more of interest away from Harlington? Your father and I think that you might wish to go to London, to the Hobcourts' for an extended visit. I should miss you so, but it is not fair to you to continue on in this way. Do you see, now, what fairness is? I do not think it fair that I needs must be deprived of my eldest daughter, yet I would not be unfair to you."

"Oh, Mamma," chortled Meg. "You always manage to make your point. I had almost forgot that I had ever mentioned fairness."

She paused and thought a moment, her deep-set eyes alive with speculation.

"Why, yes!" she declared. "I think it a perfectly splendid idea. London is exactly the place for me! You know, Mamma, I think I can do in London what is denied to me here in Harlington."

"Oh, dear, I have a premonition that I shall not at all like what you have in mind!"

"And just what do you think I have in mind that is so awful?" asked Meg, grinning.

"Dearest, it is so obvious. But what I cannot fathom is just where you think you can find what you seek."

"I am not too bad with my hands. I daresay I am at least a match for the milliners and the mantua-makers we patronize when we go to town."

"Oh, no!" exclaimed Lady Elizabeth with true shock in her face. "You cannot mean it! You, my daughter, to

11

stitch and sew. My dear, it is legend the pittance that seamstresses of that ilk earn—and I will not have you live-in under some shop. It is unthinkable!''

"Well, I hardly intend to! What I meant was that I am sure that I can foist off horrible creations on plump, innocent matrons with the best of them— 'My dear madam, it is just exactly what is needed!' '' Meg began acting the part of a dress-making shop's proprietor. '' 'Positively, I do assure you. Now allow me to just add this small bow. So! Now come to the mirror and see if it does not add just the right touch of color to the ensemble. Oh, madam, what a delight for your husband— Oops! Er—your gentleman friend' ''—and Meg started to giggle. "*Re*ally, how shocking!" she gurgled.

Lady Elizabeth could not repress a light burst of laughter. "Oh, dear, how naughty of you! I am sure you would sell *me* the shop! Do you intend then to ask your father to set you up? I warn you he will not hear of it. He would clap you in Bedlam, be sure.''

"No, Mamma, I would not dare to ask such a boon from him.''

"Do not tell me you intend to be a salesperson, a mere shopgirl. Do not, I insist, for I shall not hear of it.''

"No, not at all.''

"Then what, pray tell, *do* you intend?''

"Why, I thought that I might be a superior sort of salesperson. I am sure that I should have no trouble at all dealing with the nobility. One of the exclusive shops. Some proprietress must have need of assistance if she is successful and has more clients than she can give attention to. If she is occupied in showing styles to a duchess, she would hardly foist a common shopgirl off on a countess. She must employ someone with great presence—someone like me, I should think. I am sure I should make the countess every bit as pleased with me as the duchess may be with my employer.''

"Oh, yes! I agree with you there. For sheer presence,

no one can hold a candle to you. But, in all truth, I do not like it, and I know your father will never let you go to London if he had the slightest suspicion of your plans."

"Really, Mamma, he does not have to know. And you need not worry; I can take care of myself."

"I daresay. But think, child, if you do this thing, you can never expect to marry well. Once it comes out that you have been a modiste or some such thing, the only offers from the gentility you may expect to receive will be offers of carte blanche!"

"Oh, pooh! I will cross that bridge when I come to it. Mamma, please let me do this! I must do something! I cannot sit about all day in London, simpering at tea parties and gushing at entertainments while I die inside of sheer boredom. If it is my fate to marry, I will marry; but, in the meantime, until fate recollects that I am waiting, I would be busy at something."

"I suppose if I insisted, you would not do it," her mother mused. She sighed and said, "The thought of my daughter mingling with shopgirls—in fact, being one herself—is, at the least, extremely distasteful to me; but I cannot forbid it with a clear conscience. Harlington is no place for you; but, in London, I tremble at the thought of the scrapes you could get into out of sheer boredom. I am sure of it, for you are very like your grandmother, and until she settled down with Grandpoppa, as I have heard, a merry time was had of it. The next time you speak with my poppa, you may ask him about it. Do not fear that you will sadden him; there is nothing he likes better than to reminisce about his days with her."

"Then you will give me your blessing?"

"Yes, Meg dear, but reluctantly. And I will give you what is probably of more immediate use to you. I shall prepare a letter for Lady Hobcourt. Please try to get on with her. I know the two of you are constantly at daggers with each other; for what reason, I cannot fathom. She will assist you and, I hope it will not be needed, provide you with protection. If memory serves me right, I do believe that somewhere in that vast estate her husband left her is an interest in Madame Celestine's—you know the shop, dear; we have visited it often enough. It might be the very place for you. Between Amelia and Madame Celestine I am sure you will be well looked after." Suddenly she broke off. Then, "Really, Meg, everything would be so much simpler if you would only accept Mr. Mac-Tavish."

"Mamma, please!"

"Very well, dear." She sighed. "Be nice to Lady Amelia and, for both our sakes, not a word of this to your father."

"Oh, thank you, thank you, Mamma!" exclaimed Meg, throwing her arms about Lady Elizabeth's neck. "You are the best mamma I ever had!" she declared with a giggle.

"Yes, I daresay; and before this is over and done with you may well think me the worst you ever had!" she remarked drily as she kissed her pert daughter lovingly on the forehead.

Chapter Two

When Lady Amelia's message arrived, informing the Millers that her carriage would call for Miss Miller, Sir Samuel was somewhat incensed. He went about grumbling and grousing over their London friend's highhandedness. He kept on insisting that his carriage was every bit as fine as the Hobcourts', if not finer, and could have made the trip in just as grand a fashion. After all, it was *his* daughter and he was certainly wealthy enough to provide for his own flesh and blood. He needed no assistance from the Hobcourts.

Lady Elizabeth and Meg, hiding their smiles of amusement, immediately went to work, petting and cosseting the head of their household and soon brought him, if not to an appreciation of Lady Amelia's hospitable gesture, at least to a grumbling acceptance of it.

On the following day, as Meg was taking leave of her parents, her father slipped a packet of banknotes into her hand with these words: "There's three hundred m'dear, and don't spare the horses. You have a good time! If you see you need more, you tell me. Don't let me catch you without a feather to fly with. Now," he said, giving her a squeeze and a kiss, "there's my girl! You let us know how you get on."

Her leavetaking of her mother was somewhat more subdued. It was as though Lady Elizabeth seemed to know that her eldest-born and favourite was come to an important crossroads in her life, and that nothing would be the same for Meg, ever again. Mother and daughter both wept a little as they caressed each other.

Meg stepped into the Hobcourt carriage with mixed emotion. Relief at being able to get away from Harlington battled with the sadness of parting. London, only nine miles away, was not very far, but it was a different world and a different life. This time she was not going there as a country-cousin sort of visitor; this time she was going there, if not permanently, to at least become an active partaker of cosmopolitan life before she left it again.

The Hobcourt town house was indeed a mansion. It was large and there was enough of the baroque to its architecture as to give it some pretension to being a lesser palace. It certainly bespoke of wealth and its lavish expenditure, as well it might. Lady Hobcourt, as widow of one of the wealthier men of the kingdom, must have been quite the wealthiest woman. Sir Daniel Hobcourt had been a baron, whose original holdings had been quite modest; but, by a fortunate chance, he had, in the face of tradition, turned his hand to commerce, to all manner of ventures, and had prospered beyond all expectation. His son, George Amwell Hobcourt, had succeeded to his father's title but not to his wealth, all because of Sir Daniel's failing to give to his testamentary matters the same attention he gave to his business dealings.

It was quite plain to all that Sir Daniel's will, if challanged in Chancery, would have been set aside as being inequitable to his heir, George, but the latter was, at the age of twenty-three, quite satisfied with his lot and content to remain an heir of his formidable mother. Despite Lady Hobcourt's awe-inspiring manner to the world at large, she doted on this fair-haired young man with the laughing blue eyes; and it was quite understandable that Sir George, provided with all that money could buy and with all that charming and handsome demeanor could claim, could see no reason to seek a change in his circumstances. In fact, there was at least one very positive advantage in this status of favorite pensioner. One thing he was not prepared to undergo was the transition from untrammelled bachelorhood to the restraint of matrimony, and he found his lack of immediate legal access to the funds of his father's estate a great deterrent to all but the most persistent of the opposite sex. So he flitted from scrape to scrape, seemingly invulnerable to any snares laid for him in Hymen's cause and was well on his way to being a legend and a byword in the *ton*.

In early days, Lady Amelia had not paid much heed to the gossip concerning her offspring's activities, but as time passed and it seemed to her that there was no letup in Sir George's frenetic entertainments, she could not help becoming concerned. She had no great respect for men as a class, holding them all of little account; but she had expected more of her son. Let him pluck the wild flowers as he may, yet, at least, carry out his responsibilities as a Hobcourt. It was no great thing she hoped of him, merely to marry and beget an heir. Of course, marriage was not, in her opinion, to be a means of dissipating wealth, but rather a way to augment it. In short, she expected George, whatever his extrafamilial interests were, to marry an heiress and provide for the continuation of the Hobcourt line. She was less than satisfied that George was giving any thought to the matter and was in a mood to bring him to heel, if not to book, for his expenditures had become monstrous of late. It was only fit that he live apart from her, in bachelor quarters of his own, but she wished he would spend more time there and not, as she suspected, in the one or more gilded cages he was keeping for his ladybirds, heaven only knew how many. No, she was fast coming to the conclusion that George must change his ways.

Lady Hobcourt's appearance, as she received Meg in the grand parlour, was quite in accord with the appearance

17

of her edifice. She was dressed in magnificent taste, but not the best. Her silk morning dress, garishly striped, was not at all helped by the floral trimmings superimposed on the vandyked borders. It was certainly colorful; in fact, it was color run riot on this majestic, large-framed woman. Her very black hair, dyed, emphasizing the fine lines about her grey eyes, was caught up under a turban which very skillfully carried on the stripes of her dress. The ensemble must have cost a small fortune in precision tailoring; and, as though there could be any doubt of her ostentation, she wore a multistranded necklace of dark amber and her fingers glittered with the jeweled rings clustered on them. The effect was baroque in the extreme but on such a grand scale that it was quite an imposing spectacle, all told. Meg felt the strongest impulse to raise her hand as a shield to her eyes.

With an effort she restrained the impulse and greeted Lady Amelia, planting a cool kiss on the equally cool cheek presented to her. It was not her first encounter with Lady Amelia, for she had visited her in the past on many occasions in company with her mother. Even as she handed over her mother's letter, she felt, once again, a feeling of antagonism for this close friend of her mother's.

Lady Amelia accepted the letter and, without opening it, sent Meg off in company with a maid to see her room and get comfortable before coming down again.

Meg was anxious to see her hostess' reaction to the contents of the letter and therefore did not tarry. She was back in the grand parlour before an hour elapsed. Upon entering, she was surprised to see that Lady Amelia was busy at a writing table, examining what could only be a ledger, the so very important letter beside her still unopened.

Lady Amelia looked up and closed her ledger with a sigh. "I have been examining the books of account of a firm I have some interest in. They think because I am a woman they can cheat me at their pleasure. They will soon learn differently. It continues to amaze me the contempt in which all men hold us women when it comes to business. Hmph! Well, here is a group"—she slapped the ledger—"that I shall see in the Fleet Prison before they are very much older.

"Well, enough of that!" she exclaimed and, in a friendly tone she continued. "I hope you left your mamma and your pappa well."

"Yes, milady. Mamma's letter I am sure will say as much," responded Meg, hinting at the letter.

"Yes, I daresay. Well, Beth has a lovely hand. I shall save the letter for later when I can enjoy it."

"Oh, no!" exclaimed Meg with consternation. "Please read it now!"

"Why, whatever is the rush, child? A letter between friends can hardly be of such concern. No, I shall read it in my own time."

"I beg you, Lady Amelia, to read it now! Part of it concerns me and—er—I think it will be of interest to you."

"You always were Beth's favourite and, I daresay, she need not have worried that I shall not look after you. Beyond that what more could there be?"

Meg was quite exasperated. "If you open the letter and read it, I am sure you will find out." The acid note was unmistakable.

A little bit of stiffness appeared in Lady Amelia's posture.

"Miss Miller! I am not accustomed to anyone taking such a tone with me! Well, that is what comes of it! No breeding, no breeding at all! You should know your place, young lady, and respect your betters. I will not be browbeaten."

"Nor will I!" declared Meg. "I beg your pardon, Lady Hobcourt, for any breach of good manners which you believe to have suffered from me. Perhaps I have been impertinent, but nothing more, and for you to fly up in the

19

trees so! Well, I shall not trouble you further. I know you have always decried my mother's lack of taste for marrying my father. To even hint at it in my presence shows a far greater lack of breeding than anything I may have done. Farewell," she said, getting up.

It was quite obvious that Lady Amelia was completely unprepared for such an outburst. Miss Miller, a petite merry brunette, had always seemed to her a funloving girl, though somewhat lacking in spirit. She had marked that her son, widely renowned for his wit, had never seemed to get the better of her on the few occasions that they had been in each other's company, but the complete lack of interest on Meg's part in her son she had credited to a demure, feminine reticence with which she had no patience. It could never occur to her that George could be anything but irresistible to any and all members of her sex.

"Well, I never!" gasped Lady Amelia, making a tremendous effort to retain her composure. "Now, wait one minute, young lady! How dare you! Your mother shall hear of this! Such behaviour! Outrageous! Positively— positively—"

"Odious?" suggested Meg, not at all daunted by the explosion of exclamation points.

"Y-yes, odious," finished Lady Amelia weakly. She remained staring at her visitor, nonplussed.

"You see, your ladyship, it is as I feared," said Meg in a businesslike manner. "I did not think we would get on together for anytime at all. I did not object when Momma suggested I stay with you, because I thought her appeal for your assistance to me might have made things different between us, but—"

"Appeal? What appeal? I know nothing of— Are you in some sort of trouble, Meg? No, do not say that you—"

Meg burst into merry laughter, cutting her short. "Oh, dear no! Nothing of the sort!"

"Well, then, what is this all about?"

"If only you would read the letter! It is all in there, Lady

Amelia, and if you had done so from the beginning, it would have saved us these past twenty minutes of scratching at each other.''

By this time, Lady Amelia was fully aware that this was a different Meg Miller than what she had known; and she wondered at herself for never having taken the trouble to know the girl. But it was understandable. What was one to expect from such a common father, no matter how highly bred the mother might be?

Apparently, however, she should have expected more, for here standing before her was no sweet, shy miss. Indeed, she knew very well how thoroughly the sweet manner of Lady Elizabeth deFranche Miller—she never thought of her without including her family name— disguised a will of steel. It was that very facet of Beth's character that had first attracted Lady Amelia and finally acted as the cement to an enduring, and close, friendship. There were very few people, of either sex, who could withstand the impact of Lady Amelia's abrasive manner, but Elizabeth had surprised her. As sweet and demure as one could wish, yet once having made up her mind about something, no matter how scathingly, how rudely Lady Amelia pressed her, Lady Elizabeth, still all smiles, calmly maintained her stand, turning not a hair.

Now, here before her, was another cut from the same cloth. Meg had not turned a hair at Lady Amelia's menace; instead she gave as good as she had gotten— perhaps she had given more, because the petty altercation had left Lady Amelia shaken while Meg, ready to accommodate, but equally prepared to continue the contest, seemed to hold the field. No, there was nothing particularly sweet about Meg. At the moment no velvet covered her steel—an improvement, thought Lady Amelia, over her mother's soft demeanour—and she appeared to be waiting for Lady Amelia's next overture.

It came and it was one of peace—or accommodation, rather. Lady Amelia reached for the letter.

"As you say, my dear, I should have read the letter. Permit me to do so now." And she began its perusal forthwith, leaving Meg baffled at the sudden change in the climate.

There was silence in the room as Lady Amelia read on. Every now and then her head lifted from the paper in her hand and she gazed upon Meg, studying her. At last she finished, folded up the letter, and placed it on her desk.

"I am surprised at Beth! You know, do you not, that this idea of yours is complete nonsense and I shall have nothing to do with it? A shopgirl—that is all that it amounts to!" And she folded her hands in her lap as a signal the topic was closed; nevertheless her eyes were sharp and they watched the young lady's face intently. "Now, your mother has placed you in my charge and we shall seek to learn how we may entertain you. As for this"—pointing to the letter—"we shall speak of it no more."

"Indeed we shall, milady!" challenged Meg. "Mamma believed as you do, at the beginning, but you see I have come, and with her approval, reluctant though it may be. I cannot blame you for refusing me, but do not think that I am defeated. I am *not* in your charge, being long past the age when I must look to older hands to be responsible for me. I am of age and responsible for myself."

"And how old is that, may I inquire?" asked Lady Amelia.

"I am three and twenty!"

"Of course, you do not look to your father for your support, I daresay," she remarked caustically.

"That is uncalled for, Lady Hobcourt, and well you know it. *Sir* Samuel will always expect me to look to him—nay, he will insist on it—and surely, you must know, there is no denying him."

"Aye, I'll say that for him. But what says he to this silly project of yours?"

Pain appeared in Meg's eyes and she cast them down.

"We have not told him," she murmured.

"I thought not! Were he to know, your mad scheme to become a mantua-maker's shopgirl would be less than smoke, I'll be bound."

Meg said nothing.

"So I have you, there! Your plan has not been so well laid after all. If I were to inform Mil—er—Sir Samuel, it would be the end of it. You see, you were not at all prepared for that," triumphantly remarked Lady Amelia with all the air of an instructress who has found a lack in a prize pupil.

Meg lifted up her eyes and she could not hold back the tears of frustration that welled forth. "No, I am not prepared for that. I did not think that you would deny so close a friend to you as Lady Elizabeth is."

And Lady Amelia Hobcourt knew, without further qualification, she had quite met her match. No, the child was quite right. To Beth—and to this extraordinary child of Beth's—she knew she could deny nothing. So there it was—the cards had all been played and she, the much-vaunted Lady Hobcourt had been quite defeated at all points.

It was there that Lady Amelia began to concoct a scheme of her own. The beginnings of it began to flit through her mind, but she held it back so that she could give her full attention to Meg.

"I begin to see how it is; you will not be denied. Very well, after you have spent a week with me renewing old acquaintances and, perhaps, making new ones, I shall prepare a letter of introduction to Madame Celestine. I can assure you, you will have no trouble. What salary are you going to demand? I have little doubt it will be every bit as outrageous as this little chat we have just concluded."

"Oh, no! Please do not do that, I pray. It will spoil everything, Lady Amelia. It will be bad enough hiding from acquaintances as it is, without parading myself all over London." Meg's remarkably rapid transition from pathos to enthusiasm was not lost on Lady Amelia.

"And no letter! I must do it without your help. It will be enough to know that you do not disapprove. I wish to make my own way. If I cannot convince Madame Celestine to take me on, how may I expect to convince ladies to buy the dresses in her shop?

"And speaking of dresses, milady, I am sure that I can put you into something ever so much more chic than that—that—"

"Monstrosity? Say it, child; I understand," Lady Amelia said with a smile. "You see, dear, this is my war dress. I understand that the red savages in our late lamented colonies do paint themselves up and don all manner of ornaments just before battle to put fear into the hearts of their opponents. Well, that is what this horrible creation of mine is all about—to instill awe into the hearts of the men of business I have to deal with this afternoon. Awe-inspiring, is it not?" And Lady Amelia hoisted her huge frame up out of her seat and did a graceful pirouette, sending the riot of colors she was wearing into a positive frenzy. "They do not know what to make of me."

"Oh, oh, indeed!" cried Meg laughing merrily. "But I do not think it goes to work the same way with females."

"I think not. I could see that it put your back up immediately you cast your eyes upon it. Well, to get back to your venture, if that's the way you want to go about it, I suppose I may not gainsay you. But I am sure there is plenty of time before you begin. I may not tarry longer—those filching associates of mine, you know. Please make yourself comfortable and I will see you at dinner. I think we have much to talk about and I am sure that I must get to know you better."

Chapter Three

Lady Amelia Hobcourt did make an effort to become better acquainted with her young guest, and to the extent of her own interest, she was quite satisfied with the results. The faint idea that had flitted through her mind during their first conversation had become appreciably stronger. She had never doubted its feasibility; but to discover that Meg was so much more than she could have hoped for in a daughter-in-law filled her to overbrimming with smug satisfaction.

Here was a young lady—the more she came to know her, the less she could see in Meg any sign of Miller blood. As surely as friend Elizabeth was a deFranche, so too must this sprightly creature be one. No, there was nothing plebeian or gauche about Meg deFranche-Miller in Lady Amelia's eyes. Meg was certainly not of the first stare for beauty; yet, withal, she was charming to a degree. She carried herself as a tiny duchess might. Her bearing was erect and her manner direct. Without coyness, without simpering, Meg's wit sparkled throughout their conversations. Lady Amelia found herself enjoying their daily walks and the times they spent just sitting and chatting. She went to some pains to use these occasions to learn more about this girl, her outlooks and opinions, and, of course, her prospects. About this last she did not find the going easy, not wishing to reveal how deep was her interest. She was well aware, now, that behind those bright dark eyes dwelt a mind at least as acute as her own.

To avoid any risk of offence she contented herself with gleaning those bits and pieces that occasionally surfaced in the course of their conversations. These, together with her own knowledge of the Miller fortune, were more than enough to confirm her in her own opinion, and to bring her scheme of seeing George and Meg united in marriage to full bloom.

By the end of Meg's first week with her, Lady Amelia was fretting over her inability to win Meg away from her foolish desire to sample the life of a London shopgirl. It aggravated her frustration to have so charming a guest and not be able to show her off to the *ton*. Second thoughts came to her relief with the assurance that it was just as well, if not exceptionally fortunate, that Meg resisted all her importunities to meet her friends and acquaintances. It would be utter nonsense to suppose that only she, Lady Amelia, was privy to the information that Meg Miller was bound to receive a major portion of the Miller fortune by bequest and that her marriage portion could be nothing less than exceptionally respectable. That had all been thoroughly bruited about at the time Sir Samuel Miller had received his knighthood.

Yes, it was far better that Meg remain ensconced within Hobcourt House unbeknownst to all. Then, George must come to call—and that very soon, she thought, making a mental note—and with all his personal beauty and address on display, he must soon win Meg's hand—and a goodly portion of the milling trade along with it!

When Sir George received the summons from his mother to call upon her, Tuesday next, to renew his acquaintance with an attractive young lady-visitor of excellent prospects, he frowned. It was not his idea of pleasure to have to partake in a gab-fest with some blushing miss, and he would have ignored the note had he not known that a number of his accounts were coming due and would be presented for payment shortly. It was not an auspicious moment to gain her displeasure; therefore he resigned himself to the sacrifice of an hour of his time. He sent an answer that it would be his pleasure to call and signed it, "Your obedient son."

"I am sure Sir George will be along at any moment," declared Lady Amelia uncertainly. "Yes, he must have been detained by some business at the last minute."

Meg shrugged. "It is of no moment, milady. I am sure we are perfectly content to sit here awhile before tea. A day sooner or later for his calling upon you can be of no great importance."

"Er—yes," said Lady Amelia. "Well, but I am sure he will come. While we wait—you do not mind, I am sure, for you have not seen him in some time, I believe?"

"I think it was two years ago. Mamma and I came into the City to shop and we stayed here with you."

"Yes, yes, I remember. It seems to me that you and George did have your heads together a time or two. I am sure I heard the sound of merriment, also."

"Oh, dear!" exclaimed Meg with a little chuckle. "What sharp ears you must have, milady! I had hoped to disguise it, but I see I have failed. I do hope that George was not aware of my lack of manners."

"Your lack of manners? I do not understand you, Meg. A little laughter between two young people is a thing to be expected, I should think," remarked Lady Amelia, masking with an effort her avidity to learn more. It was in her mind that perhaps fate had already taken a hand and the business was well started.

"Oh, really; it was too bad of me—but George was quite out of his wits at the time; and you must admit it was laughable to an extreme."

"If you will but tell me of it, I should be able to judge it better, my dear." Lady Amelia's smile was quite forced.

"Well, milady, it would appear that your son had fallen afoul of two 'angelic blond angels'—his very words, I assure you—and could not decide which of them to pursue. He—he," Meg continued, unable to repress an occasional giggle, "he presented me with his quandary and after reading off an impressive listing of the charms of these two birds o' paradise, he, in all seriousness, asked me what *I* should do were I *he*!" Meg was giggling irrepressibly now.

Lady Amelia's eyes shot sparks as, through clenched teeth, she grimly asked. "Yes, dear? And you said . . . ?"

"I said I should pursue both. In the event that I failed with one I might not be so unfortunate a second time. He—he nodded in agreement and—and *thanked* me!" Meg laughed outright.

Lady Amelia smiled coldly, but her heart was lead within her breast. Her son, George, to bring such matters before a young maiden fresh from the country was outside of enough, but he must use feathers for brains to bring them to her for *judgement*. Oh, George, how could you be so imbecilic! It was too much for Lady Amelia.

"That my son should be such a sapskull!" she exclaimed aloud.

Just at that moment there was a rap on the door and the "sapskull" entered.

"Ah! Good day to you, mother o' mine!" sang out George cheerfully as he advanced toward Lady Amelia. "How beauti— Eh! What's this?" he exclaimed, reaching for the ornate quizzing glass pendant on his chest. It was a remarkable chest, bowing out in the manner of a pouter pigeon, obviously padded, and the overall effect augmented by the corset he was wearing to achieve the nipped-in waist. One would not have been surprised to hear the creaking of stays, and Meg was quite startled that one so young as George should see any need of them. Nor could she see anything to admire in the tilt-back, chin-up way in which he held his head. The strained attitude was insured by a very stiffly starched neckcloth fixed in the Oriental style, and it gave him all the appearance of a small boy trying to peer over a high white wall. She wondered that Lady Amelia should be so blind to the freakishness of her son's taste.

George Hobcourt, at the risk of crushing his neckcloth to utter ruination, stared down at Meg.

"Oh, it's you!" he said with unmistakeable contempt. "How do you go on, Miss?"

"Quite well, George," responded Meg, making no attempt to hide the amusement in her eyes as she stared back up at him, her dark eyes opened wide.

With repressed fury Lady Amelia intervened. "I am sure you remember Meg deFranche-Miller, my son!"

"Meg?" said George, making a face. "Of course, Meg! How do, Meg?" His tone of voice was flat and his manner truly insufferable.

"Meg do well an' all, yer lardship," mocked Meg. "Lor'! Them fancy duds o' yer 'Onner fair put her in stitches!"

An angry red flooded George's countenance. This contrary wench, only knee-high a cockchafer and already overlong on the shelf—what had she to say to anything? May she rot on the shelf, he thought, with that viper's tongue of hers! Why must his mother entertain this miller's brat, in any case? And how was he to explain such a departure from grace to his fellows at the club?

Lady Amelia, very dissatisfied with her son's behaviour, decided to call a halt to the hostilities and suggested that Meg might wish to retire to her room to rest and refresh herself for tea. Meg was only too happy to leave the field to mother and son, and gracefully withdrew.

The door closed behind Meg, leaving silence in the room. Lady Amelia gazed at her son, and there was an expression of disenchantment on her face. Sir George looked at his mother, one eye-brow raised in inquiry which did nothing to lessen the supercilious appearance of his expression.

Slowly, very slowly, Lady Amelia began to shake her head. Sir George, for perhaps the first time in his life, began to feel strangely uncomfortable in the presence of his parent. With some uncertainty, he attempted to smile.

"Are you feeling out of spirit, milady?" he asked.

"Most certainly I am," replied his mother, "and I am regarding the cause of my indisposition at this very moment!"

"Surely not me!" exclaimed Sir George in unfeigned surprise. "I cannot have displeased you!"

"You most certainly have!"

"Because of that chit of a girl?" he asked.

"George, I have never in my life seen you so ungracious—and that it should have been in the presence of the daughter of my dear friend, Lady deFranche-Miller—I—I have no words to express my displeasure and my disappointment."

"Oh, come off it, Mamma! This Meg Miller"—he grimaced—"truly a name fit for a bawd! Meg, indeed! What can she expect with such an ungenteel name? Well, it is no better than she!"

"It is to be deplored, my son," retorted Lady Amelia, her tones growing grim, "that Miss Miller is not of the best blood as one might wish, but she is of gentle birth for all that—and what is more to the point, she is my guest! As such you will treat her with the greatest respect and decorum.

"Now understand me, George!" Her voice grew menacing, "If you ever dare to address her again in less than your most gracious manner, we shall have, you and I, a discussion at length you will long remember, I assure you!"

Sir George frowned. This was certainly an unlooked for reprimand and it cut him to the quick. He was his own man and did not relish being brought to book by anyone. Of course, one *must* make allowances for one's mother. Repressing a heated rejoinder on the tip of his tongue, he attempted to humour his mother, grown suddenly so formidable. He was at some pains to do so, for her eyes were glittering angrily.

"Oh, very well, madam, but really—a miller's brat! You ask a great deal of me! Nevertheless, I shall respect your wishes—only do not put me to the task more than can be helped, I pray. Now, if you will excuse me, I have some friends waiting and I must be off." He began to stride towards the door.

"You are *not* excused! Come back here at once! I have not finished with you!"

Sir George, with his hand on the doorknob, turned, and with indignation, exclaimed, "What the devil is it now? I am sure it can be of no great importance, and I must not keep Rounceford cooling his heels; he is not one to brook such an assault upon his patience."

"Adrian Rounceford, indeed! He may await you or not, for all I care; you will remain with me until I have finished what I have to say to you. Now then, take your seat. Do not tarry at the door; you waste your own time!"

Sir George came back into the room and took a chair with ill grace. Once seated, he tugged on his gold watch-chain with its many tinkling seals, made a great business of consulting the ornate timepiece which emerged, gave a huge sigh, and finally settled down, favouring his mother with a look of exaggerated expectation.

Lady Amelia, ignoring his insolence, fired off a broadside that well nigh foundered him with dismay.

"It is time for you to marry," she proclaimed.

"What!" he exploded.

"I am quite sure that you heard me. It is high time that you gave consideration to the task of finding yourself a suitable wife. Lord knows but you have had ample time to sow your wild oats. Now you must give over this school-

31

boy style of living, settle down, and take your place in respectable society.''

''B-but this is nonsense! Sheer and utter nonsense! I am only three and twenty. There is plenty of time yet before I need do anything so drastic! Wh-why Adrian is almost nine and twenty and still a bachelor!''

''And just what has Adrian Rounceford to say to perpetuating the Hobcourt name, may I ask? Frankly, I do not care for Rounceford a ha'penny's worth. Oh, yes, I know well enough that he is considered a nonpareil at gaming and all sorts of crackbrained frivolities; but as to his character and general behaviour, he is indeed something a great deal less than that! Rounceford marry? Hmph! I should say not! Have I not heard that, at this very moment, his engagement to that daughter of Lord What's-His-Name—Daphne, is it not?—is broken off? It comes as no surprise to me. I should like to see the gentlewoman who'd have 'im.''

''Just because I have in some way—I don't know how —put you up in the boughs over something—I do not know what—is no reason for you to disparage one of my closest friends.''

''Oh, enough of your friends! It is you we are discussing, and I will thank you to remember that. Now, about your marrying—''

''To blazes with my marrying! I have no intention of marrying—yet!''

''I think that I shall have a deal to say to *that*! And I shall say it right now. You, my lad, have become excessively expensive of late. Now, I have never begrudged you anything these many years, for I believe a young gentleman should have every opportunity to enjoy whatever it is that young gentlemen enjoy before they needs must give their attention to more serious matters. Well, you have had as much time for your escapades and your flirts as should satisfy any normal man. Now it is time for you to realize that you are fully grown. You are,

32

after all, the head of the house; act like it!''

"But, Mamma, I have hardly done anything at all. Why—why, I am just starting to enjoy things!''

"Just starting! I should say not! I do not know how many mistresses you have supported, but if you have not given carte blanche to at least a dozen, may I never say another word! And to carry on with more than one light-skirt at a time is more than enough!''

"Who is carrying tales to you?'' demanded Sir George.

"I need no tale-bearers where you are concerned! Your peccadilloes are so well known that I must be deaf and witless not to be aware of them. Besides, am I some schoolroom miss not to be able to understand the bills that I pay? Must I seek chapter and verse from you when I see bills for women's clothing and women's jewelry? What do you take me for? Just beginning? Indeed! Do you think we are made of money? I have said nothing of this before, but I have often wondered, on seeing some bit of fluff, whether or no the clothes on her back were paid for out of Hobcourt funds. Well, I say no! No more!''

"And I say it is none of your business!'' stormed Sir George.

"None of my business!'' cried Lady Amelia. "This is your mother? How dare you!''

"All right! All right!'' exclaimed George, breaking out into a cold sweat. He had never seen his mother so angry before, at least not with him. "Let us leave this. Anything for peace! I promise I shall give some thought to marriage. There, does that satisfy you?''

"It is a beginning,'' said Lady Amelia, smoothing her ruffled feathers. "Now, I have just the girl for you and, if you know what is good for you, you will seek her out without delay.''

George frowned. "You go too fast! I merely said I would think about it.''

"Well, you go too *slow*, I think!'' retorted his mother. "She is quite a prize and I will not have her snapped up by

33

a stranger whilst you are *thinking* about it.''

"And just who is this prize you have in mind for me?''

"Meg Miller.''

"Meg Miller!''

"Will you cease your shouting! Must you proclaim your intentions to the world?''

In a voice only slightly subdued in force, Sir George protested, "My intentions, indeed! I have no such intentions and well you know it. Meg Miller? Pah! It is enough you insist upon having her here as a guest. I can assure you *I* will make no boast of the fact. You cannot be serious! Why, her face is almost common, and for all she is shapely, she is a midget! And how the Creator managed to gather so much acid into so small a goblet—well, He is noted for His miracles and Meg Miller must be one of His most wondrous!''

"Do not blaspheme! And surely there must be some wits in you; after all, you are my son. Do you never look beyond face and figure? Is every woman to count with you only as a paphian?''

"Oh, do not make me out such a rakehell! But do give me credit for taste—and the Miller girl does not tempt me in any way.''

"Oh, you fool! Do you not know that Miller, her father, is worth some two hundred thousand pounds for all their modest style of living? And do you not know that Meg is their firstborn and best-beloved? How well-favoured must the husband of Meg Miller be when the Miller fortune continues to grow by leaps and bounds? Must I lay it out for you upon a slate? There are only three daughters, and Meg is bound to inherit the greatest share. I am not Lady Elizabeth's friend for nothing, you know.''

"Well, all I have to say is that that female viper will need every penny and more if she is to find a husband. Of one thing be sure—that poor dupe will not be me.''

"If that is your last word, then hear mine,'' retorted Lady Amelia, drawing herself up. "You will pay court to

Miss Miller with a view to making an offer or''—she reached into a drawer and withdrew a thick packet of papers—''you can pay your own bills, starting with these!''

Consternation appeared in Sir George's face. ''What!'' he cried out indignantly. ''How in Hades do you expect me to do that? You have got all my money!''

''Yes, and it is a good thing! I begin to doubt that your father intended it in any other way. In truth it is your money by rights, but *I* have it. The day that Meg Miller agrees to become your bride, I will prepare for you to take over the Hobcourt holdings. It will be my wedding gift to you.''

''Never! Keep it and do what you will. Why, if I were to find myself in a sponging house tomorrow, I should not acquiesce in this scheme of yours!''

''Even in a sponging house money is required to dwell there. No, I daresay you will not be in one for very long. It will be the Marshalsea for you! Do not come to me if you find the society of penniless debtors somewhat less select than that you now enjoy.''

Sir George forced a laugh. ''Now, Mamma, you do it too strong. What would be said? The scion of Hobcourt in gaol for debt! Why, we should be the talk of the *ton*, and you would not care for that!''

''Never you mind what I care or what I do not! I have told you how it will be. Think on it. I say no more.''

''You are really serious? But why? This Miller female cannot be so important to us. We are not poor—or are we?''

''No, we are not poor, but add any large portion of the Miller fortune to the Hobcourt estate and you, my son, may well become the wealthiest man in the kingdom. I should think marriage to Meg a small price to pay for so great a distinction.''

Since Sir George had never in his life turned his hand to anything productive and had always been given whatever he desired, or the wherewithal to obtain it, he was perfectly satisfied to continue in this way of life. He could see no reason to pay any price at all for the gain of added wealth, certainly not the price of his freedom. Yes, marriage to Meg Miller was more, much more, than he was prepared to pay for anything. But his mother, as she sat there regarding him with eyes grown strangely cold, was suddenly not at all familiar. That she could bring herself to threaten him with debtor's prison—well, he did not believe her to be serious for a moment; but, nevertheless, he thought it the best part of discretion to appease her.

With a sigh of resignation he said, "Very well, milady, I am as ever your obedient son. I will do as you wish." He bowed.

"Believe me, my son, you shall not regret it."

I assuredly shall not, you may be certain, said George to himself, but the Miller chit may well do so before she is much older.

Strange as it may seem, she was truly christened Meg. As it happened Samuel Miller chose it. He had thought Meg Miller was a most appropriate name for the little black-haired mite. She was born the daughter of a miller, and what could be more fitting? By the time Meg made her appearance, Lady Elizabeth was "Bess, m' love," and neither she nor her husband ever thought he should prosper so well or rise so high. When it became obvious that the name of Meg was less than appropriate for a young lady of wealth and station, Meg had lived with her name some seventeen years or more, and was so thoroughly Meg Miller that no one gave any thought at all to its being changed, least of all the party most affected.

But now her name was indeed a problem on a different score. Meg, in company with her momma, had patronized Madame Celestine's a number of times, and couturières were noted for their memories where affluent clients' names were involved. There could be no question but that

Meg could not apply for a position at the Madame's establishment as Meg Miller. Certainly her name had to be changed. She did not think her appearance so striking that Madame Celestine would recall her on sight, and she was hopeful that if she selected her costume with an eye to appearing inconspicuous, yet in reasonably good taste, her connections might remain unknown. It was of the first importance to her that this be so, since all of the fun, all of the achievement promised by this adventure would be dissipated if she failed to carry it off on her own merit.

And she had another reason. She could not trust Lady Amelia not to tip the wink to Madame Celestine. She did not see how she could keep her identity a secret at the shop for very long, but at least she hoped to keep it concealed long enough to learn whether or not she could secure the position she sought without assistance. She needed a new name and she had to move quickly.

"Peg" was a natural and comfortable substitute for "Meg," and she decided that the family name of Mannering, which she borrowed from the works of the recently created baronet, Sir Walter Scott, would confer just the right air of upper-middle class to her new identity. On the very next day, with every intention of foiling Lady Amelia's interference, garbed with taste but not expensively, she slipped out of Hobcourt House and set out for the Burlington Arcade.

The shop of Madame Celestine would, after more than a score of profitable years, have still been entirely in the hands of its founder and proprietress, Madame Celestine D' Erblay, an émigrée, but for an error of judgement. When Napoleon began to overrun the Continent, making his name synonymous with opprobrium in the hearts of *les anglais*, Madame Celestine had panicked; and, believing that anything French would rot upon her shelves, had bethought herself to fill her racks with only the materials and styles of Britain. Being short of the necessary funds

37

for these emergency purchases, she had appealed to Sir Daniel Hobcourt, the well-known financier, for financial assistance. Her emissary, of course, was no less than Lady Amelia, her very good customer and friend. She could not have chosen better. Although as a result the money was provided, the loan was too generous, and only by granting a silent partnership to Hobcourt was Madame able to meet her indebtedness. In the end the arrangement turned out to be quite satisfactory to all parties. With the passing of Sir Daniel, Lady Amelia succeeded as partner and turned out to be an alter ego to Madame, seeing eye to eye with her on most matters of business. As they were of an age, they got along famously and the shop continued to prosper.

It did so well through the years that when Lord George Cavendish came to build his Burlington Arcade—"to give employment to industrious females"—Madame had no great difficulty in being amongst the first of the original forty-seven leaseholders.

The Arcade was new to Meg, it having not been in existence when she had last visited London. In fact, it had not been opened more than four months previous, and the signs of its recent construction were still prevalent. The smell of new plaster and the tang of freshly laid-on paint became evident as she began to walk along the covered way.

Being so tiny, she had some difficulty threading her way through the crowd of shoppers, but she could easily make out the shop signs displayed on high. It was not long before she espied her goal. She was within steps of the shop's entrance when a sudden, sharp blow on her shoulder sent her reeling. She would have fallen had not a strong arm caught her up and pressed her close.

Dazed more by the unexpectedness of it all rather than by the shock of the blow itself, she remained motionless for a moment, her face close against a white, lavender-scented shirt front. It was a surprisingly pleasant position to occupy—but what must he think of her! She pushed

38

herself out of his arms and looked up to thank her saviour. But she quickly changed her mind.

It was an impudent face that was looking down into hers. It was not a handsome face, but one that might, for its ruggedly strong features, have been a most interesting face were it not looking so smug. The easy grin with its display of white teeth seemed to dare anyone to wipe it away.

His brown hair, as the fashion of the day dictated, was parted in the middle and flowed in soft waves onto his forehead. His tall, broad-shouldered figure was neat and trim. Meg, despite her annoyance, was not immune to his attractiveness.

He bowed slightly. "My dear young lady, I am honoured to be your partner in this waltz, but methinks you were less than maidenly modest in the manner in which you have conferred the honour upon me."

Meg lifted an eyebrow in a perfect match to his supercilious air and, as she rubbed her aching shoulder, said, "And may I say that your overly enthusiastic reception of that honour smacks more of the bumpkin than the gentleman!"

"Would you rather I had let you take the fall?" he asked, somewhat nettled.

"I would rather you had looked where you were going! It would have served me better—or is this your way of bringing yourself to the notice of young ladies?"

Stung, he drew himself up and said stiffly, "Adrian Rounceford has no need for such exceptional conduct. I beg your pardon!"

Meg felt that she had gone far enough and nodded acceptance of his abrupt apology.

She turned away from him, but he stepped in front of her, blocking her path.

"Allow me to escort you, Miss—er . . ."

"I am Peg Mannering and there is no need—"

"Oh, but there is! You never can tell when some lout

39

with his eyes in the back of his head may knock you down again,'' he said, grinning.

If his grin had been less of a leer, Meg would have told him that she had already arrived at her destination but his look made her blood boil.

"Very well, Mr. Rounceford, please do.''

They proceeded for a dozen paces, side by side, when upon reaching Madame Celestine's shop, Meg turned to him.

"Thank you very much, Mr. Rounceford, for your protection.'' And with a grin she walked briskly into the shop.

Mr. Adrian Rounceford, for once in his life, was left standing; put all to sea by a female—and by one who stood barely as high as his chest. He remained where he was, his mouth open in astonishment, his left hand on his hip, his right held up to his chin.

"Well, by damn!'' he muttered under his breath.

As Meg stepped into the shop she was pleasantly surprised; the interior was almost as bright as day. Despite the fact that the shop windows opened onto the covered promenade of the Arcade, a profusion of gaslights spread a pleasing brilliance throughout, picking out the colorful displays of materials and dresses. The shop walls and panelling were wrought in the Classical style, and their ivory-whiteness appeared to soften the shadows, giving an airy look to the place and moderating the effect of the imposing lintels and mantels with which the walls abounded.

A young woman, not much older than Meg, came up to her.

" 'Ow can I sarve 'ee, momzelle?'' she inquired, attempting a French manner and accent completely at variance with her Cockney pronunciation.

"I wish to speak with Madame Celestine,'' said Meg pleasantly.

40

"The Madame is very busy," responded the girl, taking in Meg's costume and making a business of looking behind her to identify Meg's nonexistent abigail. Not finding one, her expression immediately stiffened into one of hauteur, showing quite plainly that she did not believe this newcomer to be worthy of Madame's attention, which was reserved, exclusively, for the wealthiest and loftiest clientele.

"I am sure she must be. That is why I have come. Please inform Madame Celestine that Peg Mannering has come to assist her, and that if she can spare a few minutes to me before I enter on my duties, I should be grateful."

The girl frowned in puzzlement. " 'Ere now, I never 'eard o' that! Er you bammin' me?"

"My dear young lady, time is precious. Madame will not thank you for keeping me waiting."

The girl sniffed, fluffed about, and departed.

The shop was busy. Without exception the customers were quite wealthy or at least accustomed to the trappings of wealth. The richness of their costumes and the manners they affected indicated no less. It amused Meg to observe the languor and the excessive condescension which the ladies affected in their conversations with their attendants, the shop people, and even with their friends. In attempting to appear worldly, Meg felt they overdid it and only managed to appear dull.

Here and there she noted a few male members of the gentility. They gave her pause, for she could not understand their presence in a shop for ladies' wear. Her observant eyes soon gave her the answer. Identifying the females they were attending, it took little thought to understand. Invariably the women were quite young, quite pretty, and excessively loud. Their titterings, as well as their commands to one and all about them, rang throughout the shop. Meg smiled to herself as she thought of Sir George as a possible patron of Madame Celestine's.

Her attention was diverted by the approach of a woman

41

whom she recognized immediately as Madame Celestine herself. Inwardly she hoped that the proprietress' recollection would not be as acute as her own.

"Ah, *mon enfant*, what is this I hear?" Madame gushed. "You are my new assistant? I have no knowledge of this!"

Even as she spoke, Madame Celestine was examining Meg very carefully.

"You look ver' familiar. We have met? Perhaps you have been to my shop before? No!" She shook her head in answer to her own question, and gestured at Meg's apparel. "That is not from my collection. It is not bad, but it is not good. The ribbons, the leetle flowers, they are *de trop*, you understand?"

"Indeed I do, madame, but it would not serve for your assistant to be as well dressed as you!"

Madame Celestine's eyes widened and she peered intently at Meg, who remained standing calmly by with a pleasant smile on her lips.

They made an interesting pair. Both women were of the same height and, at the moment, each had adopted an air of challenge as both realized that a contest of sorts lay before them. But the resemblance went no further. Madame's stocky build was accentuated by her overwhelming bust. Her fashionably blond hair was gathered under a green, lustrous turban topped by a small ostrich plume. Her pelisse, of the same metallic, glistening green as her turban, covered a simple, white, muslin dress. All in all it was a rich-looking costume; and the turban, distinctly *démodé* by some eight or nine years, just kept her appearance from being in the height of fashion without diminishing its elegance.

Meg's simple costume fitted her slim figure well, and its color was admirably flattering to her black hair and fresh complexion. She had on a Spanish pelisse of red-dotted cambric to which she had added a tiny rosette of ribbons at the high neck and three red organdy rosettes down the closure of the garment. The effect bordered on the inelegant yet had an ingenuous air about it. In effect, both Madame and Meg were dressed to a purpose.

"Mademoiselle, who sent you? How could you know? I did not know myself until this very minute that I needed an assistant. Suddenly, the work, it is too much! But you—I do not need! Thank you for coming." And she turned away.

Meg, trailing behind her, exclaimed, "Madame, you *do* need me! Look at what has happened in your shop and you only turned your back on it a few moments! Is there no one of your staff who can keep your patrons interested, besides yourself?"

"Que diable!" cried Madame Celestine with fire in her eye. "It is true! But where can I find another such as I?"

"Why, me, of course!" declared Meg.

"And just who are you?"

"Peg Mannering."

Madame Celestine looked up at the ceiling and shrugged her shoulders with Gallic emphasis. "Ah! Peg Mannering!" She nodded her head vigorously. "This tells me all! Now, I do not have to know anything more!" She gave Meg a little push. "So, because you are Peg Mannering, who I never heard of, I am to make you my assistant? I am indeed honored! Now, go away, *ma petite* Mannering, you are a bother to me and I have work to do."

Meg had no doubt that if she mentioned her connection to Lady Hobcourt, her reception by Madame Celestine would quickly warm up with enthusiasm, and she was sorely tempted to do so. But she resisted the temptation and instead began to study the prospective customers, some of whom were showing signs of impatience over the lack of attention they were receiving from Madame Celestine.

She set her sights on one great lady who was trying on a cardinal mantle without having the slightest idea of how to carry it. The shopgirl, by her side, was pretty close to tears; for every time she tried to adjust the wrap so that it would not sag so distressingly, her reward was to have her hands slapped away, accompanied by a sharp admonition to "Leave off, there!"

Meg went right up to the irritated customer. "A thousand pardons, milady. I am Madame Celestine's assistant. That is a charming wrap you have selected, but it takes a little getting used to. Just let me set it right, by your leave."

She snatched the mantle from the shoulders of the lady and, before anything could be said, deftly wafted it over her own shoulders, catching one fold of it under her arm. With a charming flip of her right shoulder, she laid back the right side, so that her shoulder and breast were free.

"*Voilá!*" she said with a smile and a pirouette. "It is not quite my size, milady, but it will be absolutely adorable on you. May I?" she asked, whisking the mantle from her shoulders and holding it spread out in invitation.

Madame Celestine, who had been about to intercede, relaxed and, with a smile of approval, turned away to wait on someone else. As she did so, she murmured to herself. "It would appear that *la petite* Mannering is right. I needed an assistant, *et voilá*! I have one! But how comes she to know that if I did not know it myself? And where did she come from? *Eh bien*, we shall have a talk, *bientôt*, little one!"

Chapter Four

Evening was come, not that the falling darkness in the streets was at all apparent to the inhabitants and habituées of the arcade shops. The amount of daylight filtering in during even the brightest part of the day could not illumine the interiors without the aid of the new gaslights which were lit the very first thing in the morning and extinguished the very last thing at night.

In Madame's shop the last customer had departed and the shopgirls had gone up to their dormitory, except for the few who lived out-of-doors. Only a few lamps were still lit. In their light, Meg was donning her cloak preparatory to taking her leave. As yet, Madame had had no word with her, and she could not help wondering if she had succeeded in winning the position. In her own mind she was sure that she had done, at the very least, as well as any of the other girls, but she realized that only Madame could have the final word. Now that her first day was over, she kept a careful eye on Madame, trying to read in her aquiline face, that had not a sign of the plumpness of her figure, some token of approval.

As for Madame Celestine, she had made up her mind quite early in the day that "that one, *la petite* Mannering," would not get out of her sight before she had had her talk with her. If she did not have Miss Mannering as her own special assistant before "that little one" had left the shop, then Celestine D' Erblay was not the woman she

45

thought she was. Now that they were alone, she would commence.

"So, you are leaving, mam'selle?"

"Yes, but I had hoped to speak with you before I left. I have enjoyed this day in the shop and I would like to return tomorrow."

"You are so young, yet you have of experience more than you have years. How comes this? Where have you worked before? Perhaps your *maman* was a couturière, *non*?"

"No," said Meg, shaking her head.

"*Non*? You say *non*, but to what do you say *non*? You *are* experienced, but your *maman* . . . ?" Madame shook her head questioningly.

"Yes," Meg agreed with a smile.

"Ah, *bien*! And where have you become so wise in the ways of the modiste at such an early age?"

"But, Madame, surely it is not exceptional that at my age a female is conversant with fashion and fabrics."

"Hmph!" snorted Madame. "Your first day in the shop and never, not once, do you come to me to ask what shall you sell to this one, what material shall you suggest to that one. In my shop I have girls and, after five years, still they must come to me with their questions until I am exhausted. Ah, but you, *ma chère*, not once! And yet you have no difficulties with the patronage. Why, I have seen the ladies merely smile and nod when you mentioned the price. And such prices!"

"But, Madame, I was not sure of how much to charge. Surely if I was in error, you would have said as much when I brought the reckoning to you for your approval."

"Who am I to argue with one who values my efforts so highly, especially when the customers only smile and do not object? No, my little one, you have a flair and I am very pleased."

"Oh, thank you, Madame!" cried Meg. "Then you will take me on as your own assistant?"

"But all my girls assist me!" objected Madame. "Why do I have them if they do not?"

"Why do you? From what you have just told me, I doubt very much that they assist you. It appears that you assist them!" Meg pointed out.

Obviously Madame Celestine had not thought of it like that before, and to hear it so stated not only raised Meg even higher in her estimation, but "gave her furiously to think" as she would have put it.

She looked at Meg in an appraising way, resting her forefinger on her cheek. She nodded her head slowly and said, "You have a head on your shoulders. Yes, you would make for me an excellent assistant."

"Then you do engage me?" asked Meg, delight shining in her eyes.

"Ah, now you go too fast! There are things we must discuss first." Madame Celestine held out her hand. "You have a letter of reference for me?"

"N-no!" stammered Meg, now discomposed. "I had not thought it to be necessary. After all, you did say I am capable. What more need there be?"

Madame Celestine regarded this girl she had hoped would be an asset to her establishment with disappointment. "I do not understand. You come to me for to be engaged, but you do not have a reference. *Incroyable!* It is not done! I do not know you!"

"But, Madame, I will be industrious. You will have no cause to regret it."

"And honest, too? How do I know this? Because you say it is so? How naïve! You cannot have had experience."

Meg cast her eyes down. "No, Madame, I have not had experience," she admitted regretfully, and then looking up, she appealed, "But you have seen—"

"*Non, c'est impossible!* Mam'selle, Madame Celestine's is, of all shops, the most exclusive. That is not only because I, Madame Celestine, am here—and without me

47

there would be nothing—but because everything in the shop is of the best. There are no finer seamstresses, no finer attendants, employed anywhere! I, Madame Celestine, say so. And you, *mon enfant*, while I like you and would have you with me, who can say who you are or what you are? Non, *ma pauvre*, it cannot be. *Alors*, I cannot engage you; *c'est fini*."

"If I brought you such a letter, you would hire me, then?"

Madame Celestine shrugged, "Perhaps! But do not think such a one from any bourgeoise is all that I require. *Mais non*!" she admonished Meg. "It is not good enough for Madame Celestine. You have no experience? Then I shall require a recommendation from a lady of the highest; *enfin*, one that I know. So you see, it is hopeless—and, *ma petite*, I am desolated, for if it could have been, I should so much have wished to have you with me in the shop."

Meg was disappointed. She had hoped not to have had to reveal her identity; yet, with Madame Celestine so insistent upon a reference, she could see that she had no choice. She must make application to Lady Amelia to provide just such satisfaction as Madame Celestine demanded. It was, nevertheless, a wonderful feeling to know that in any case she had qualified in Madame's eyes and strictly on her own merits. She sighed as she resigned herself to making use of Lady Amelia's good graces.

Madame Celestine, mistaking the sigh for a sign of discouragement, patted Meg on the shoulder.

"Why do you not go to some other dress shop, something less exclusive, less particular? Stay with them a year—say six months—and if you do well, then come to me, *eh bien*? I will suggest such a place."

"Thank you, Madame, but no. I will work here or nowhere. It is the best shop and I will not have less than the best!"

Madame Celestine threw up her hands and grinned.

48

"How brave! How determined! But"—she shook her head—"I fear I shall not see you again."

Meg grinned back. "You shall, never fear. I shall see you at nine o'clock tomorrow morning."

Madame Celestine merely shook her head again and, as she closed the door behind Meg, she murmured, "*Bonne chance, ma pauvre petite.*"

When the door of the shop was unlocked the following morning, Meg stepped inside and marched briskly up to Madame Celestine. The latter had just indulged herself in a gargantuan yawn and was still attempting to dispell the last cobwebs of sleep from her eyes. She came suddenly alert at the unlooked-for appearance of Miss Mannering, a brightly smiling Miss Mannering who was waving a sealed envelope under her nose.

Madame was thunderstruck; she had been sure that their conversation of last night had quite ended the matter. For this one—of no experience and *le bon Dieu* only knew of what antecedents—to persist in this farce was becoming tiresome. It must cease!

She snatched the letter from Meg and, without glancing at it, waved it in Meg's face.

"Mam'selle, you go too far and you begin to try my patience. It was not for nothing that I informed you only the best people—"

"Madame!" Meg was not smiling and there was enough of a command in her tone to bring Madame Celestine to an abrupt stop. "You are becoming quite trying yourself. You asked for a reference and I hand you one that cannot be bettered. Do you read it? No, you do not even look at it. You are just like Lady Amelia, who also believes she knows what a letter contains before she reads it!"

Madame's eyebrows shot up at the mention of Lady Amelia.

"And who is this Lady Amelia?" she demanded.

"Lady Hobcourt; I was sure you must be satisfied with any recommendation from her ladyship."

"Do you mean to stand there and tell me that this is from Lady Hobcourt?" she exclaimed, flourishing the unopened letter about.

"I do not mean to stand here and tell you anything at all! One has only to open the letter and read it. If that is too much to ask, I must beg you to return it to me—and I will return it to her ladyship."

Disbelief was writ all over Madame's countenance as, muttering something very French under her breath, she examined the seal and finally opened the missive. It read:

MY DEAR CELESTINE:

This will introduce Miss Peg Mannering, an unexceptionable young person in every way, and who is, in a manner of speaking, my protégée. I do not wish to dictate to you and therefore will only say that if you find her suitable for the shop, I shall not object to your engaging her; any arrangements between Miss Mannering and yourself to be at your discretion.

AMELIA, LADY HOBCOURT

Madame Celestine looked up from perusing the letter. "I do not understand. You have this letter all the time and you do not show it to me, *comment*?"

Meg shook her head and laughed, her black curls dancing merrily. "I did not have it yesterday. I did not think I should need it. I obtained it last night."

"You were at Lady Hobcourt's; you have entrée there?"

"What does it matter, Madame?" asked Meg in her turn, becoming slightly irritated.

Madame Celestine raised a hand to her forehead in bewilderment and then brought it down to the letter in her hand.

"But this is so strange! She does not say I *must* hire you."

"Of course not! I would not have it so! If you do not want me, there is no more to be said," Meg stated flatly, knowing full well that she had quite gained her goal. She could not help feeling thrilled at the prospect.

"You go too fast! Just who are you?"

"My mother is an old friend of Lady Hobcourt's; but what has that to say to anything?"

"Yet you come to work here?"

"Lady Hobcourt does not object; do you?"

"*Non—non*—but . . ."

Meg did not care for this turn in the interview, and steered the proprietress back to the business at hand.

"How much shall I earn, Madame?"

At once Madame Celestine was the woman of business again. Her eyes narrowed and she looked at Meg shrewdly.

"Again you go too fast, little one! Perhaps I cannot afford to hire you."

"But perhaps you can!"

Madame Celestine was a businesswoman before all else, and Meg was something she knew she needed in her business. She was not about to lose the opportunity over a matter of a few shillings. She had seen what the girl could accomplish and knew she would be worth a premium. Her best shopgirls—and they could not hold a candle to Miss Mannering—received some £5 the quarter, an excellent wage.

"I think that I can afford ten pounds the quarter. I know it is a great deal, but I do not think that I shall lose by it."

Meg blinked in surprise at the mere pittance she was being offered, for the sum, even at year's end, was but a tiny fraction of the funds her father had placed in her hands at parting. She wondered if it were too small a sum to agree to.

51

Madame Celestine had believed herself to have gone as far as she could to make such a magnificent offer. For the expenditure of so much money she expected to receive a handsome return from Miss Mannering's efforts. It is not surprising, therefore, that the look of dismay, as she thought it must be, came as a shock to her. She had thought to win the mademoiselle over at once.

She considered the young woman carefully. The letter from Lady Hobcourt had no true bearing on the present situation. It was a sufficient reference to permit her to notice Miss Mannering; but as a recommendation it was at best lukewarm. So it was entirely up to herself to determine the fate of this surprisingly forceful young woman standing before her.

Madame Celestine bethought herself of how many of the women who had come in yesterday merely to browse —and she knew them well—had left with some purchase. No, she could not countenance doing without *la petite*. She could never find such a one in a thousand years. Girding herself for the effort, she went to the extravagant length of increasing her original offer by £10.

Meg noted the great strain in Madame's face as she made this advance. The £10 rise appeared to exhaust the older woman.

Meg decided to accept. It was not a living she was after, and it was quite obvious from these negotiations that nothing like what she could live on was to be forthcoming.

Madame Celestine's very cordial response confirmed the bargain and Meg was able to take her leave. No, she would not join the other girls in their sleeping quarters upstairs. To Madame's great disappointment she explained that she had already made arrangements to live out-of-doors, arrangements which were eminently satisfactory to her—and she left before Madame Celestine could pursue the matter further.

By the end of the third week of Meg's stay with her,

Lady Amelia found herself at her wit's end. It was no use whatever to push Sir George. As he had pointed out when she had remonstrated with him that he was doing nothing to further himself in Meg's good opinion, "The gel's never about! How can I do anything when I can never lay eyes upon her? Dammit, is she here or ain't she?"

As to Meg, there was no talking to her; she was in the highest spirits. Out to the arcade at daybreak and never back before tea, Lady Amelia had almost as little opportunity to talk with her as did her son—and then she must sit by and listen while Meg regaled her with the follies and foibles of the women of her set. She had to admit that it was amusing, because many of the objects of Meg's sharp wit were intimate friends of hers.

But she did make up her mind to see that Meg was brought into a more docile frame of mind so that she could devote herself to more gentle pursuits, particularly that of receiving the attentions of Sir George. With that in mind, Lady Amelia sat herself down at her writing table one afternoon and dashed off a note to Lady Elizabeth. "Dashed off" may have been how she would have described it, but the many crumpled sheets of foolscap littering the floor after she had finished attested to something quite different.

As it turned out, her effort was in vain. Lady Elizabeth's response, as it pertained to the problem uppermost in Lady Amelia's mind, was disappointing in the extreme. She wrote to say that as long as Meg was not endangering herself in any way and was being diverted by her adventure, she saw no cause to interfere. She assured Lady Amelia that her daughter was in constant correspondence with her and that she, Lady Elizabeth, was following the latter's new career with consuming interest.

Lady Amelia was sadly disappointed to see all her hints, all her innuendos, blithely ignored. Well, if Lady Elizabeth had forgotten how a wellborn young lady must comport herself before the world, she certainly had not. It

53

was a matter of great wonder how the status of Meg's birth improved proportionately as Lady Amelia's understanding grew of how great Sir Samuel's fortune truly was.

In any case, Lady Amelia still had one string, at least, left to her bow. She would speak with Madame Celestine; surely between the two of them they could find some way of dissuading Meg from continuing in her questionable occupation. When the quarter came to an end she would be reviewing the business with Madame Celestine; then it would be time enough to take up the matter of Meg.

But she never got the opportunity.

The arcade was busy. The Duchess of York's introduction of the German fashion of Christmas gift-giving had become extremely popular in London, and the shops all over town, especially the exclusive ones located in the Burlington Arcade, were reaping great benefits as the holiday approached.

The shop's clientele was a highly favored one. The holiday spirit had loosened pursestrings and the holiday spirits had loosened tongues. The result was extraordinary clamor and great confusion in the shop. It was lent a particularly ribald note by the presence of a number of gentlemen of means and their mistresses whom they were escorting. It would be difficult to say who behaved in the poorest taste: the ladybirds flirting outrageously and flaunting their charms, or their well-bred, high-born escorts who constantly egged them on.

Meg was not amused.

The shopgirls held back from these raucous groups for fear of becoming butts for their merriment. Madame Celestine had her hands full with her regular customers; so it was left to Meg to attend to the holidaymakers. She found it distasteful, but bent to the task coolly and with confidence.

She did not try to bandy words with them, but in a most businesslike manner she saw to it that the articles of clothing they wished to see were duly displayed for them and properly fitted.

One young man, quite deep in his cups, ventured to pinch her as she went by. She stopped and turned upon him a look of such glittering contempt that he sobered up on the instant. She was not bothered further.

As Christmas Day came ever closer, the shop began to roar, rather than hum, with activity. It was not an easy time for Madame Celestine's people and tempers were beginning to fray.

A light snow had fallen that morning, but nothing of it could be seen from the shop windows, of course. The people passing to and fro along the promenade were well wrapped against the cold, making the shop feel all the more cozy in the warmth issuing from the three blazing fireplaces.

Meg looked up from her work to see two gentlemen and a lady enter the shop—at least, she thought her a lady until she looked again. Meg had been long enough in the shop now to distinguish between the respectable people and those of the demimonde. One further glance was all she needed to know that the ''lady'' was a cyprian of the first stare, expensive and notorious.

When she turned her attention to the two gentlemen, she was in for a surprize. They were both familiar to her, being none other than Sir George Hobcourt and Mr. Adrian Rounceford! Even as she wondered which was the escort and which the friend, the danger of her identity becoming disclosed began to gnaw at her.

Panic began to rise within her, for Sir George, she was sure, had no idea that she was masquerading. She could hardly depend upon him not to unmask her; in fact, she did not doubt but that he would take great pleasure in doing so, there being no affection existing between them. To avoid any risk of exposure, she put down the accounts that she was working on and withdrew quietly from the showroom where she busied herself inspecting some of the garments

55

that the seamstresses had brought to various stages of completion in the workroom.

Meg, at three and twenty and despite her countrified existence, was not just out of the schoolroom by any means. For all her mother's soft charm, Lady Elizabeth had made sure that her daughter was come to an understanding of that which made men what they were and women what they were, or she would never have permitted her daughter to visit London under the circumstances.

In Harlington, although Meg had not been accounted a belle, she was never, after the age of sixteen, free of the attentions of the local swains. Foremost amongst them had been Colin MacTavish and, while she had encouraged them to a point and indulged in mild flirtations, none of her beaux had made any impression on her heart. If anything they had encouraged in her the belief that men were a deal less than the beau ideals they believed themselves to be. Any woman, she felt, could do what she wished with any man so long as she had her wits about her and went about it the right way. Nothing in her Harlington experiences had occurred to contradict this feeling.

It is needless to point out that seeing Hobcourt and Rounceford in the company of Mrs. "Cherry" Pye, the well-known courtesan, did not raise either of the gentlemen in her estimation. The former could not sink any lower and, she was sure, the latter was no better than his friend. She intended to have nothing to do with either of them. It was, therefore, disconcerting to Meg to receive a message from Madame Celestine to come to the showroom at once and attend upon important customers.

Meg put down the dress she was examining and rose with a sigh. She had a very good idea who the "important" customers were; the son of Lady Hobcourt, Madame Celestine's sleeping (silent) partner could be no less. She took a deep breath and braced herself for the ordeal.

As she parted the draperies which opened onto the

showroom, she noted with relief that George's back was turned towards her, and Madame Celestine was engaged in exchanging pleasantries with all three.

She came up alongside George without him noticing her. Madame called out. "Ah, *la petite* Mannering! She is here! She will see to your wishes. Do not worry! She is of the most capable."

Naturally all of the party turned to view the newcomer, allowing Madame to slip away unnoticed.

"Oh, I say!" exclaimed Sir George, turning his lorgnette on Meg. "What the blazes are you doing here?"

"I am employed here, Sir George—and there is no need for such an elaborate exhibition of amazement," she responded in a menacing tone, trying to glare him into silence.

It was a wasted effort. Sir George began to sputter, and Meg was sure that his very next words would let the cat out of the bag if she did not take more positive measures to shut him up. She stepped close to him so that her skirt fell over his boot and came down as hard as she could on his toes, at the same time hissing, "Shut up, you fool!"

Sir George let out a yelp of pain and then gritted his teeth as he fought off an almost overmastering impulse to grab at his injured limb. Since it was more important to maintain his dignity before the flashy female, he remained standing there, breathing heavily through his nose, effectively muffled.

Mr. Rounceford cocked an inquiring eye at this strange exchange of civilities, but otherwise showed no sign of having noted anything exceptional.

Mrs. Pye, on the other hand, frowned in annoyance that the attention of even one of her gallants should be diverted from her attractive person for an instant. She immediately exclaimed, "How very tiresome of you, dear boy! I had no idea your acquaintance was so extensive. It is dreadfully hot in here; I do not think I shall buy a thing. Come, let us go!"

"Oh, I say!" George protested. "She's not just any-one, you know—ow-ohh!" he howled as his tender toes received another hard crunch.

Rounceford chuckled. "I should think not, George, old thing! To say the least, she appears to have an extremely forceful way with her. She must know you only too well," he concluded with a laugh.

"But stay!" he exclaimed suddenly, although Meg had made no move to leave. Nothing could have dragged her from the spot, not until she was assured that George would say nothing to embarrass her.

Mr. Rounceford was scrutinizing her carefully. "Have we not met before this, Miss Mannering? Why yes, I am sure we have!"

"Well!" cried Mrs. Pye with undisguised indignation. "If this is not the coziest, I am sure I do not know!"

"Yes, indeed, madam, you are quite right," said Meg with a charming smile as she turned to Mrs. Pye. "These gentlemen have only the merest acquaintance with me. I think we can dispense with them. If you will be seated, I am sure I can show you something quite tempting in a bonnet, or perhaps a gown. Everything in our shop is of the first stare for fashion as I am sure you will agree."

Mrs. Pye appeared mollified as she took the seat Meg offered. Sir George and Mr. Rounceford arranged them-selves, one on each side of her, and put on expressions of the utmost boredom. Mrs. Pye, very pleased with the arrangement of her admirers about her, began to primp as she surveyed the shop. It was quite obvious to the most casual observer that she thought herself a queen to be attended by two such highly fashionable gentlemen. Her interest was now engaged to be sure that everyone else in the shop was aware of her distinction.

Meg could barely suppress a smile at the pretension so obvious in the heavily made-up albeit pretty face. She had not a doubt that the bizarre creature could never resist any of the shop's wares so long as they were brightly colored or glittered, and she went off in search of just such delicacies.

"Who is she?" demanded Rounceford of Hobcourt.

By this time Sir George was having second thoughts about revealing the identity of their attendant. Although his poor toes still ached, it was not their discomfort that dissuaded him.

With blazing clarity the rudiments of a plot had come to his mind—one that appeared to be a perfect solution to two of his problems; namely, how to satisfy his mother that Meg was not fit to be his wife, and how to get his own back at Meg so that she would never again dare to demean him.

"Not here, Adrian, old boy! Tell you about her later. Everything!" he said with a grin and a knowing wink.

Rounceford raised his eyebrows and gave a slight nod.

"And what is so interesting about that female?" demanded Mrs. Pye. "Hmph! A mere chit! No bigger than a schoolgirl and no more up to snuff, I'll be bound!" she said with annoyance. That another female was to be discussed in her presence was not to be borne—and a mere shopgirl at that, was truly insufferable.

"Yes, yes!" Sir George agreed hastily, sensing a stormy tantrum in the wind. "Exactly so! That is why we will not discuss her further. Ah, here she comes now, with some very pretty things, Cherry!" he cried, hoping desperately that he had succeeded in diverting her thoughts.

He had, or rather Meg had. Her arms were laden with what appeared to be a glittering mass of sequins and multicolored fringes that defied the eye of the beholder. Meg said not a word, but gracefully let the gown slip out to its fullest length. She presented it, shimmering blindingly, before Mrs. Pye, whose eyes started to glaze over with cupidity.

Sir George brought up his lorgnette, his face the picture of distaste, while Rounceford, after one look at the gown, began to study Meg's expression.

Meg was the very picture of the correct dressmaker's

attendant, her slim frame slightly bent at the waist, emphasizing the expression of encouragement on her face. A grim smile played over Rounceford's features.

Suddenly the air was filled with "oohs!" and "aahs!" from Mrs. Pye. She stood up and snatched the glorious creation from Meg's arms and held it up under her chin, one hand pressing it close to her body.

"Oh, it is too *delightful*!" she squealed as she posed herself before the two gentlemen. "I must try it on!"

"Oh, I say, Cherry—" Sir George began to remonstrate, but he got no further, for Mrs. Pye had gone off to the changing room without giving Meg a chance to follow.

George wheeled on her. "What do you think you are doing?" he demanded, his choler mounting.

Rounceford chuckled.

Meg looked at George coolly. "At Madame Celestine's we try to match the gown to one's disposition, and we invariably succeed."

"*Touché!*" cried Rounceford, who was obviously enjoying the contest.

"*Touché*, my sainted aunt! Just what is Madame asking for that disreputable mess of fish scales?"

"We had thought to ask three hundred pounds, but I am sure you may have it for two hundred and fifty, we shall be so pleased to get rid of it. I do believe it is giving the shop a bad name. Lady Slade ordered it despite all that Madame could do to discourage her. But one sight of it was even too much for Lady Letty. Do not despair, Sir George; Mrs. Pye will probably tire of it after wearing it a time or two."

At which Rounceford remarked, "I can see there is little love lost between you two. It interests me greatly to know the cause of it."

"I have no greater acquaintance with Sir George than I have with you, sir; therefore I think your interest an impertinence of the first order. But please be assured, Mr. Rounceford, I shall cheerfully serve any lady friend you may be pleased to escort here with the same pleasure I have served Mrs. Pye.''

She smiled, dipped into a slight curtsy, and went after her client.

Rounceford turned to George. "A cute bit of goods that, Hobcourt; though I should think not in your usual taste.''

Sir George looked at his friend in disgust. " 'Pon my word, Adrian, *I* am a connoisseur! Can you doubt it?''

Adrian smiled, and there was a touch of contempt in his tone as he replied, "If yon Cherry pie is an example of your taste, yes I can.''

"Oh, come now! You will admit she is a fine figure of a woman and with a face to match—and a high flyer to boot!''

"Aye, a most decorative piece, indeed—and after the Mannering female finishes gilding your precious lily, she will be a sun goddess in a veritable blaze of glory!''

"Drat that female! You know, Adrian, I cannot help but think that she is trying to plague me!''

Adrian's white teeth flashed as he laughed in his friend's face. "I am surprised that *you* should think so. It was abundantly clear to me from the first. What the devil is between the two of you?''

"Not here. I will tell you about it later, over a brandy.''

"Do not put it off! We are alone. Heaven only knows when Cherry will have finished! I do not think that horrible gown is all the Mannering girl will put onto your account.''

Sir George groaned.

"Come, let me hear about it, man! We have time and to spare,'' commanded Rounceford.

"Oh, very well.'' George paused to extract an ornate snuffbox made of gold, topped with a rich blue sapphire. Dexterously, he flipped it open with one hand, his little finger extended, and proffered it to Adrian.

61

Rounceford shook his head. "I cannot abide the stuff nor the way it dusts all over one."

Sir George shrugged. Very delicately, maintaining his little finger in its extended state throughout the manipulation, he transferred a generous pinch to his nostril and sniffed sharply as he tossed his head back.

Almost immediately he began to scrabble at his pockets. Desperately he whipped out a handkerchief and applied it to his nose just as the grandfather of all sneezes exploded and shook him with a blast that rattled his teeth.

Adrian let out a sharp bark of laughter.

Sir George, eyes tearing, his immaculate neckcloth stained and reduced to sorry wrinkles, looked utterly woebegone. In watery accents he mumbled, "Never can get it down. It's the sneeze, you know. Blows it all out again, confound it!"

Chapter Five

Adrian Rounceford took his half-blind friend by the forearm and led him over to a pair of seats against the light-colored wall.

"Here, be seated old man. If that is the best you can do with snuff, I do not wonder that I have never seen you use it before."

Sir George took out a tiny gilt brush and began assiduously to remove the remains of snuff from his pale-blue waistcoat.

"I am not a fool!" he declared. "Can you imagine what an imbecile I should look at the club? But I was sure that I had it down properly, or I should never have tried it here. Did-did anyone observe me? Anyone we know, do you think?"

"You may rest easy. There are only women about, and they are too interested in the wares and in their own gossip to give heed to us. You may rely on it; we could not be more private. Now then, what have you to say about *la petite* Mannering, as our Gallic friend refers to her?"

"*La petite*—pfah! Nothing *petite* about that one, let me tell you. Meg Mannering—"

"Meg? I distinctly recall her name to be Peg!"

"Meg, Peg, what matter? What is your strangely intense interest?"

Adrian's eyes appeared to be focused on something far away. He said nothing for a moment. Then, with a slight effort, he brought his attention back to Sir George.

"My interest? My pleasure, perhaps! A likely bit of goods, I think. No beauty, of course, but yet tempting. As you know, George, I have been at loose ends these days. Since my falling out with Daphne, I have been of no mind to fix my interest with anyone; but, now, I am of a mind to do just that."

"Do not say that you are looking to tie the knot!" exclaimed Sir George as he nodded in the direction of the changing room to which Meg had gone to assist Mrs. Pye.

"Do not be more daft than you can help, you bufflehead! In the plainest words, I seek to mount a mistress —and yon tiny baggage may be exactly what I seek. What think you, or are you similarly so inclined, my friend?"

George blessed himself silently. His scheme was developing with practically no help from him. He cried, "Never, dear boy! My sweet pastry Pye is all that I can handle for the nonce. So you are truly interested in Miss Mannering?"

"So I have said! How well do you know her? Could you act as—er—go-between?"

Sir George gave vent to sardonic laughter.

"Now, who is the bufflehead? You have seen the airs she puts on with me. You shall have to rely on your own resources—but I do not think you will find any insurmountable obstacles in your path. What sort of ménage à deux do you have in mind for her?"

"Miss Mannering is too much beforehand—so she strikes me—to warrant anything less than a carte blanche."

"Carte blanche!" Sir George exclaimed.

"What, may I ask, is so astounding about that?"

"Oh, nothing," said George with a snicker.

"Obviously you know something I do not. Out with it, old man!"

"Really, Adrian, if your pocket is so well-lined . . ." A canny glint came into George's eyes as he let his remark hang in the air.

"I daresay it is sufficiently well-lined for my purposes, but what is that to you, or anyone for that matter? I am not a fool about money."

"I did not think you were, and therefore I will let you in on something you should know. A way to Mannering that will put no great strain on your pockets."

"I am all ears, my friend. Say on! You have my complete attention."

"Very well. Listen carefully! This girl, for all her pretensions of being quite up to the knocker, is far from it. You see, she dotes on 'romance'!" He pronounced the word as though it were obscene.

"You cannot mean it!"

"So help me, Adrian, it is the truth! She positively gorges herself on novels—all that romantic tripe—she breathes it! I tell you I know! Oh, yes, I quite agree that, upon appearance, she is a taking little thing; but I have no taste for schoolgirl prattle." As he said this, George was studying his friend with some apprehension. It was necessary to portray Meg as an easy mark, but if he overdid it, Adrian, the man of the world, might find the bait without sufficient charm to tempt him.

Rounceford stared back at his friend vacantly. He was turning over in his mind the "facts" that George had presented to him, but George need not have feared for his plan. The conclusion that Adrian was coming to could not have fitted in better with George's hopes.

Adrian's face relaxed and he grinned in a knowing manner. "I begin to see what you are trying to tell me. This need not be a prolonged affair so long as I go about it the right way."

"Exactly!"

Rounceford's grin broadened. "Shall we say a cozy little nest for a fortnight or so?"

Sir George grinned his approval.

"Yes," continued Adrian, "I should like that very much." He put his tongue in his cheek and looked vaguely

65

up at the ceiling. "And it is romance she wants? Well, I shall see to it that she has as much of that commodity as she could wish for!"

George was bursting with pride and satisfaction to see everything going along without a ripple. He could hardly contain himself as he asked, "When?"

"There is no time like the present."

"And you account yourself a man of address with the tender creatures? I am amazed!"

"Why, do I not make a proper appearance?"

"What has that to say to the business? Can you not conceive of a better setting than this, a dressmaker's shop, for making your overtures to her?"

"Of course I can!" exclaimed Adrian. "But where's the opportunity, man? We do not travel in the same circles. Where can I approach her, but here and now?"

Sir George was now ready to spring the trap. He was sure that Adrian was so busy worrying at the bait that he would not now hesitate to take any step to make sure of his quarry.

"In affairs of the heart," said George coolly, "one makes one's own opportunities."

"Well, that is exactly what I am about to do."

"Then you will fail," declared George, suppressing a shudder at the thought of what would befall them all if Rounceford should attempt to further his less-than-honourable intentions here in the shop.

"Don't be a fool. I shall not fail!" retorted Rounceford with heat.

"No, of course you will not fail with her on any count, old man," said Sir George soothingly. "What I mean to say is that this is not the way to go about it if you wish to keep your brass in your pocket. She is the sort that if you attempt to reason with her, you will find yourself having to come to such terms with her as will cost you far more than it need. You cannot begin here. You must sweep her off

66

her feet and never give her a chance to haggle with you. Now, you cannot do that in this place.''

''I take it you can suggest a better?''

''Indeed, I can! And, if you go about it in the way I will suggest, she will thank you for it and never think to be unreasonable about it.''

''So, I am to take lessons from you in how to manage a female, am I?''

''No, no, not at all! It is just that I happen to know the chit well.''

''Hm-m! And your advice is . . .''

''You must abduct her!''

Rounceford stared at Sir George as though he believed his friend had quite lost his wits.

''Think, Adrian! What could be more romantic than an abduction? I am sure it cannot fail. What more could a shopgirl ask for than to be carried off by a rich and handsome devil. You know, Adrian, you can play the part to perfection; and just think how you will reap the benefit of the adventure!''

Adrian pursed his lips in thought for a moment. Then he nodded. ''Yes, it could be great fun. Thank you, old chap; I do think that I shall have a go at it. But stay! Just how does one arrange these things? Do you know?''

''Oh, it should not be too difficult. It was quite the thing in the days of our grandfathers. I say, why not do it by the book? You know, use the novels themselves to guide you. I understand that they are full to the brim with abductions. In that way you will be able to proceed exactly in the way Miss Mannering will expect of you.''

''Capital! Can you lend me a volume or two?''

''Burn my britches! I don't have such drivel by me! Go to Sam's. I am sure you will find what you need there.''

''Sam's?''

''You know the shop—the Royal Library.''

''Oh, that one! Good idea. I shall go there right off! I

say, you won't mind it if I leave you now?"

Very magnanimously, George waved him away. "Go to it!"

Rounceford strode away. Suddenly he stopped, wheeled about, and came back.

"Oh, now, really! This is ridiculous!" he exclaimed. "Who ever heard of a more nonsensical business—and, furthermore, just how am I supposed to get her to come along with me?"

Sir George sighed. It began to appear that friend Adrian was having second thoughts. He threw himself into the breach without hesitation. Anything for a friend!

"You don't get her to come along. This is an abduction; you—er—you just take her!"

Adrian was horrified. "By force! What if she should struggle and cry out? I say, do you think she bites?"

"Gad, sir, do not say that you quake and tremble at the thought of a female, small and weak as a mere babe! Have no fear; she will not fight you off. She will be as gentle as a lamb. After all, you will be making her fondest dream come true."

"Do you really think so?" asked Adrian weakly.

George assured him of his complete confidence in the matter and in his friend's ability to carry it off without a hitch.

Adrian was still not satisfied. "But I still do not see how I am to get at her. Where the devil do shopgirls live, anyway? I cannot be expected to abduct her in broad daylight, right from these premises, no matter how much she may desire it."

"Hm!" murmured George. "A very good question, that. Wait here! I'll be back in a jiffy."

Sir George turned and left. Rounceford was disconcerted to see him approach Madame Celestine and enter into conversation with her. They spoke together for a few minutes and then Sir George returned to his friend.

Rounceford was beside himself with anxiety as he pounced on his friend.

"Are you mad? Why could you not have waited? I might just as well have asked Miss Mannering, herself!"

"Collect yourself, Rounceford, and give me some credit for wit, do! I merely told the good Madame I was interested in one of her girls. I was properly devious about it and asked her where she hid them after their day's work was done. She was quite gracious and most informative. It would appear that they have sleeping rooms somewhere abovestairs—"

Rounceford groaned.

"Except for a few," continued Sir George, "such as the petite Mannering, who lives out-of-doors."

"Oh, good! And where does she live?" Adrian asked eagerly.

"Well, I could hardly ask her that, you blockhead! Devil take it, man, it is of no importance! All you have to do is await her at the end of the day. She must leave by the entrance to the arcade."

"Yes, of course; you are quite right. Thank you, old chum; I will get on with it now. Only—"

"What else can there be?"

"Well, I had not thought it would be quite such an undertaking."

As Sir George watched his friend leave the shop, he smoothed his neckcloth, brushed lightly at his shoulders —and grinned.

With Christmas and St. Stephen's behind them, and the new year before them, traffic in Madame Celestine's establishment was at a low ebb. So few and far between were the calls at the shop that Madame Celestine's constant refrain was to the effect that it hardly was worthwhile to keep the shop open. Her work force, including Meg, were, however, quite thankful. The respite from the hurly-burly of the holiday season was very welcome; and the girls in the shop and the girls in the workroom spent the hours relaxing in gossip and in holding tiny parties.

Madame Celestine was no hard taskmaster. Although she expected her people to work, and work diligently, when the orders were flowing; in the present doldrum of activity she refrained from harassing her staff and looked the other way when their behaviour bordered on the hoydenish.

At the end of one such day, Meg was feeling fatigued. To her, the inactivity, coupled with the boredom that accompanied it, was more exhausting than any day she spent thoroughly occupied. She did not regret its conclusion and, as the other girls drifted off to their sleeping room, she went about, assisting Madame Celestine with the shutters and extinguishing the lamps. When they were both satisfied that the shop was secured for the night, Meg donned her cloak and arranged its hood for protection against the cold winter's evening.

"*Eh bien*, Peggee; tomorrow you must come with me to see Lady Hobcourt. She is my *commanditaire*."

Meg had some acquaintance with the French tongue, but this word meant nothing to her. She looked her puzzlement.

"She is my sleeping partner," explained Madame Celestine, making a wry face. "Your language is *exécrable*! *Oui*! she is my sleeping partner, but not in bed, you understand. It is in the business."

"I know. She has invested, but she does no work."

"*Oui*! Well, tomorrow we meet so that she sees how goes the shop. I wish you to attend with me. Since you have come, I am amazed! Business has never been so good. Always you are charming, always you are chatting with the ladies, and always they buy. What you cannot sell has not been made! Even that abomination of gold lamé for the Cade woman which, after we went to so much trouble with it, she refused. Oh, Lady Hobcourt will be most pleased when I tell her it has been sold!''

Meg chuckled to herself as she imagined Lady Hobcourt's face when she found out who had been billed for the gown.

''Well, it is late, *mon enfant*. Perhaps you should stay with me tonight? *Non*? Then go quickly.''

Meg stepped out into the covered promenade. A cold wind was racing through the arcade, carrying with it wisps of dry snow from the light fall they had had that day. She drew her cloak snugly about her and proceeded down the lonely way.

As she passed along, the lights from the shops that lined the way began to flicker out and the gloom in the arcade deepened. It was with great relief that she arrived at the archway which served as the entranceway and stepped out onto the street. She was later than was her wont, and the available hackney cabs were considerably reduced in number. In fact, there were only two vehicles. The nearest was a private carriage—a gleaming chariot with a beautiful matched pair of bloods in harness. The horses were in fine fettle and impatient to be gone, for they stamped and snorted, holding their place only because of the tightly held reins in the hands of the coachman. Standing alongside of it was a tall figure wearing a Wellington-styled top hat and a many-caped driving cloak. Meg paid the group little attention, for just beyond she espied a single remaining hackney.

She started to pass the first vehicle, but got no further. A smelly something draped itself over her head, completely blinding her and half-smothering her in its folds. A pair of powerful arms encircled her and she was whisked off her feet and thrown roughly into the chariot so that she landed with a thump on the sumptuous leather seat cushion. Even as she fell, she heard the door slam and the coachman signal to his horses. The chariot lurched forward and they

71

were dashing away into the deepening dusk before she had caught her breath.

Although the carriage was remarkably well sprung, its headlong darting through the streets of London, with their many twists and turns, rendered her insensible to all but the necessity of hanging on for dear life to her seat. Confined within the folds of some coarse material, she had particular difficulty, nor was she made any more comfortable by the smell of grain and the choking dust that threatened to smother her. It would appear that she was swathed within the confines of an old, well-used gunny sack.

The violent swaying of the carriage defeated her attempts to maintain her equilibrium, and her various and painful encounters with the walls and floor of her prison quickly assured her that her captor was suffering a similar fate as every now and again his muttered oath would signify. It did her heart good to hear these signs of his discomfort; but the horrid sack soon had her choking and gasping. Under its restraint, try as she would, she could not get free of it. As quick as a thought, the very next time her hand contacted her captor, she pinched what she could with all her might.

She was immediately rewarded by hearing a sharp gasp. Assured of his attention, she called out, "Are you trying to stifle me? Free me at once!" and broke out into a fit of coughing.

Hands quickly came to her assistance, lifting the sacking, but they were inordinately clumsy and fumbled helplessly when the sack had been lifted not quite clear of her shoulders. Her arms now free, Meg sharply slapped away the "helping hands" and finished the removal herself.

She emerged from the sack dusty and disheveled, and her untidiness contributed as much to her subsequent ire as did any of the rest of her predicament.

She shot a furious glance at her companion. He was

wearing a mask, but it did not hide the grin with which he was regarding her.

"Just what do you think you are about?" she demanded. "Who are you? Where are you taking me?" Even as she spoke, she was dusting herself off with vigour and attempting to bring her tresses into some semblance of order.

"Be easy, my love." His voice was mellow and his smile charming; and to Meg, they were elusively familiar. "We are on our way to Tunbridge Wells, where everything is prepared for us. In due time I will discover myself to you, but for now we have a drive before us of an hour or two. I am sure we can spend that time in an interesting fashion." With that he reached over and drew her close to him. He was very strong and Meg was quite helpless in his arms. His lips sought hers and he pressed her close.

Startled though Meg was, she could not help admitting to herself that the sensation thus produced was pleasant to a degree—but the circumstances were decidedly unpleasant and she wanted none of it. She remained passive in his arms until he released her, and then she swung up her hand and slapped him smartly across his cheek.

"What the devil!" he cried as he drew back, startled. "What did you do that for?"

"That is the least you can expect when you force your attentions on a lady!"

"You—a lady? Hah!"

"Yes, a lady! Why are you doing this? Do you intend to ravish me?"

"Good lord! What do you take me for? Of course I have no such intention. I have merely abducted you."

The very collected manner in which he made the statement rendered Meg speechless with amazement. But only for a moment.

"Merely abducted me! What are you, a madman? Do you not realize that this is England and that it is the year of our Lord eighteen hundred and twenty? If you are not mad

73

then you must be a villain! You intend holding me for ransom!''

He saw great humour in that and laughed heartily. ''Ransom, indeed! I am sure all the worldly wealth of Peg Mannering would not pay for my stickpin!''

Meg breathed a sigh of relief. Obviously, if he knew her only as Peg Mannering, he could have no idea of the wealth she had access to as Meg Miller. Yet, this made the business stranger than ever. He had forced a kiss on her, but claimed no evil intent. And if ransom was not his purpose, then why all this? Any puzzle was a challenge to Meg, and this one was no exception despite the trying circumstances of the moment.

''Then why have you abducted me?'' she demanded.

''I was sure you would find it romantic,'' he responded in a tone that would brook no contradiction.

Meg could not believe her ears.

''How old are you, sir? I should take you for thirty.''

''I am nine and twenty!'' There was a slight note of indignation in his voice as he corrected her.

''Nine and twenty, and you would have me believe that a gentleman—at least, you dress like one—and one who must be up to snuff if he has his wits about him—would indulge in such a missish prank as this? You, sir, have been reading too many novels—and what is worse, believing them!''

Rounceford, for it was he, of course, looked very annoyed. He flushed under his mask. Something was definitely wrong. This was not the flighty ninny he had been led to believe she was. She was accusing him of the very thing that friend George had claimed was the affliction she suffered from. He began to have misgivings, and his composure was disturbed. But the venture was begun and, if Miss Mannering turned out to be the woman of spirit he had thought she was from the beginning, why so much the better. It might turn out to be a more expensive frolic than George had deemed, but he was quite sure that he could satisfy the demands of a London shopgirl.

"You do read novels?" he asked uncertainly.

"Why, yes, every one I can get my hands on. I find them quite diverting; childish, but amusing nevertheless."

"Oh!"

"Oh?"

"I had thought that being addicted to romantic literature, you would have found this abduction exciting and—"

"If *you* had read your novels, you would have learned that only villains abduct young females. The heroes *elope* with them! Are you, then, a villain, Mr. Rounceford? You are certainly no hero!"

Chapter Six

"You know me then?" Rounceford was extremely discomfited. With his identity discovered, the possibility of a graceful exit from the affair disappeared; and he was beginning to feel that this dauntless little female was become a great deal more than he had any desire for.

"Of course! How could I help but? I have only been at Madame Celestine's a matter of weeks. The few gentlemen I have seen there in that short time must be easily remembered."

"But I am wearing a mask!"

"True, but your voice is distinctive and, coupled with your figure, your graceful bearing, and your perfectly beautiful teeth—"

"Spare me the details!" he exclaimed, but he was not ill-pleased with her comments upon his physical attributes. It encouraged him to proceed. "Miss Mannering, I fear that I have made a cake of myself in your eyes and I would beg you to forget my foolishness so that we may deal with each other in a better fashion. We might start again from the beginning."

"That would be more than a little difficult as we must be halfway to Tunbridge Wells by this time."

"Hardly that! My nags will go with the best, but we are not a league beyond the outskirts of London yet."

"What is the hour?"

Mr. Rounceford reached for his timepiece. "It is well past ten. You were late coming out, you know."

"How very bad of me! I do apologize for having kept you waiting," remarked Meg with scathing irony. "Well, in any case, I cannot go back. I should not arrive before midnight."

"Oh, there is no need for you to go back. I am sure we shall deal extremely well together. I shall make you quite happy."

"Then it is an elopement?"

"An elopement! What do you take me for? A Rounceford wed to a shopgirl? I should say not!"

"Well, then, it must be that you intend to ravish me," declared Meg matter-of-factly.

"Devil take it, girl! Is ravishment all you have on your mind?"

"Believe me, Mr. Rounceford, it is certainly not the least thing I have on my mind at this moment. But, pray, what am I to think? You claim it is not the one nor the other. What else is there left? Of one thing I am sure, and that is there can be nothing honourable in your attentions to me."

"All I ever intended is that you live with me for a while at my place near Tunbridge Wells. I am sure it would be quite pleasant and I will see you well recompensed. Who knows, if afterwards, I may not be able to arrange a marriage for you? Something better, I am sure, than you can achieve on your own."

In the dimness of the carriage, Meg's eyes began to glitter in anger. She hunched herself back into her corner of the seat to be as far away from him as possible.

"So you see," he continued in a reasoning tone, "you need not be afraid of me; I meant you no harm." He paused. "Well, what do you say?"

Meg said nothing.

"Come, come, Miss Mannering, you cannot find anything exceptional about such an arrangement. I am not unattractive and I can easily afford you."

"Do not be so sure! I am quite expensive."

"Ah, that is encouraging! I am pleased to see that you are not new to this game. I feared that you might be. One does not expect to find a taste for reading in one's heart's delight."

"Just how did you know that I read and what my taste in literature was?" she demanded.

"Why, why, er—I guessed!" he answered lamely. Damn the girl, he thought, must she be forever challenging? What could there have been between her and Hobcourt?

He felt enough of a fool already and was not about to lower himself further in her eyes by admitting any part of Sir George's assistance.

"I still doubt that you can afford me," she stated flatly.

By this time Rounceford was beginning to feel that there would be words between George and himself the very next time they met. He remembered quite well his friend's assurances that this escapade need not be expensive.

"Well, I am not accustomed to haggling, my dear. What sort of arrangement do you have in mind?"

"I am not accustomed to haggling either, Mr. Rounceford; in fact, I am never concerned about money matters at all. My terms, if I accept, are quite simple: no restraints!"

"I do not understand," said Rounceford, frowning.

"It is very simple. There shall be no restraints upon me in any way. I shall be free to spend; I shall be free to look where my fancy is best pleased; and I shall be free to end the arrangement at my pleasure. And why do you not remove that silly mask?" she shot at him.

For some time now the going had been much smoother, but of this Rounceford was completely unaware. He sat there as though turned to stone.

He was trying to collect his thoughts. The proposition he had just given ear to was so completely beyond any expectation, so completely outrageous, that he was rattled beyond belief. To gain time, he reached up to the laces of his mask and made a business of undoing them.

He was so long at it that Meg lost patience. She moved over the seat to him. "Here, let me do that! You seem to be all thumbs," she said as she nudged his hands away from the tie strings.

"You have made quite a tangle," she continued close to his ear. "I am getting it undone now."

To all intents and purposes she was now in his lap, her body pressed close to his, the delicate scent of her hair pervading his nostrils and sending riotous images racing through his mind. He knew then that he wanted her above anything and made up his mind to have her—but never on her terms!

The mask was coming loose when the carriage lurched suddenly. Almost without thinking, his arms came about her to steady her. For a moment she lay passively in his arms, looking up into his eyes. He bent over to plant a kiss on her lips—and the partially loosened mask slipped down over his mouth! His eyes opened wide in frustration.

Meg smiled, then she began to giggle. Finally she burst into hearty laughter. Adrian appreciated as fully as she what had gone forward—and what had not. His frustration gave way to the humour of the situation, and his laughter, somewhat muffled by the mask, joined hers.

Still giggling, Meg disposed of the flimsy bit of silk and handed it to Adrian. "There now, let that be a lesson to you!" she said, resuming her seat in the far corner.

"Thank you, Miss Mannering. Indeed, it shall be!" he declared ruefully as he tucked the mask into his pocket. He sank back and stared straight ahead. They drove on in silence for a bit.

He looked over at his companion. He could barely make her out, sitting primly erect, her reticule on her lap. He found it remarkable that she still had that article in her possession, for she had not been handled with any nicety at all. He was sure another female would have been petrified, would have dropped it and screamed in panic. It would appear that Miss Mannering was just not any girl at all.

He could not help feeling intrigued by her. Here they were, quite companionable—had she not assisted him with the mask? He winced as he thought of his roughshod and callow scheme. It was quite apparent to him that Miss Mannering was a woman of experience, not easily flustered. Well, he was not without experience himself, and he should be pleased to demonstrate the fact to her. He turned to address her.

"Well, my dear, have you made up your mind?" he asked.

"About what?" she responded in return. Her tone was natural, evincing not the slightest concern.

"About what we were discussing a moment ago."

"There is nothing to make up my mind about. I told you how it must be."

"You cannot mean it! Why, that is like a carte blanche forever! It is unheard of! I would sooner marry you; it would be less expensive.

"Then we do not agree?"

"Absolutely not!"

"What is to be done then?"

Rounceford was beside himself with anger. She was too outrageous in her demands for him to have anything more to do with her. The sooner he could get rid of her the better.

"I will see you home," he replied coldly and prepared to signal his coachman. Before he could rap on the glass, her hand was on his arm.

"You cannot do that! It is too late!" she cried.

"Of course it is not!" he exclaimed in annoyance. "I will have you back in London by midnight. Rest easy!" He reached to the window again. Again her hand stayed his arm.

"And just what do you think Lady Hobcourt will say to

80

you upon learning that you have forced me to accompany you at such a strange hour?''

Rounceford looked at her in astonishment. Very deliberately he lowered the window and called out to his driver, ''Joseph! Rest the horses!''

Immediately the chariot slowed its wild run and soon came to a halt beside the road. Joseph leaned down and asked, ''Shall I walk them, sir?''

''Please do, Joseph.'' He shut the window and turned to Meg. ''Now why in the world would Lady Hobcourt have anything to say when she can know nothing about it? She can hardly be concerned over the doings of a dress-fitter!''

''Oh, but you see, I am her houseguest,'' explained Meg, all sweetness.

''H-houseguest? Hobcourt! You!'' cried Rounceford. ''Who the devil are you, anyway?''

''Meg Miller.''

''Oh, do come off it, Miss Mannering. I think you are better off with 'Mannering'; 'Miller' is in such low taste. Now stop trying to come over me and tell me exactly what Lady Hobcourt's concern is with you. But do not think I shall believe anything you say!''

''It can hardly make a difference now, sir; the damage is done. If it is your wish to believe that I am not who I claim to be . . .'' She shrugged with indifference. ''You may take me home, but it must be to the Hobcourt's, where I am staying—and you must be prepared to accept the consequences.''

''Now, Miss Mannering—''

''Miss Miller, if you please!''

''Very well, then. Miss Miller, pray tell me how you come to be a guest of Lady Hobcourt and yet be employed as a shopgirl.''

''I am not a shopgirl. I will have you know that I am assistant to Madame Celestine.''

"I am impressed no end. It still does not explain your presence at the Hobcourts'!"

"Lady Amelia is sleeping partner to Madame Celestine. I-I wanted to see what it was like—working for wages, that is—and she consented."

Adrian nodded sagely. "I see. That explains it."

For the first time since the mad flight had started, Meg relaxed.

"You understand, then?" she queried.

"Well, not exactly," he replied as he began to puzzle over the part that George had played in foisting Miss Miller upon him. He shook his head. "Are you some poor and distant relation to the Hobcourts? It makes no sense, else."

"I most certainly am not!" cried Meg with indignation. "My connection with the Hobcourts is through my mother. She and Lady Amelia are friends of very long standing."

"And who, may I ask, is your mother, that she should have so high-flying an acquaintance?"

"Lady Elizabeth Miller."

"Oh, now you do it too brown by far! I can imagine that it must be Lady 'Bess' to go with daughter Meg." He laughed.

Meg humoured him and laughed in turn as she remarked, "Yes, and I am sure you will find my father's name as amusing. He is Sir Samuel, and Lady Bess, just as you might think, does call him Sir Sammy on occasion."

Rounceford laughed again. "Very good, very good, indeed, Miss Miller. Sir Sammy Miller—" He came to a stop as a thought not at all to his liking came to him. "Sir Samuel Miller," he pronounced slowly and the blood drained from his face.

Suddenly he turned upon Meg and demanded, in accents completely free of levity and scorn, "Tell me at once! Are you the daughter of The Miller?"

"Yes, he is a miller," replied Meg, puzzled at the

82

sudden intensity of Rounceford's manner.

"Are you his daughter, Sir Sam Miller's daughter?"

"I daresay I must be since he is my father, a fact I have already pointed out!" she retorted, beginning to be irked. "If it will help in any way, I am his eldest daughter."

Rounceford stared at her with pain in his eyes.

"Oh, what have I done!" he exclaimed, clapping his hand to his brow.

"Abducted me, so you have said," Meg responded helpfully.

He turned to her and he appeared distracted. There was a glazed look in his eye.

"Is your father truly The Miller?" It was as though he was begging her to deny it.

"He is a miller. He has been a miller all of his life and I have never heard that he was ashamed to admit it."

"No, no! You do not understand. 'The Miller' is a sobriquet; it means—are you familiar with the cant of pugilism?"

"No."

"Well, a mill is a fight and a miller is a fighter. You see, it is a play on his name—"

"You need not draw me pictures! But what is the point of all this? Pappa is no fighter, he is a lamb—a huge sort of lamb, I must admit—but nevertheless the kindest, gentlest—"

"That may well be how a beloved daughter may see him, but I can assure you the *ton* does not! He is The Miller and with good reason."

"Oh, you cannot be speaking of Pappa. I have never seen him raise a hand—"

"Well, I have and it was a hand I shall never forget. It was at the club, about four years ago. He was just Sam Miller then; a new member. Recommended for membership by Lord Charningham; accepted sight unseen on his lordship's vouching for him—a most unprecedented piece of business. Old Charny was wily as a fox; knew your

83

father hadn't a chance if anyone saw him beforehand. As it was, we were all shocked when we got our first look at him. I shall never forget it!

"There he was, larger than any man had a right to be, and dressed up to the nines, but like a country cousin. Needless to say, everyone snubbed him; and he must have been demmed uncomfortable, but he never let on.

"D'Arbuthnot—you have heard of Tommy D'Arbuthnot?" he broke off to ask.

"No, I have not, but do not stop!"

"Well, Tommy is a corinthian of the first water, a nonpareil if there ever was one. Quite before the world at any sport, an excellent hand with a gun or a sword, fists, too. Trouble with Tommy, he has got a violent temper and one that he has no trouble at all in losing.

"Well, he let it be known that the club was no place for tradesmen and that he, for one, was not going to stand by and let it become one. His opportunity came when, in passing, Mr. Miller brushed against him. Mr. Miller brushes everyone he passes; there just is never enough room for a gentleman of his size.

"Tommy cried out, 'Sir, you have jostled me on purpose!'

"Mr. Miller apologized humbly but disclaimed the intent.

"Tommy retorted, 'Then you call me liar!'

"I saw what Tommy was about and stepped forward to dissuade him. I believed it would be sheer murder for Mr. Miller to have been forced to meet young D'Arbuthnot on the field of honour.

"But your father put up his arm to bar me, and it was like a rock. He looked at me and said, 'Thank ye, son, but this gentleman's quarrel, if that is what he wishes, is with me.'

"He then turned to D'Arbuthnot and said calmly, 'If it's a duel you seek, sir, I will not oblige you. I fear duels and they prove nothing. Since I have already apologized and, too, since I am no hand with weapons, you may consider your honour satisfied and mine destroyed.'

" 'Why, you yellow cur!' snarled Tommy, and he raised his hand for a buffet. As fast as Tommy could strike, your father, for all his great size, was faster. His huge hand flashed out and grabbed Tommy by his shirtfront. Then, with his one hand, Mr. Miller thrust him high up, as far as his arm could reach. It was an astounding display of strength, and that he gave no sign of it being a strain awed us all.

" 'Now, sir, that I have your undivided attention, know this! I am a man of easy temper and will harm none who do not harm me; but you, sir are not mannerly'—he gave him a little shake—'and this is true of all the rest of you gentlemen. Now, I am here, a bona fide member by right, and I will remain one by might, if necessary. You had all best learn to live with that fact.

" 'As for you, sir, praise your god that I have not lost my temper—and if you see fit to send lackeys to horse-whip me, choose only those you can spare, for then I *shall* lose my temper, and after I crack their skulls I shall come for yours!' With that he merely opened his hand, and D'Arbuthnot came crashing to the floor.''

Meg let out a little cry. "My pappa did that? Oh, how bad of him not to have told us!"

"Wait, I have not finished! Mr. Miller was the first to Tommy's side. He picked him up and set him on his feet as though he were a babe. Then, with a worried look in his eye, he asked, 'Did I hurt ye, son? I did not intend it.'

"Tommy just remained motionless, eyes staring and mouth agape—a classic picture of astonishment. Mr. Miller then went on to offer to pay for any damage he might have caused to Tommy's wearing apparel.''

Rounceford was smiling as he finished the tale. Meg, her eyes sparkling and her lips parted in a smile, looked adorable. She touched something within him and he was stirred.

"Pray tell me how it all came out," she begged enthusiastically.

"From that time your father became known as The Miller. Everyone in the club accorded him every respect and most of us came to value him as a colleague and a friend. Some did, perhaps, because they were afraid not to; but most, I believe, because they found him a gentle and easygoing spirit, second to none in generosity, yet shrewd as need be."

"And you?"

"I had never thought I should look up to a miller, but Sir Sam may ask anything of me!"

The warmth of the young man's esteem for her father pleased her immensely.

"Oh, lord!" exclaimed Rounceford, "how can I ever look Sir Samuel in the eye again?"

"Yes, it would be embarrassing after forcing his dear daughter into a life of ill repute!"

"Here now, I never forced you into anything!"

"Then how, pray tell, do I come to be in your chariot, unattended and at such a disreputable hour?"

He gritted his teeth and snarled, "How was I to know you for a gentlewoman? For that matter, what father would permit his daughter to enter upon such a menial life if he had any choice?"

Meg said not a word.

He looked at her intently. "It is apparent, I daresay, that you are in this pickle as deeply as I am. I am willing to wager a monkey that Sir Samuel knows nothing of how you have been spending your time in London." Receiving no response, he pressed on. "I cannot believe that either of your parents are in town with you."

Again Meg said nothing, but she stirred uneasily as though her seat was suddenly too warm.

"Well then," declared Rounceford with smug satisfaction, "There we have it!"

"What do we have?" snapped Meg. "Here we are,

close to midnight, sitting in a chariot heaven only knows where!—and I am hopelessly compromised, not through any fault of mine. How can I have a shred of reputation left after this?"

He gave her a worried look, being sure she would burst into tears next. He sought hurriedly to take her mind off her troubles.

"Well, I am in the same boat, you know. It is not at all the thing to ruin a lady."

To his surprise and relief she giggled. "I daresay you will survive it, however."

He grinned shamefacedly. "How terribly absurd of me! My apologies, Meg; but we *are* in an embarrassing predicament. I cannot think what we are to do about it."

Meg yawned. "Ho-hum, I wish there was someplace we could retire to. I am too exhausted to think clearly. I *have* had quite a day!"

"Yes, I know, and I am sure you will never let me forget it. Well, we cannot tarry here any longer or the horses will go stiff with the cold." He put his head out the window and called, "Joseph!"

"Sir!"

"Let us continue on, but there is a change of plan. We shall not go to my lodgings; instead take us to the Countess."

"But it is so late, sir; surely she'll not be receiving."

"Never mind, it will be all right! We will rouse only Jamieson and he will arrange everything."

"As you wish, sir!"

When he drew back from the window and settled himself down, he saw that his companion was curled up on the seat fast asleep. The chariot started up and he devoted the next few minutes to studying Meg.

She looked so vulnerable lying there that it tugged at his conscience that he should have acted the perfect villain to her. In fact, it was quite a turmoil he had cooked up for the both of them, and the solution to their troubles—the only

87

solution—was nothing he could have wished for. She was charming and, under other circumstances, likely to prove a bit of fun, but his birth was too high to sanction any closer connection. Yet what else was there to do?

He was strongly tempted not to interrupt her repose, but matters could not be left in the condition they were. Something had to be done to extricate themselves from their embarrassment. It was imperative that they agree upon an action that would protect them both from the whiplash of gossip. If it ever came out that Adrian Rounceford had degraded a gentlewoman, he would henceforth be labelled a cad and a rake, and the Rounceford name would ever be pronounced with a knowing leer. As for Meg, no matter how spotless her reputation had been before, her chance of a happy marriage would be dimly remote. If married she would be, no doubt some down-at-the-heels rogue could be induced, for something more than the price of his indebtedness, to tie the knot with her. It was too unsettling to ponder all this unpleasantness by himself. He leaned over and nudged Meg awake.

"Are we there?" she asked sleepily as she sat up rubbing her eyes. She was still very weary.

"No, it is yet some distance; but, before we do get there, we must come to some understanding. Things being what they are, we shall be destroyed if we cannot find some way out of this maze."

"I cannot think! What do you suggest?"

Adrian took a deep breath. "I shall have to marry you."

Meg blinked. Now, she was wide awake. She began to chuckle.

"Miss Miller, this is hardly the time for levity. I must ask that you treat the matter seriously."

Meg began to laugh and Rounceford became angry.

"What in heaven's name do you find so comical?"

"You!" she chortled.

"I am only trying to do what is best for us!"

"I only think it so funny that now, willy-nilly, you must

needs act the hero and change the abduction to an elopement."

Rounceford frowned as he tried to comprehend her meaning; then, as it dawned upon him, he smiled.

"It is ridiculous, is it not?" he acknowledged with a half-smile. "But what would you have? You must agree that marriage is our only hope. I brought it all about, and so I must make amends, whatever the cost. You will have to marry me."

Meg's eyes narrowed a bit.

"*I* do not have to do anything, sir! And I cannot see that I must require so great a sacrifice from *you*! I would not have you—nor anyone—a martyr for my sake."

"What is this talk of martyrs? All I am proposing is a marriage of convenience. In fact, it can be exactly what you yourself demanded."

"I demanded? How dare you say that when I have never discussed marriage with you!" cried Meg.

"You did say that you wished no restraints," countered Adrian. "You expressed yourself as wishing to be free as your fancy might direct—and, oh yes, you were very expensive! Well, it can be true for each of us. After all, that is, in essence, a marriage of convenience."

"No, thank you!" exclaimed Meg with indignation.

"I say, that is being awfully contrary! Those were your terms and I am agreeing to them. It is the least I can do."

"How very correct you are. It is the least you can do, indeed! Do you know, sir, how very insulting you are? My terms! Why, I would not marry you if you were the last man on earth!"

"But-but, what have I said to put you up in the boughs so?"

"This night you have played the fool to perfection. Now, you must needs be the greatest simpleton as well! Had you so much as a ha' penny's worth of brains in your skull, you would know that I was only drawing you on. For you to think for an instant that I could make such demands for such a purpose—why, you must really believe me to be a harlot. I find you insufferably insulting to an extreme!''

Meg terminated her accusation in sobs of anger and huddled in her corner of the seat, as far away from Adrian as the confines of the vehicle would permit.

Adrian was nonplussed. He sat frozen into immobility while he tried to understand what she had found so objectionable in his offer. Why, any other woman, with even greater claims to gentility, would have rushed to accept him, a Rounceford. She should have been honored; yes, and humbly grateful as well, that he should condescend to her to so great an extent. It would have given him the greatest pleasure to have stopped the carriage and put her out on her own; but that, of course, was unthinkable. Things were bad enough as it was and there was still a hope that the situation could be saved. To be accounted an abandoned villain—what would his grandmother, the Countess, say? What would his cousin Marcus say? And Lady Daphne, would she ever speak to him again?

Lady Daphne! He groaned as he thought of Daphne. What a monstrous coil to find oneself enmeshed in. It had only been a lovers' quarrel, soon to be made up. Now, he had put the finishing touch on their love. He could not have Daphne if he married Meg; yet, if he did not, such a decision must make him the loosest fish in Daphne's eyes—not to mention the impossibility of his explaining this escapade in such a way as to gain his fiancée's approval. So there it was! Marry Meg he must!

He looked over at her. She was asleep, a tiny heap from which an occasional sob still escaped. Well, he thought, she is too distraught. A good night's sleep will bring clearer thinking the next day and she will see the uselessness of it all, that she must accept him with good grace. He was sure she was only being coy.

He could not be happy at this way to resolve their

problem and as he settled down to rest, he entertained a faint hope that a less drastic remedy might be found.

The chariot drew up to a large, dark building and came to a halt. It was well after midnight and the only light, other than that of the moon, was provided by the coach lamps.

Joseph rapped on the glass behind him.

"Mr. Adrian, if you will hold the horses, I will seek out Jamieson."

"Vey well, but do not make any noise. I have no wish to rouse the household," Rounceford said as he descended from the carriage and went to the horses' heads.

In a little while, Joseph returned with an elderly man of great dignity which even his attire—nightgown, robe, and cap—did nothing to diminish.

"Ah, Jamieson! It's good to see you. How is the Countess?"

"Very well indeed, sir. But she is not in residence at the moment."

"That is too bad. I had wished to speak with her. Where is she, then?"

"At Bath, sir. She took a sudden notion that the waters here were not on a par with the springs at Bath," remarked Jamieson with a slight smile.

Rounceford smiled back at the old family retainer. They both knew that her ladyship was forever travelling about in a never-ending search for the health which she claimed to lack, but which no physician had, as yet, ever been able to overlook.

"Then the house is closed?"

"Oh, no, Mr. Adrian; the Earl is visiting."

"I begin to understand why the Countess went to Bath. So Cousin Marcus is here. Well, it will be an annoyance to have to put up with him, but it cannot be helped."

He gestured toward the carriage. "I think you had best

91

arrange for one of the womenfolk to attend upon the young lady.''

With no change of expression Jamieson answered, ''Yes, sir. I have already done so. A room is being prepared.''

Rounceford stepped around to the other side of the chariot. When he returned his arms were full of a small, still-sleeping female.

Jamieson stepped forward, his arms outstretched. ''Shall I relieve you, sir?''

''No, it is quite all right. She weighs no more than a feather. Lead on, pray.''

As they proceeded into the building, Adrian bethought himself that the burden in his arms was not at all an unpleasant one. Marrying her might not be all that great of a sacrifice after all. Thinking along such lines, he pressed Meg closer.

She sighed in her sleep and her hand came up to rest lightly on his shoulder.

Chapter Seven

The next morning, as he expected, Adrian encountered his cousin in the breakfast hall, seated at table, quietly perusing a newspaper as he enjoyed a cup of coffee.

"Good morning to you, cousin!" was Adrian's greeting to the young man, whose attire and grooming were impeccable, not a whit less than his own.

"Why, cuz, what a delight for my tired eyes! When did you arrive? I knew you were in London, the last I heard. I cannot conceive how you could leave a warm bed at so early an hour to make the journey here before the day is well begun—nor why!"

"Well, one does what one must when one has to."

"Oh, I say, is that remarkably clever? It sounds witty, but I cannot make heads nor tails of it. If it is, you know, I should like to remember it to use at the club."

"It is a certain thing that your wits have not kept pace with your years," countered Adrian with heat.

"Oh, now that *is* clever, Adrian, old chum! Yes, that one I must remember."

"Leave off! I know you of old. You are trying to get my back up, but you shan't succeed this time. And what brings you here? I had thought you were in Paris. I suppose your pockets are to let again," he concluded with sarcasm.

"I really do not see why you must take that tone with me," replied the Earl of Marchford with mock indignation. "You are in league with Grandmamma, I do believe.

I had no more than put my foot in at the door, than she comes charging down upon me, her walking stick raised on high for all the world like a cavalryman's saber—I swear she uses that demmed weapon for everything but walking—'Not a penny, you rogue! Do you hear! Not a penny shall you have!' she shouts. I ask you, is that a proper way to welcome a cherished grandson? I had only come to inquire after her health.''

Adrian smiled. "Only her health, cousin?"

Marcus smiled in turn. "Well, I was sure she could let me have a century or two. She does have more than she knows what to do with.''

"Hmm! It is just as I thought. Did you get it? If you failed, it will be for the first time."

The Earl looked sheepish. "Yes, I got it all right, but at a price. She let me have a century on the condition that I did not follow her to Bath!''

Adrian gave a shout of laughter and the Earl joined him. They clapped each other on the shoulder and it was moments before their merriment subsided.

Finally Adrian shook his head and said, "Come, cousin, it won't do. I cannot believe that you left your Parisian pleasures merely to bedevil our respected grandparent over a matter of a hundred pounds. I am well aware that when you claim to be without a feather to fly with, it is entirely for our old dame's benefit. I begin to suspect, too, that she enjoys this pecuniary jousting as much as you do. So tell me, what brings you to these parts, eh?"

Marcus smiled. "Ah yes, cousin, it is indeed witless of me to think I can ever lead you up the garden path. I am sure I have never met anyone who is a patch on you for nosing out all my little misdeeds.''

Adrian ignored the remark. "Why have you come?"

Marcus gave vent to an extravagant yawn and slowly crossed one leg over the other as he leaned back in his chair. He lifted up his cup to Adrian and said, "Excellent coffee, old man, truly excellent! Do try some. One must hand it to the old lady; she does everything in great style."

"You are not in any greater trouble than usual, I hope?" Adrian persisted.

"This would be the last place I should come to if I were! It is enough to be read out of the family each time I merely attend her ladyship. Really, Adrian, it is too much! It is I who am the head of the family. How would she like it if I threatened to expel *her* from our illustrious ranks?"

"Like as not you should have to present her with a new stick to replace the one she will have broken across your pate! You know, Marcus, you may as well tell me. You cannot put me off, although I will admit that as you grow older you become ever more skillful at persiflage and evasion."

"Nor can *I* ever forget Cousin Adrian and his persistence on a hot scent. With you, it is ever view halloo and away. I say the coffee is quite good, is it not?"

"To the devil with the coffee! Why have you come?"

Marcus sighed. "Really, Adrian, I had no reason to believe that you would be here—or I should not have come."

"Good God, man! What are you hiding so desperately?"

"You will not laugh?"

Adrian shook his head and looked up to heaven in vexation that was only partly feigned. "No, I shall not laugh."

"I have come back to England to find me a wife."

Adrian stared blankly at his cousin.

"You-you are going to get m-married?" He started to chuckle.

"You promised!" stormed Marcus good-naturedly.

But nothing could stem the torrent of mirth that issued forth from Adrian. "You-you seeking a wife? I will send for a physician, at once. One of us must be out of his head!" And he continued to chuckle while his lordship grinned back at him.

95

"Do I intrude, gentlemen?" asked a cheerful young voice, and Meg stepped into the room. She was looking very well. There was color in her cheeks and her jet-black eyes sparkled to match her gleaming black hair. It was cropped and tightly curled à la titus except for the larger curls falling upon her neck. Her muslin dress was without ornament and high-waisted in the modified Empire look. It was olive green and had the high neck of the current fashion. It was attractive on her, and it was the only dress she had with her.

The eyes of both gentlemen turned as one to focus upon her. They both rose from their chairs and accorded her a bow. Until Adrian spoke she was not perfectly sure which one of them had been her escort—or captor—of the night before.

It was puzzling, even startling, to find two such similar gentlemen. They were of a height; they were of an age; their features bore a marked resemblance; and, at first glance, they could easily be mistaken, one for the other.

"Good morning to you, Meg. How very nice you look. I hope you slept well?"

"Good morning, Mr. Rounceford, and thank you. I am quite refreshed."

"Allow me to present my cousin, Lord Marcus Rounceford, the Earl of Marchford. Marcus, this is my fiancée, Miss Miller."

It was now Marcus' turn to stare; but it was only for an instant. The disbelief in his eyes quickly gave way to scorn, and the laughter which followed was caustic in the extreme.

Meg turned with shock to face her "betrothed." She was out-and-out furious at Adrian's presumption and would have loved to give him a setdown that he would never forget, but the presence of the stranger dictated discretion. As Adrian's affianced, no explanations would be required; whereas, if she were to deny the connection, how could she explain her presence there? It was not in the best of taste that she had gone with him to Tunbridge Wells unchaperoned, but that would call forth only head-shaking amongst the gossips, for engaged couples' departures from what convention demanded were never seriously denounced. And so, though she seethed with anger, she did not gainsay Adrian.

Lord Marcus was exclaiming, "No, no, cousin, I cannot let you get away with a clanker like that! Your fiancée, indeed! And what of Lady Daphne?"

Adrian was plainly uncomfortable. His hand rose to his stock in a nervous gesture. "Lady Daphne and I have come to an understanding not to understand," he muttered.

"And so what must you do, but turn for solace to this—this—"

"Be careful of your tongue, milord. Miss Miller is a lady!"

"Oh, come now!" laughed Lord Marcus. "The next thing you will tell me is that she is some distant connection of Sir Samuel, The Miller, but I have beat you to it."

"His daughter, to be exact," declared Adrian, beginning to fume.

Lord Marcus slapped his knee in glee. "Adrian, you are a card! Really, old boy, there is no need for this flummery. I know that mum's the word; Daphne will never hear of it from me. Now, tell me about this Miller business; is that your story or hers?"

"Gentlemen!" cried Meg, but they ignored her.

"I told you, Marcus, that there is nothing left between Daphne and myself. You may accept it as the truth that I shall wed Miss Miller," Adrian declared in deadly earnest.

"Gentlemen!" cried Meg. Again they ignored her.

"Very well, I shall not contradict you," said Marcus placatingly. "You are going to marry this person; so be it. It is rather sudden, you know; quite shocking, in fact! Tell me truly, who is she?"

"Gentlemen!" cried Meg. The quality of her voice was light. It was not of such strength as to make itself heard over the deep voices of the two men; but the plate she brought crashing down upon the table put a sudden lull to their conversation. Both men stopped and turned to stare at her.

"What's this!" exclaimed Lord Marcus. "Bit of temper, wot! Girl, how dare you interrupt your betters, and in such fashion?"

"My betters have better manners than to ignore a lady, milord!"

Marcus turned to his cousin in indignation. "You shall have to instruct this person in the proper forms of etiquette. She is a forward baggage. Now really, Adrian, you cannot mean to marry this—this—"

"Do not say it, Marchford," interjected Adrian angrily. "I warn you, you have said too much as it is!"

"Well, *I* have not!" declared Meg. "Milord, know this! Had I been prepared to wed Mr. Rounceford, meeting you, his close connection, must have dissuaded me from such a match. As it is, I am not promised to him nor shall I ever be!"

She turned upon Adrian. "You, sir, are as witless as your cousin if that were possible. Your behaviour is even more to be condemned than his!"

"Bravo! Bravo!" cried an elderly lady as she made her way into the room, followed by a blond young lady who was much the same age as Meg. "My very words to both of them on many an occasion!"

"Grandmamma!" exclaimed Lord Marchford.

"Daphne!" cried Rounceford.

"Meg!" cried Daphne and rushed over to her.

"Daphne! Is it really you?" cried Meg, embracing her.

"Well, bless my soul!" exclaimed the dowager Countess of Marchford.

For the next few minutes the breakfast hall was filled to

overflowing with a babble of confused conversation as everyone attempted to satisfy their curiosity. Needless to say, as each individual tried to pursue his or her particular interest, no one, in the uproar, was able to make heads or tails of anything at all, least of all the Countess.

Finding her attempts at gaining anybody's attention foiled, and feeling completely at sea, she immediately took steps to set things to rights. Raising her stick on high, like a majordomo about to announce the presence of a newly arrived guest, she brought it down sharply on the floor. Once! Twice! Thrice! and the sudden silence that followed was indeed marvellous. All eyes were turned upon her.

"Well, that is much better," she declared as she leaned on her stick with both hands. "Marcus, a chair, if you please!"

The Earl of Marchford hurried to comply.

Seated, the Countess shook out and arranged her voluminous skirts. They were of a style current some three decades past. With both hands resting on her cane, she looked about at the young people surrounding her. Her gaze finally came to rest on Meg.

The Countess, a large woman herself, who had often been described as a veritable Juno in her salad days, had no particular sympathy with, and very little patience with, diminutive members of the sex. She had generally found them to be oddly proud about their lack of height and cute to the point of making her ill. It was, therefore, a matter of intense interest to her to behold both of her magnificent grandsons, nonpareils at anything they put their hands to, being held at bay, as it were, by this fiery little female. It was a most unusual sight: nay, she could not recollect when anyone, male or female, had given pause to Marcus. She must know more about this Meg.

"There is a stranger in our midst!" she declared. "How long am I to be kept in ignorance of her?"

Adrian took Meg by the hand and led her up to his

99

grandmother. "A thousand pardons, milady! May I present Miss Meg Miller? Miss Miller is the eldest child of Sir Samuel Miller."

The Earl's eyes opened wide and he flushed crimson.

Her ladyship continued to stare at Meg. "The flour king?" she asked, without turning her head.

"Yes, milady," responded Adrian.

In turn, Meg's deep-set eyes were fixed upon the Countess. She could readily discern that the elderly lady must have been a beauty in her youth and was a woman accustomed to having her own way. Despite her imperious manner and her great age, the Countess' clear blue eyes sparkled with animation and, Meg thought, with a twinkle of humour.

"Well, Miss Miller, what have you to say for yourself? Why were you berating my grandsons so? It is really too bad of you to reduce two such fine gentlemen to the status of abashed schoolboys." And then, leaning forward a little and lifting one hand to shield her mouth from the others, she said, in feigned confidence, "How did you manage it?"

Meg chuckled. Before she could respond to the Countess, Lord Marcus stepped forward and saluted Meg with a bow.

"Miss Miller, I humbly pray that you will accept my most sincere apologies. I beg you will forgive me, although I know how difficult that must be."

Meg returned him a respectful curtsy. "Do not fret, milord, you are easily forgiven. Neither flattery nor scorn from *you* can be of any consequence," she said with a smile.

The Earl of Marchford came erect with a start. He had all the appearance of a man who had been slapped. For a moment he stood and glared down at Meg; then, with a muttered "By your leave" to the Countess, he turned on his heel and left the room.

"Well!" exclaimed her ladyship, "that has done for

Marcus! I do declare I have never seen him so thoroughly set down! Adrian! What is between those two that Miss Miller should find it necessary to affront him so?''

"My cousin merited no less, although the confusing circumstances which led to his odious conduct to Miss Miller may serve as some excuse.''

"Odious conduct from Marcus? I cannot believe my ears! What circumstances?''

"Er—well—'' began Adrian, suddenly become very flustered.

"Oh, never mind, I am sure I shall hear about it eventually. It is a good thing my coach broke down at Sevenoaks, or I should have never witnessed such a sight. To see Marchford put down, and by a female, so gladdens my heart. I am sure it will do the dear boy a world of good.''

Addressing all, she continued, "Now, I am sure that Adrian has much to say to Daphne, who was so kind to carry me back. It was indeed fortunate that she happened to be stopping in Sevenoaks. I do not know what I should have done, else.

"Go along now, and leave me with Miss Miller. I have heard of doughty females—and seen some of 'em, too— but never did I suspect to find one no bigger than my thumb!''

Neither Adrian nor Daphne made a move to comply. Adrian was standing like a stick, looking at her out of the corner of his eye, while Daphne, very pretty in a travelling outfit of a rich blue that matched her eyes, merely tossed her golden curls and became intensely interested in the lace at the end of her sleeve.

The Countess registered surprise. "What have we here? A lovers' quarrel, I do not doubt.''

"Milady, I have something of great importance to—to disclose to you,'' said Adrian.

"How truly fortunate for us all that the failure of my carriage forced my early return! What is it that you have to say?''

"I am pledged to marry Miss Miller!"

There was stunned silence in the room. The Countess stared at her grandson; then she turned her head and looked with incredulity at Meg. Daphne dropped her reticule and remained frozen. Tears welled up in her beautiful eyes and coursed down her cheeks.

"Oh, Meg! How could you!" she cried.

Meg put out a hand in protest. "No, Daphne, it—"

But Lady Daphne, after one heartsick look at Adrian, had fled.

"Well!—well!—well!" breathed the Countess. "I have seen the eighth wonder of the world! What is there about you, Miss Miller, that can put to rout two such proud and formidable persons as are Lady Daphne and Lord Marcus? I should not have believed it possible. I must get to know you better. Indeed, I must!"

"I assure you, milady, I have done nothing great. Your grandsons are, I fear, a pair of fools. Mr. Rounceford, for an instance, is suffering from a misapprehension. If he is truly pledged to wed me, his position must be embarrassing to a degree, for I am not pledged to wed him.

"As for Lady Daphne, I would not distress her for the world. She is a dear, dear friend from my schooldays. I beg you will allow me to go to her and repair the damage our very heavyhanded Mr. Rounceford has caused. Your ladyship is truly not blessed in the grandsons Fate has allotted to you!"

It was one thing for Lady Marcia, Countess Marchford, to disparage her descendants, but never in all her born days had she had to sit by and listen to such scathing remarks pertaining to two of the three young men she cherished above all else.

Meg, taking her shocked silence for assent, went off in search of dear Daphne.

"Wherever did you find her?" gasped the Countess to Adrian, the sole survivor.

"There was a bit of a mistake, you see—"

"A mistake! I should think so! But what is all this nonsense about marriage? You cannot be serious!"

"Unfortunately I am. You see, the—er—mistake was mine. Not that I was all to blame. If she had been what she claimed she was, nothing like this would have occurred!"

Lady Marcia was not only surprised at this making of excuses before ever the worst was known, but she found it hard to accept in Adrian, always correct Adrian.

"I have not the faintest idea of what you are talking about," she remarked.

"I—I—er—I abducted her."

"Yes, I am sure that you did! Now be serious, Adrian; I have enough gammon from your cousin. I do not expect it of you!"

"I am not gammoning you, milady. It is as I say—a foolish escapade on my part, but what would you have? It is done and I must bear the consequences."

"My child, I think you had best tell me everything that has occurred—and after, we shall see what is to be done."

As Adrian came to the end of his tale the Countess regarded him with a stern expression. "I cannot blame her; I cannot blame her at all. I am ashamed of you. Is that any way for a gentleman, one who is of the finest lineage, to behave?

"And for Marcus to rub salt in her wounds—no wonder the little lady was less than gracious. I marvel that she speaks with either of you at all."

Then she chuckled and cocked her head. "Game as they come, ain't she? Imagine haggling with you over terms! Hah! You can count yourself a lucky man if she'll have you on any terms.

"Well, we must see to it that knowledge of this scrape goes no further. It may be too late, but we must do what we can."

Since Adrian had already given his mind to the question

103

and come up with no better answer than that he must marry Meg, he did not have great hopes that his grandmother could do better. Lady Marcia, on the other hand, having been in the forefront of society for years, was well aware of what a bit of bluff and daring might accomplish.

"It is not so very difficult to arrange," she declared after a moment's thought. "She shall have had to be my houseguest. Ran into her in London and insisted she come back with me to Tunbridge Wells. Would not be denied the pleasure of her company. Message to the Hobcourts' delayed—you can think of some reason. There, that should cover it!—whether anyone believes it or not. Be up to you to shut the mouth of Sir George. Never cared for the fellow. This is what comes of keeping bad company."

"Never fear! I will attend to Hobcourt."

"Well then, it is settled! She has released you from your pledge; and, as my houseguest, with any luck at all our several reputations should be quite safe. You know, I think that I shall enjoy her stay with us.

"There is no need for you to attend me any longer. I am sure you have some explaining to do to Daphne. I should do so without delay."

"Yes, you are quite right. I do hope that the matter is quite settled and that we shall hear no more about it."

He took his leave and left the room.

Meg had had her fill of the Rouncefords; and, as she passed through the rooms in search of Lady Daphne, she quite made up her mind that she wanted no more of them. She felt that of two such striking gentlemen, as Mr. Rounceford and Lord Marchford were, it was shameful that the former should be so harebrained and the latter so insolent. It remained for her to make her peace with Daphne and then to quit the presence of the Rounceford family just as soon as she could. She was not overly worried about what might be thought of her flight from London. Before she ever got back to Harlington—for it was her decision to return to her family—she was sure she would think of some reason to cover her absence.

She felt a sense of disappointment after having made up her mind. As silly as the abduction had been, her captor had not been without charm, nor had the drive down been all that unpleasant. Rather, it was his air of desperate sacrifice as he made the offer of marriage that had quite set her teeth on edge and made her quiver with anger.

When she finally discovered Daphne, it was a strange scene she beheld. In a small salon, she found her erstwhile schoolfellow clinging to Lord Marcus, her blond head on his shoulder, sobbing as though she could never stop. Lord Marcus did not appear to be at all annoyed that his jacket—a marvel of exquisite French tailoring—was being ruined by its being bathed in a freshet of feminine tears. His arms held Daphne close as he murmured words of comfort in her ear.

Lord Marcus saw Meg as soon as she saw him, and sprang back quickly from Lady Daphne's embrace, an irritated look on his face.

Daphne gasped, looked about to see who had disturbed them, and turned away blushing deeply. She brought her handkerchief up to her face in a vain attempt to hide her rosy cheeks.

"I hope I have not intruded . . ." began Meg inanely. She had some hope that conventional civility might help her to get over the embarrassing and hostile atmosphere emanating from the room's two occupants.

"I believe I speak for Lady Daphne, Miss Miller," declared Lord Marcus with overt malice, "when I assure you that you *have*. However, you can easily make amends by withdrawing at once!"

Meg's eyes glittered with anger. "You Rouncefords are an insufferable lot!" she shot back.

Lord Marcus stiffened. Very coldly he stated, "You forget your place, Miss Miller!"

"I think not! Indeed, I should be eternally grateful to you—or anyone—if you can say exactly what my place is!"

"Oh, come now, there is no need for these histrionics. You have, it appears, been quite successful in your campaign to trap my cousin into betrothing you. Exactly how you managed it, I cannot say, but Adrian has fallen mightily in my esteem if the truth be known," he said, staring at her through his lorgnette with emphatic disapproval.

Resting her chin upon her left hand, which she supported at the elbow with her right hand, Meg gazed at Marchford appraisingly. A tight smile played across her features.

"I begin to think that it is inconceivable for a Rounceford male to believe that he is not the cynosure of any and all females. You, milord, cannot understand that, with regard to your cousin's avowal to marry me, I have not asked for it nor have I consented to it. To put a point on it, the very name of Rounceford has become anathema to me. Can I make myself any clearer than that?"

Lord Marchford's lorgnette dropped out of his hand to dangle at the end of its ribbon. He stared at her in astonishment.

Lady Daphne gasped. "Meg, you cannot be serious! Surely Adrian would not have said"—she interrupted herself—"but, then, how come you to be here? I—I do not understand! What *is* between you and Adrian?"

Meg answered in very dry tones, "Your lately dearly-devoted wished to confer the honour of becoming his light o' love upon me and so he abducted me."

Again Lady Daphne gasped. "Adrian? Never!"

"What balderdash is this?" demanded Lord Marcus. "It is my cousin you defame, Miss Miller!"

"Of that I am very much aware. The family resemblance is too marked to mistake," retorted Meg.

"I cannot believe it of Adrian," protested Daphne.

Marcus continued in a tone of menace, "I will have you

know my cousin is a gentleman. He would never so insult or so impose upon a lady."

"No, indeed!" confirmed Daphne, now quite indignant.

"Well, that was part of the trouble," admitted Meg ruefully. "I—I was not known to him—as Miss Miller."

"Oh?" exclaimed Marcus, all curiosity.

"What do you mean?" demanded Daphne.

"Well, that is neither here nor there. He made a most outrageous offer to me—and he would not believe me, at first, when I made myself known to him. By the time he came round, it was too late. I was hopelessly compromised."

"Oh, God! You do not mean to say . . ." cried Daphne.

Meg laughed. "No, you need have no fear on that score, my dear, not but it will make no difference to the gossips."

"You are doing us too brown, girl! We Rouncefords are more considerate than that! Adrian would never have—"

"Are you really? Then how do you account for your very recent apology to me if it was not over the very same thing. *You* could not accept Adrian's word—your own cousin and a Rounceford, do not forget—you could not accept his word as to my identity."

"Oh, I say, that is unfair!" protested Lord Marcus. "I thought he was bamming me. I thought you were—er—that is—I—I . . ." His eyes glazed over as he realized that to continue would only result in further self-condemnation.

"Milord, I wish to speak with Lady Daphne. Your presence has now become distinctly *de trop*, *n' est-ce pas*?" said Meg very sweetly.

Daphne said in a little voice to Meg, "Oh, how shocking of you, dear! I see you have not changed a bit!"

Lord Marcus, decidedly pink of face, made a little bow. "With your permission, ladies," he said and strode stiffly from the room.

"Oh, Meg, Meg, can you never learn to control your tongue? What must Lord Marcus think of you!" exclaimed Daphne, coming over to her friend with a giggle and an embrace. "But, pray, do tell me about this—this absurd business. You *were* bamming us, were you not?"

Meg smiled and looked deeply into Daphne's eyes. "Is it true? Are you and Adrian to make a match of it?"

Daphne looked down and blushed. "We—we had a quarrel. It was not important, but he became so stuffy about it that I sent him walking. But truly, Meg," she implored, placing her hand on her friend's arm, "he can be quite charming most of the time. It is just that he can be so wrongheaded at other times that I quite lose my patience with him."

Meg shook her head and sighed. "I do not think you will find my story amusing, then. I had best leave. I am sure my welcome here is nigh threadbare by this time."

"Oh, Meg, you must tell me, please—and you cannot think of leaving until you do."

"What I have to say you will not believe, my dear. Surely it is enough for you to know that I have no designs upon Adrian. You may have him—if you must—but I would not be your friend if I let you think I approved of your choice."

Daphne frowned. "Now that is too much! You might have said less, but having said as much, you must say more!"

"Very well, then. Since you insist . . ." And Meg recounted the tale of her adventure with Adrian to Daphne.

Daphne's face was buried in her handkerchief and she was weeping bitterly by the time Meg wearily brought her story to an end. It was minutes before her efforts at consolation made appreciable inroads upon her friend's torrential outpourings.

Her patience at an end, Meg finally said, "Truly, Daphne, there is no call for all this lamentation. I appreciate your concern for me, but, except for a little wear and tear and the smell from that horrid sack upon my clothes, I am unscathed, I do assure you."

"Oh, it is not that!" wailed Daphne. "That—that Adrian could be so—so fickle! It was such a little quarrel—and for him to rush into your arms—I hate him!"

Meg was startled. She looked at the bowed blond head and could not repress a chuckle. "My dear, I do not think you have quite got the right of things." She threw up her hands. "Oh, well, it makes no matter. Come, come, Daphne; you will have red eyes and swollen cheeks if you continue on in this way."

The admonition had all the effect needed. Daphne's tears ceased as she rushed over to the pier-glass to study the ravages her sorrow had wrought.

"That's better, dear. Here, let me help you. Your hair. Yes! Now, smile! Ah, charming!" And Daphne beamed. She could not help but do so upon seeing Meg, her eyes dancing merrily, standing before her with her dark head cocked, reaching out a skillful little hand to deftly coax the golden curls back into place.

A little frown gathered on Daphne's brow. "But, Meg, what are we to do? What are *you* to do?"

"I shall leave, and quickly. My taste for the Rouncefords has long since been satisfied."

"Oh, do take me with you! Please do! I—I never want to see *him* again!"

"Well, really, my dear, I can hardly take you with me. I have no carriage. But wait! You have one! Perhaps you had best take *me* with *you*!"

"That is a splendid idea! I will inform Lady Marcia—"

"Do not be such a silly goose! If we are to leave, we had best do so now, without a word to anyone."

"But, Meg, darling, that would be rudeness unforgiveable!"

"Oh, I daresay there will be a bit of a to-do when they discover us gone—but do you wish *him* to be escort. Surely you must realize that one, or probably both, of the Rounceford gallants will insist on accompanying us—and," continued Meg with a sharp look in her eye, "I would be spared Adrian's importunities about the necessity of his marrying me to save my good name."

"Oh, yes!" agreed Daphne vehemently—and then she paused as a thought struck her. "But what about that, Meg? How will you explain—"

"Silly! we ran into each other in town and went for a drive in the country in your carriage which broke down—and, after it was repaired we decided to visit my people in Harlington. Yes, it was very thoughtless of us not to let Lady Hobcourt know, but is not that the way with such scatterbrain girls as we are?"

Daphne giggled as she nodded enthusiastic agreement.

Chapter Eight

Lemmy Peterskin rubbed the black bristles on his chin as he studied the greasy, rumpled sheet of foolscap in his hand once again. Slowly he began to shake his head in disgust. All this fuss over a mort, and a wee mort at that, was beyond his ken. That she was the daughter of Sir Sam Miller, of course, made a difference; and that a £500 reward was posted for information leading to the discovery of her whereabouts made a difference that was particularly interesting to him.

But it was beyond belief that he, the great Lemmy, Bow Street's master thief-taker, should have been assigned to find and bring in a young and wealthy gentlewoman. What had he to do with eloping females? And, if that was not enough, the strict instructions regarding his behaviour, if he were successful in his search, were more than enough. It made him think back to his life as a sergeant in His Majesty's regiments with longing. If the army would have him, he'd go back in like a shot. But the grievous wounds he had suffered during the campaign that led to Waterloo had brought that career to an abrupt and final end, as it almost had to his very existence.

He began to fume as he read, once again, that he might not molest or physically restrain aforesaid female in any manner. He must, instead, inform the young lady of her father's concern and then persuade her to accompany the runner back to Harlington.

Who ever heard of ''such flap-sauce bein' served up to a

cove as kens his lay as well as me?'' he spat savagely as he recalled his argument with his magistrate. It had been long and heated, but it had been to no avail. He was given his orders and told to march!

He had marched, but he still could not see what all the fuss was about. From what he had learned during his preliminary investigation of her disappearance—he had spent most of a long night at it—it could be nought else but an elopement.

A hackney had witnessed her being enfolded in the arms of a tall flash cove, whisked into a spanking chariot with nary an outcry, upon which said vehicle had dashed off like the wind. It had been no trouble to trace its wild career through the streets of London and learn that it had headed south. Aye, that weakened the elopement theory, for Gretna Green was in the opposite direction. He had thought at first that the vehicle would ultimately circle about, but that had not been the case. Comparing notes with tollkeepers soon proved that the carriage was truly headed south, and that fact caused him some hope that a violent crime was intended. The possibility that the case might yet develop to the point where his major talents would be called for was encouraging.

As an old cavalryman, it required small exertion on his part to follow the trail a goodly distance. It led him to Tunbridge Wells before it disappeared. He concluded that his quarry had gone to earth somewhere in the vicinity and assured himself, at the same time, that the young lady would not be discovered in the pristine condition she was reputed to be in before she decided to elope.

Well, that, at least was not his worry; but he did hope that the reward would not be any the less for that eventuality.

It was fairly early in the morning when he stepped out of the doorway of the inn where he had stopped to break his fast. The low winter sun did a deal less to warm him than did the potful of ale laced with rum he had recently imbibed. He mounted up and slowly walked his horse out on to the high road.

As he plodded along, trying to make up his mind as to just how he would conduct his search, he was disconcerted by the odd thought that the young lady, for all he knew, might even now be back at the Hobcourts' in London. After all, she had not been gone above a few hours before Bow Street had been bombarded with all sorts of requests and orders concerning her. It annoyed him considerably to think that he might have lost a night's sleep in a warm bed for what could turn out to be a mere fool's dance. With a sound that was something between a growl and a grunt, he settled himself in the saddle and urged his horse on.

The road to Tunbridge Wells led south out of Tunbridge, and on this cold, crisp morning there were not a great many people using it. In fact, there was but one gentleman rider and he appeared to be in no great hurry to arrive at his destination.

Sir Arthur Winstock, K.C.B., late of the Royal Horse Guards (the Blues) had within the past week sold out his commission as major in the corps, and was now on his way to visit his family seat. It had been some years since his last visit; and, if he did not have need of counsel of an intimate nature, this particular trip might have been postponed for, perhaps, another decade. Although he was the youngest member of his family group and less wealthy than any of them, he was not indigent, or he could never have afforded his commission in one of the most expensive cavalry regiments in the kingdom. The problem, then, that was occupying most of his waking hours was not of a financial nature.

As he travelled along, he experienced a compelling desire to discuss his affairs with someone. Many times in the past, especially when standing lonely picket duty for his decimated command at some godforsaken post near the Belgian border, he had found it necessary to pass the hours in conversation. It was, indeed, fortunate for him that Cleo made an ideal partner. She was a brilliant conversationalist in that she never interrupted him; and when she did have something to contribute, her comments never consisted of more than a soft whinny or a snort, the sort of thing that one did not have to spend too much time thinking about.

"Cleo, old girl," he began. His mount's ears pricked up at the sound of her name and he was encouraged to proceed, now that he was assured of her attention. "I daresay you believe that I owe you an explanation for dragging you away from your comfortable stall to embark upon a new life fraught with uncertainty. Well, I shall tell you what it is.

"You see, the last five years have been a bloody bore! Playing soldier in the heart of London—all those ceremonies with their fancy parades and formations—never once a blood-tingling charge! Never once the slash and parry of a furious engagement! Devil take it, the Park was the only place we could stretch our legs! And even there, for the crush of lady equestrians and doddering old bucks, little more than a canter and you would be cursed for a reckless ruffian. That is not for us!

"The Frenchies were thrashed; Napoleon will not be given a third chance—and that's too bad for a lad like me—for if there is to be no more action, then I had best settle down and make the best of things as they are—and that, certainly, does not admit of prancing in full dress before the London mobs. The pretence is more painful to me than the complete denial, and so I have elected to quit it without regret, find me a wife, and begin my family. What say you to that, Cleo?"

The mare nodded her head up and down vigorously and let out a soft whicker. Her response was noted and approved.

"Good girl! You have good sense. I have always known that you have more than oats between your ears;

114

and that is what I must find in a wife. She must have sense, and, too, I would have her sensible. I want no termagant, but one whose heart I can win. If she be a beauty, I shall not object; but it really is not all that necessary, so long as her appearance is not exceptionable. That should not be too difficult to find in a young lady, I think. The devil of the matter is that I do not know where to begin.

"I will not have a London belle; they are too much before the world for my taste. Perhaps she awaits me in Bath—for that matter, Tunbridge Wells will do as well and, since my connections are there, it is as good a place to start as any. There, I shall have entrée into the best families. So there you have it!"

Having finished his soliloquy, Sir Arthur became sensible of the cold.

"Br-r-r!" He shuddered. "This crystalline air is beginning to frost my bones! Let us make speed to see my aunt, so that we may take our ease and consult with her concerning the local beauties."

With that he eased his reins slightly and the charger, ever eager, broke into an easy canter. The landscape began to slip past, and both rider and mount seemed to partake of the exercize as though it were a special treat.

They had not been travelling five minutes when Sir Arthur brought Cleopatra to a halt. He stood up in the saddle and stared hard down the road.

He could make out a small group of people at the bend, a quarter mile off. A male figure, with one hand on the bridle of a horse upon which was seated a colorfully appareled female, appeared to be making threatening gestures with his free hand.

It was enough for Major Winstock. He touched Cleo with his spurs. "Charge!" he whispered, and down the road they flew. Cleopatra had lived the past five years for just such a command. The canters in the Park and the restricted gaits of town ceremonials were never to her liking. She was a charger, bred to go at a great clip into the smoke and peril of battle. It had been far too long since she had last been ordered into the fray and she was ready for it. The pace she set ate up the distance to their objective in less time than it takes to tell.

With a firm tug on the reins, the Major brought his mare to a flamboyant stop, her eyes blazing, her forefeet pawing the air, the classic picture of a horse at war.

"What the devil is going on here!?" demanded the Major.

"Oh, please help me!" cried the young lady as she tried to fend off a burly, black-whiskered rogue from taking the reins of her well-set-up gelding.

"Never you mind, sir! 'Tis no business of yours!" exclaimed the fellow roughly.

"Then you are quite mistaken, for I have made it my business. Now leave off at once or you will have me to deal with!" commanded the Major sharply as he dismounted and carelessly tossed the reins over Cleopatra's neck. She made no attempt to wander off, but moved in closer to him, so that her mouth brushed his shoulder.

"That be a fine horse ye have, guv'nor, but I must warn ye! This be official business and you interferes at yer peril!" declared Black Whiskers, standing before the Major in a defiant attitude.

Sir Arthur looked him up and down. The man broached six feet in height and was obviously no weakling. In his belt he carried a truncheon, which he now began to finger. The Major was not above average height, somewhat small for a crack cavalry officer, but he was lithe and the well-tailored cut of his clothes did not disguise the fact.

"Then you will have credentials of some sort to show me, I believe."

Black Whiskers nodded and began to struggle through the wool scarf wrapped in a great many turns about his neck. After some difficulty he was enabled to reach into his jacket and secure his grubby wallet. He opened it up

116

and thumbed through a sheaf of dogeared papers, finally selecting one and presenting it to the Major for his inspection.

The Major accepted it and began to peruse the document.

"So, it is Bow Street, is it?" He looked at the runner sharply. "Peterskin, eh? Did you have a relation at Quatre Bras?"

"That I did not—and I should know, for I was there meself. It did for me, too. A Frenchie swiped at me cockloft, but got me in the shoulder instead. 'Twere enough to put me out of the service; but 'tis fine now exceptin' fer a mite o' stiffness, now and again." And he swung his arm about to demonstrate its healthiness.

Sir Arthur continued to stare at him in an interested manner. "Then you must be—"

But Peterskin was off again deep into his memories. "Corporal-major I were, and fer the finest fighting capting you ever did see. I tell ye, he was 'Old Nosy' hisself, for all he was a little feller—like you, sir. He had a horse like yourn, too, but it had an outlandish name. 'Cleo,' he called her."

On hearing her name, Cleo came up close to Peterskin and let out a soft whinny as she nudged at him.

Peterskin's hand went up of its own volition to pat her nose and she gave another little whinny.

"Cleo, do it be you?" he cried and he gave her a hug. Excitedly he turned to Sir Arthur. "Guv'nor, this be the horse! I swear it! The very horse!"

The Major chuckled. "You dimwitted featherbrain! Of course, it's Cleo! And just who in blazes do you think *I* am?"

Peterskin turned from making over the mare to peer at Sir Arthur. "I cain't rightly say, guv'nor, but the voice is awfully familiar."

"I should think so! Are you blind? Whatever is the

matter with your eyes that you do not recognise me, Lem? The finest corporal-major of the Blues and he doesn't recollect his commander! For shame!"

"Capting, sir? Be it really you? Aye, I collect ye, sir! It's just that me winkers ain't what they used to be."

"I can believe that, Corporal-major!"

"Sir!" shouted Peterskin, coming to attention and throwing a perfect salute.

Sir Arthur laughed. "Be at ease, friend! We are no longer in the Corps, either of us. God, it does me good to have found you at last! I have been looking for you for years. Why did you not await my return—"

"I beg your pardon," broke in a sweet feminine voice, "but it is cold and I—"

"A thousand pardons, ma'am!" exclaimed Sir Arthur, doffing his hat and bowing deeply. "Allow me to introduce myself. I am Major Sir Arthur Winstock, late of His Majesty's Blues. How may I serve you?"

He looked up at her as she sat gracefully at ease in her saddle. He found himself being contemplated by a pair of large, clear, violet eyes. The face from which they peered was no less lovely, being oval and framed in a wealth of brown hair that made her tiny beaver hat appear like a vessel tossed upon a shiny sea of brown. The phrase "breathtaking vision of loveliness" had never before seen use by Major Winstock, but now it began to resound through his mind in endless refrain. He could have kicked himself for not having paid attention to her sooner. He jumped to take her horse's bridle out of Peterskin's hand. "My most abject apologies for not having waited upon you before this!"

"Major Winstock, thank goodness you happened along! This—this person insists upon my coming with him. He is terribly mistaken. I am not—could never be— this Meg Miller"—she enunciated the name with distaste—"whoever she may be. I have told him that I am

118

Lady Honoria Dalrymple, but he will not believe me! It is very upsetting to be so accosted."

"I am sure of it, milady. Give me a few moments and all will be remedied. Have no fear. I know him well for a fine old soldier."

He addressed the runner. "Now then, Lemmy, what is this all about? Why are you annoying the young lady?"

" 'Tis me duty, sir! Me orders is to find the young lady and purs-purs—I'll have it in a jiffy!" He dived into his bulky muffler once again and resurrected his wallet. He quickly found the document he required and after shaking it open, he peered closely at it. "Ah, there 'tis—'persuade her to return to her father'! There be a spankin' reward fer the sarvice!"

"Who is her father?"

"Sir Sam Miller, sir!"

"Oh, that Miller! But this lady claims to be Lady Dalrymple!"

Peterskin winked at his former commander. "What she claims and what she is needn't be the same thing. But rest easy, sir, I'll have the truth out of her."

"Well, before you begin, let me inspect your orders."

Peterskin handed the document to the Major, who began to examine them with care. As he read on he would, now and again, raise his head to study the young lady. When he had finished his examination of the papers, he was smiling broadly.

"Milady, I hope I shall not trouble you if I request that you dismount. It will help to clear up matters."

Peterskin took the bridle from the Major, who went to assist Lady Honoria. She slipped so easily out of the saddle that the Major's assistance, which consisted of catching her in his arms, was highly questionable as to its necessity; not that either of them appeared to regard it. For a moment they stood in each other's arms until the lady, blushing, disengaged herself. The Major appeared to be

119

discomposed and covered the sudden wave of emotion that swept through him with a laugh.

Turning to Peterskin, he asked, "Well, does Lady Dalrymple fit the description?"

Peterskin scratched his head and sighed. "She ain't no wee mort. I does beg yer pardon, yer ladyship. I was only trying to do me duty."

"How you could be so mistaken, I shall never know!" declared the Major. "Milady's stature is just right, not unbecomingly short. Her hair is not black, but a lustrous brown. And her eyes, Peterskin, note her eyes! They are not black, but are of a heavenly shade of violet. In short, old friend, she is quite a dream and could never be anything so prosaic as a 'Meg Miller.' Surely you can appreciate how exactly fitted is the name Honoria to milady. Do you not agree?"

Peterskin merely looked at the Major and grinned. Lady Honoria moved uneasily, trying for an appearance of unconcern.

"There, then that is settled! Milady, allow me," said the Major. He turned to her and made a step with his hands.

She thanked him and permitted herself to be remounted.

"It will be my pleasure to see you safely home," offered Sir Arthur.

"I do not wish to trouble you. You have been more than kind to me, a perfect stranger, already."

"Then you must be kind in turn and allow me this pleasure."

She gave him a lovely smile of consent, and the Major turned from her to his mount. Once up on Cleo, he called to Peterskin, whom he discovered moving off the road into the thicket that bordered it.

"Corporal-major! I have not dismissed you!"

Peterskin came scurrying back and stood at attention at the Major's stirrup.

"Lem, I have sold out the service and I am at loose ends for the moment, but I have need of you. I promised you before you received your wound that if we were ever parted, it should not be through any fault of mine. Now that I have found you, I would have you take my shilling. I may not be able to offer you as much adventure as Bow Street—although chasing after fallen wenches is not my idea of a cavalryman's duty—"

"Begging your pardon, sir, but there's some as may disagree wi' ye!" remarked Peterskin with a broad grin.

Lady Honoria turned her head away to hide a smile.

Sir Arthur grinned, too, even as he shouted, "Silence in the ranks!"

"Well, how say you, Lemmy?" asked the Major.

"Ah, sir!" cried Lemmy, his eyes alight with pleasure. Then his face fell. "But, Major, sir, I cannot take yer shillin' just yet. You wouldn't want me to quit in the middle of a fight—er—that is, I have me orders, sir! You'll understand."

"You mean this Meg Miller business, I take it?" Peterskin nodded.

"Well, then, let us see Lady Dalrymple home safely first, then you can tell me all about the Miller case—and we will turn our talents to it, you and I. Yes, that should be quite interesting, I think. After we have cracked it, I will arrange to have you mustered out. Will that arrangement be agreeable to you?"

"Sir!" shouted Peterskin, once more coming to stiff attention.

"Well, then, Corporal-major!" barked Sir Arthur.

"Sir!"

"Mount up!" commanded the Major.

Lady Honoria, who was vastly entertained by the ongoing exchange between the two men, was startled to hear the order. The only horses available were the Major's horse and her own mount. She became flustered at the

121

question of whose mount was about to be shared with the rough fellow.

An ear-splitting whistle from Peterskin and a responsive grin on the Major's face quickly put her fears to rest.

A crashing about in the underbrush heralded the approach of a large creature, and out from the thicket broke into view a fully accoutered mount. It was a beautiful steed, quite the equal of Major Winstock's Cleo. A slashing scar marred the perfection of the well-groomed stallion's flank. It must have been a grievous wound, and caused one to wonder how the animal had managed to survive it.

"King Willie, as I live and breathe!" cried the Major.

"Right you are, sir!" said Peterskin with a grin as, despite his big frame, he effortlessly mounted. "Old Will and me—dismissed the service at the same time for the same cause. We might not be all the crack on parade, but we gets along."

The Major laughed. There was something so satisfying in the picture that Peterskin on King William presented that Lady Honoria smiled, too.

"Corporal-major, ten paces to the rear!"

"Sir!" And, grinning with delight, Peterskin fell behind.

"Now, milady, we are at your command," said the Major gallantly, and they moved off at a walk.

Lady Honoria was more than pleased, now that the impasse with the Bow Street runner was got over, to have such a handsome and dashing gentleman escort her home. She was intrigued with his cheery manner and the way it contrasted so with the unflinching austerity he demonstrated when acting the iron military man.

With her he was completely at ease; and, after some few minutes of riding alongside each other, exchanging commonplace pleasantries, she was surprised at her own relaxed feelings in his company. Being a beauty, she had never had to exert herself to any extent to attract the attention of young gallants, nor had she ever experienced a wish to do so, but Major Winstock affected her strangely, indeed.

She put herself out to be pleasant to him. In fact, she attempted to be charming beyond anything she had ever been before, and was very happy to observe that the effect upon the Major was all she could have wished.

In turn, Sir Arthur was sure that never before in his experience had he encountered so lovely, so delightful a girl—and he believed himself to be a great judge of feminine beauty and charm.

The result was easily calculated. They succeeded in bewitching each other to such good purpose that not twenty minutes later they each were sure that they had met their partner for life. But having so recently become acquainted, and knowing so little about each other's background and prospects, a certain natural caution prevailed between them.

The bantering that they indulged in was going along at a great rate when a travelling carriage, fully equipped with two footmen and four ponderously powerful Clydesdales, slowly passed them headed north. Feeling full of fun and drunk with giddy romance, he called out to Peterskin, "Hi, Lemmy! Yon coach may contain your quarry!"

Peterskin responded with a "Ho!" and whirled King Willie about; then, shouting "Charge!" he was off in a thundering rush of hoofbeats after the coach.

The footmen, seeing this wild madman charging down upon them in the best cavalry style, immediately raised up loaded fowling pieces and let fly at him. Peterskin's hat was whipped off, but it in no way slowed him up.

He shouted, "Halt, there! King's business, dammit!"

Sir Arthur groaned. "Oh, lord! Now, we are in for it. I did not intend for him to take me at my word. Excuse me,

123

milady." And he, too, whirled his horse about and charged after his henchman.

"Cease fire, you rogues! Lemmy, break off and return! At once! That's an order!" he shouted.

The coachman applied his whip to his horses; but they, like the coach, were built for endurance not for speed. The only effect was to shake the vehicle until the footmen had all they could do to hang on, much less reload.

Still shouting, "The King's business!" Peterskin came up to the leaders and gradually brought them to a standstill.

The Major came up with a rush and quickly dismounted. He stepped over to the great carriage and drew open the door.

"Ladies, do not be frightened, I beg you. A mistake has been made by my groom; he has overreached himself."

Even as he spoke, he could see that there were three passengers within, all women. One by reason of her drab appearance he judged an abigail. The other two were gentlewomen, both young; one a strikingly opulent blonde, the other a dainty but vibrant brunette. The blond young lady was a beauty, but at the moment quite fearful. The little brunette appeared unafraid and was regarding him with a stern look from her flashing dark eyes.

"Allow me to introduce myself. I am Sir Arthur Winstock, and I hasten to reassure you that no harm was intended."

By this time Peterskin had come up and was staring in at the young ladies. He nudged the Major, who ignored him.

"Please accept my regrets for this untoward incident. If there is any way I can make it up to you, you have only to ask."

"We will ask no more of you, sir, than that you shut the door and allow us to proceed—and, Daphne, don't you dare to swoon!" cried the dark-haired girl.

"Pst! Capting—I mean Major, sir!" whispered Peterskin so loudly that the ladies in the coach could hear

Here's Max.

The maximum 120mm cigarette.

Great tobaccos. Terrific taste.
And that long, lean,
all-white dynamite look.

"Max, I can take you anywhere."

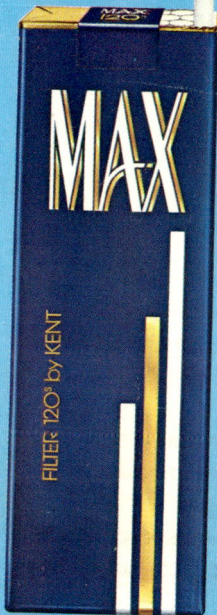

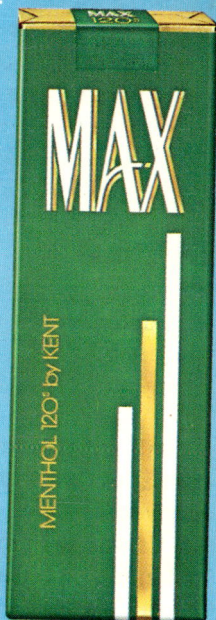

MAX

FILTER 120's by KENT

MAX

MENTHOL 120's by KENT

© Lorillard 1976

After all I'd heard I decided to either quit or smoke True.

I smoke True.

King Regular: 11 mg. "tar", 0.6 mg. nicotine;
100's Menthol: 13 mg. "tar", 0.7 mg. nicotine
av. per cigarette FTC Report Nov. 1975.

The low tar, low nicotine cigarette.

© Lorillard 1976

him quite plainly. "If that ain't the wee mort, Meg Miller, I—I'll eat King Willie!"

"You may inform King Willie he need have no fear. I *am* Meg Miller. How do you come to know me?" asked Meg pleasantly.

Chapter Nine

Sir Arthur Winstock stood transfixed. Not for a moment, when he had promised to assist Peterskin in his search, had he believed that they would be successful. He had thought that they would jaunt about the countryside for a respectable period of time, looking here, making inquiries there. He did not doubt that, in the very near future, the missing heiress would turn up married—or otherwise—and the matter would no longer be the concern of Bow Street.

He could not have been more astonished to find the object of their quest so quickly and in so unprecedented a manner. He was completely confounded, and to add to his confusion he could see that the young lady in question was no hoydenish scapegrace. It was beyond his imagination to expect it from a miller's daughter, but she was as cool and poised as would do credit to one of greater age and nobility than she had any claim to. For some moments he remained silent, not knowing how to proceed.

Meg smiled at him. She sensed his embarrassment, but did not understand its cause. He was a pleasant-looking gentleman, undeniably handsome in fact.

She found him interesting at first sight and would have liked to become acquainted with him. But at the moment, the prospects were not too brilliant. As long as he was going to stand with one foot on the step in stunned silence, neither their acquaintance nor her journey would get any further. She decided to begin the exchange.

"Sir, I do not know what business you have with me, but allow me to present my friend, Lady Daphne Colworth, whose carriage I share. Now, pray tell me exactly why you have interfered with our journey."

"Er—Miss Miller, you must realize that you have been discovered, and I must ask you to accompany me," explained Sir Arthur, feeling slightly uncomfortable under her inquiring gaze.

Miss Miller continued to look at him for a moment before she asked, "Why in the world should I?"

"You have been the object of a search by Bow Street."

"How amazing! Are you then a Bow Street runner? I had not thought to find one so respectable!"

Major Winstock laughed. "No, no; you mistake me. *I* am not a runner. It is my groom that is."

"Why, that is even more marvellous! Is this a new craze amongst men of fashion, to have a runner for a groom?"

"No, indeed! He was my—but that is a long story and we are wasting time." He turned to Peterskin. "I do not know why I should conduct the business when it is your responsibility. Carry on, Corporal-major!" With that he stepped back to make room for Peterskin to approach.

The runner drew himself up into his concept of an official attitude and drew near.

"Miss Miller, I be from Bow Street, name of Peterskin, not Peter-skin. I'm the heir, not the hide, if you foller me."

Meg laughed. "Oh, yes, I do! How awfully clever! You know I have never met a Bow Street runner before. I am absolutely fascinated. It must be very dangerous work and you must be very brave."

Peterskin floundered. No one was chummy with runners, especially not the people they were sent to apprehend. He had never encountered the like before and he was completely at a loss. He fell back a step and looked askance at the Major. The latter grinned back at him encouragingly.

"Ma'am, me orders is to persuade you to accompany me to Harlington so that ye may be returned to the bosom of yer family."

He was extremely proud at having been able to contribute that particular phrasing. It was not in his orders, but he felt it gave the proceedings a definite air and must go far to persuade her.

"But I need no persuasion, Mr. Peters-kin. That is where Lady Daphne and I are travelling to."

At the beginning of her statement, Lemmy's face lit up with the thought that the reward was practically won. It fell when it became clear that his offices were completely unnecessary and he was to be done out of it after all his trouble.

Major Winstock, having known his man for many years, could appreciate his great disappointment. As for himself, well, here was an interesting young lady come to hand. It could be an opportunity that he might regret if he let it pass him by. His mind began to race to discover some pretext for prolonging this meeting as much for Lemmy's sake as for his own interest.

"Miss Miller, I fear we have some exceptional circumstances here, and I am sure you will agree that the middle of the highroad to London is the last place to try to resolve them. I am on my way home to visit what family I have left. You will honour me if you and Lady Daphne will agree to accompany me there. We could then—over tea—discuss what is to be done."

At that point the abigail sneezed, and Lady Daphne, who was not immune to the Major's charm, immediately seconded his suggestion, remarking that it was as she feared. Her woman, Bales, was coming down with a cold, having complained of a hoarseness earlier, and there was still all the journey before them.

Meg shook her head and chuckled. "This has been an adventure to end all adventures. Well, I can see nothing for it, Daphne, but to do as the gentleman suggests. We have lost so much time and I have become so chilled that the prospect of a steaming cup of tea is too tempting to resist.''

The coach was closed up, the coachman directed to swing the vehicle about—which he managed, due to its great size, only with great difficulty, Peterskin having to go to the horses' heads to make the turning and the wheeling as nice as possible—only to come to a halt again so that all could be introduced to a very annoyed young lady by the name of Honoria Dalrymple. Of course, being of the neighbourhood, Lady Daphne had some slight acquaintance with her and immediately offered her a seat in the coach.

Lady Honoria, suffering from prolonged exposure to the icy air, was forced to accept. She would have dearly loved to continue the ride, stirrup to stirrup with Sir Arthur, but it came to her that teeth achatter were not conducive to engaging in light-hearted pleasantries, and when Meg remarked, ''Oh, your poor nose must be frozen; it is so red!'' she quickly surrendered her mount to Peterskin and stepped into the travelling carriage.

It was not out of the goodness of her heart that Meg had made the remark. She had found Sir Arthur to be of more than passing interest, and she did not think it particularly equitable to that interest that he be left in the company of Lady Honoria solely.

Now that all the ladies were safely in the coach, away from his presence, she could give herself over to some reflection on the topic of Sir Arthur without being disturbed by the thought of another female absorbing his attention. Giving only half an ear to the chatter of her companions, she closed her eyes to consider just how the late scandal would affect such a gentleman's feelings for her. Her immediate conclusion was that it was certainly something a girl could not ignore.

As they progressed along the road back to Tunbridge Wells, Lady Daphne and Lady Honoria immediately struck up a conversation. If Meg had paid them closer attention, she would have been brought up to date on a great variety of tidbits concerning the more reprehensible activities at the spa. But this was only preliminary to the topic that Lady Honoria wished to pursue.

"Major Winstock said they were searching for her," said Lady Honoria, lowering her voice and nodding at Meg, whose eyes were still shut. "Should she be permitted to share the carriage with us? Who is she?" she asked, her violet eyes wide with curiosity. "What awful thing has she done?"

Lowering her voice, Daphne responded in tones of great sympathy, "It is not what she has done, but what has been done to her!"

Lady Honoria's eyes opened wider still. "Do tell!" she exclaimed.

"Oh, but I dare not! I have said too much already!"

"Indeed, you have!" broke in Meg wearily. "But do not hesitate, on my account, to reveal all. It is obvious that if both the good Major and his 'hide-nor-heir' henchman know so much about it, I cannot but believe that it is hardly a secret any longer. I am sure Lady Honoria will treat the matter with as strict a confidence as it has already received. Well, Daphne, why do you hesitate—is it because you fear to reveal gallant Adrian's role in it?"

But for this attack on her beloved, Daphne would have forborne continuing the topic. Now, although she blushed with confusion, she declared, "Oh, I am sure Adrian is not to be blamed! After all, Meg, he could not have known who you were. It is really asking too much to require a gentleman to recognize a lady when she is not being a lady— Oh, dear! That is not exactly what I meant!"

Meg burst into laughter. "I know what you meant, but I think you had best tell Honoria all about it before she expires with curiosity and is given to imaginings of the most horrible kind."

Daphne proceeded to regale Honoria with the details of

the previous night's happenings, taking every opportunity to make it clear that Adrian had truly been taken in. Meg listened to it all as a stranger might and found the recital even more distasteful than the original experience had been. With a dry comment every so often, she attempted to ameliorate the effect; but she soon gave it over as a thankless task. It was a bad business and she had yet to reap the bitter crop it was bound to produce.

Daphne had done her work well and Honoria was entranced with it all.

"How very romantic!" she cried. "An abduction, in truth, and by Mr. Rounceford, too! Are you sure he was not in love with you?"

"How could he be?" demanded Daphne indignantly. "It was all a mistake and he was being very noble about it!"

"Honoria," said Meg, "I do not know you well enough to call you a goose, but be assured it is in my mind to do so."

"But to receive an offer from Adrian Rounceford!" protested Honoria. "Under any circumstances I should have accepted!"

"Would you?" asked Meg, and there was a hint of bitterness in her voice. "You think he must come to love you for easing his conscience? I say never. He must always hate you for the constant memory of his misdeed that you would be to him. As for me, I can never have any but the least regard for a man who has acted the noodle so completely."

"But think of your reputation, Miss Miller. What of that?"

"Well, I had thought to salvage it; but now with Major Winstock to contend with—and heaven only knows how many others—I really do not know what is to be done about it."

"Speaking of Major Winstock, I have heard mention of him," remarked Daphne, "but for my life I cannot collect in what connection. Do you not find him a most attractive gentleman?''

"Oh, I should like to be abducted by *him*!'' gushed Honoria.

"Then you must expect to be disappointed, Lady Honoria, for I suspect the Major has too much sense to oblige you.''

"Well, if it had been me, the story would have had a different ending,'' declared Daphne with a very superior air.

"I daresay!'' retorted Meg. "You are in love with Adrian and he knows you for a lady to begin with—and, when all is said and done, this entire sorry affair came about only because you and he had a falling out!''

"I do not love him! I hate him! I am sure I have never loved him!'' cried Daphne petulantly.

"What is this? Oh, please tell me! Did you and Adrian come to words over Miss Miller?'' asked Honoria eagerly.

"Of course not!'' Daphne exploded indignantly.

"Now that would be beyond everything!'' declared Meg. "Please, Daphne, before ever such a story makes the rounds, you must make the way of it quite clear to Lady Honoria or we shall never hear the end of it!''

And so, unpleasant as was the task for her, Lady Daphne had to explain in detail how it was that Adrian and she had been at cuffs with each other. Meg had all she could do to repress her laughter as she listened to a tale of Adrian's having insisted on wearing a pea-green jacket to Almack's when Daphne was bedecked in pale blue. As the jacket was George Hobcourt's suggestion, it is needless to point out that Sir George was, right along with Adrian, in Daphne's black books as well.

The little cavalcade finally turned off the highroad and proceeded along a drive of some extent before coming to a stop at the door of a large, ornate house.

Lady Honoria was helped out of the coach by the Major and he escorted her to her door beyond earshot of the coach's occupants.

"You have been so kind, Major Winstock," she said, looking up into his face with a charming smile.

"It has been a pleasure to serve you, milady. I shall look forward to the early renewal of our acquaintance," said the Major, letting himself drown in two pools of violet light and enjoying every moment of it.

"I—I, too, Sir Arthur," she murmured, lowering her head and blushing prettily.

Major Winstock took her hand and pressed it. "Then I may call upon you?" he asked.

"Do you live nearby?"

"We are practically neighbours. I wonder that we have not met before—if not at the Wells, then in town. So lovely a young lady would have the town at her feet."

"My father has been ill and we have only returned from Dorset quite recently. We have not been in the way of attending functions in town, but he is now much recovered and we have taken this house so that he may have the advantage of the waters." She paused as a thought came to her. "In fact, in a fortnight's time I am giving—or rather my mamma is—a dance. I—I hope you will come." It was slightly odd, that! But a moment before, such an entertainment had not been dreamed of; and it could be relied upon that her good mother had not the faintest inkling of the sponsorship to which she had been so suddenly elected.

"Bony and his Imperial Guard together could not keep me from it!" proclaimed the Major gallantly.

"But I have no idea where to send the invitation," she protested.

Sir Arthur was not one to stand idly by for two weeks when such a prize was in the offing. He was determined to take every advantage to forward his interest. He saw his opportunity and took it.

"If I may call upon you tomorrow, it shall be my pleasure to provide you with the fullest direction."

She held out her hand and smiled happily. "Tomorrow, then," she said as the door was opened behind her by a footman.

The Major pressed her hand, raised it to his lips. "Tomorrow," he murmured. She nodded and stepped into the house. The door swung shut and the Major stood staring at it a moment.

Finally he turned and descended the steps, fighting an idiotic impulse to leap into the air and click his heels in wild elation. Instead he put on a sober expression to mask his feelings as he stepped up to the coach and peered within.

"Ladies, we are not more than half an hour from our destination. Are you comfortable?"

"We should be more so if you would join us, Major Winstock," said Meg with a smile of invitation.

Sir Arthur would have preferred to be alone with his thoughts, but he could not decline without giving offense. Surrendering his mount to Peterskin, he climbed into the coach and took the seat left vacant by Lady Honoria.

There was silence in the coach while it started up and they resumed their journey. Major Winstock began to relax, and soon a pair of violet eyes beguiled him into a dream of the future. But, alas for him, Fate in the form of Miss Miller would not have it so.

"Major, you have never satisfied my curiosity. How comes it that your groom is an agent of Bow Street? Am I to understand that you are engaged in similar employment?"

"Er—ah, I beg your pardon? You asked . . . ?"

"Corporal Peterskin; he is a Bow Street man?"

"Yes, he is; but not for very much longer. He returns to my service as soon as he completes this last assignment."

"I see! Then he was your servant at some previous time?"

"Not exactly. He was my corporal-major before Quatre Bras. He was wounded there and I went on to Waterloo. I have not seen him since that time until I found him this morning. In fact, we had not met but twenty minutes before you happened along. I have elected to assist him until he can free himself of his present service."

"And, somehow, this service concerns myself?"

"Yes, it does. Your father has offered five hundred pounds for your return. Peterskin was the fortunate agent to draw the case."

"Oh, dear!" exclaimed Meg. Then with a sigh she said, "If only Pappa had refrained, I should have been able to sneak home with no one the wiser. Now I blush to think of what will be said of me. Meg Miller will become a byword in the mouths of the *ton*. The abduction, in itself, will not have been half as bad as the consequences which now must follow."

"You were abducted? By force? You did not elope?"

"My dear Major, how do you account for my being here, else? I assure you had I eloped there would have been one less bachelor in the world!"

Major Winstock was plainly puzzled. Miss Miller appeared to be anything but a young lady who had undergone so frightening an experience. He was amazed that she could so calmly discuss the harrowing business, especially as she seemed perfectly aware of how it must redound against her reputation.

"But you seem so—so unruffled, to put it mildly," he protested. "It must have been a terrible ordeal! Were you harmed in any way?"

"I will admit it was decidedly inconvenient—and having a dusty old sack over one's head is not conducive to pleasant conversation."

"Were you not even frightened?"

"Now, Major, I had not thought you to be a sapskull! Of course I was frightened. Would not you have been?"

Sir Arthur was taken aback. It was most unusual for a

gentleman of his address to be spoken to in such a forthright fashion by a young female of any station. Oddly enough, he did not find himself put off by her manner, only surprised.

"I beg your pardon, but I cannot imagine myself in any circumstances that might compare. All the same, I marvel that you can speak of it so calmly."

"Oh, do not doubt that I should dearly love to indulge myself in tears," said Meg, her lips starting to quiver. She drew a deep breath and got herself back under control. "I pray, let us speak of something else—or you will soon find your arms full of a weeping female," she added brightly, forcing a smile.

Sir Arthur frowned with concern. "I think it an atrocious business!" he said as he reached over and patted her hand consolingly.

It was the last bit necessary to break through Meg's tight control of her emotions. The brave front she had so successfully maintained up to this point was now shattered, and she clutched his hand, holding it tightly as she sat erect with tears streaming down her cheeks.

Lady Daphne looked helplessly on, distraught by the spectacle of Meg, self-reliant Meg, a picture of despair.

Meg's anguish, before so completely masked and now so completely revealed, reached to Sir Arthur's heart, and he could not withhold his good offices even if he had wished to. He signalled to Lady Daphne, who arose and exchanged seats with him.

What he was about to do, once he was beside Meg, the Major could not have said. In the event, it was enough that he was there. Meg fell into his arms and Sir Arthur patted her shoulder while he supplied her with his handkerchief. He received a watery thanks and an apologetic sob.

It was some little time before Meg regained a sense of the impropriety of her being in the gentleman's arms. She pushed herself away and brought her weeping to an end.

She dried her eyes and with a sunny smile, she addressed the Major.

"I beg your pardon, sir, for behaving so badly; but, you see, I did warn you that it would happen."

"My dear Miss Miller, I will oblige you by not referring to the matter again if you will but answer me one question. Who was the damnable villain who perpetrated this outrage?" The Major's anger was only thinly disguised.

"No, that I shall not tell you. The business has gone far enough and—" Meg stopped in midsentence, for her glance out the coach window showed her that they were coming to a place she was only too familiar with. The slowing down of the coach, preparatory to turning into the grounds, confirmed the fact that this was the Major's destination.

"To where have you brought us? Why here, of all places?" demanded Meg, looking at the Major with indignation.

"Oh, heavens!" exclaimed Daphne.

"Whatever is the matter?" asked the Major. "This has ever been my home. You will be welcome here, never fear. It is the residence of my great-aunt Marcia, dowager Countess of Marchford."

"Oh, no!" cried Meg, staring at him in horror. "It cannot be! Pray do not tell me that you are a Rounceford," she implored.

Sir Arthur, very puzzled, said uncertainly, "Although I do not share the name, I have the honour to be of the blood. What troubles you so?"

Meg was suddenly cold and distant. "Major, you will do me the greatest favour if you will leave us now, so that we may resume our journey to Harlington."

"Now that is beyond reason! Your coach would never reach London before nightfall."

"I believe there are inns aplenty along the way."

"It is not to be thought of. You must and shall have an

137

escort. It will be my pleasure to accompany you, but it is already too late, today.

"Furthermore," he continued, "there is a mystery here and it is not difficult to surmise that the Rounceford name is concerned in it. We shall not stir until it is made clear to me."

He turned to Daphne. "You, Lady Daphne, are connected with my cousin Adrian, I believe. I vaguely collect that you and he are promised. Am I correct in that?"

"No!" cried Daphne with a sniffle. "He considers himself pledged to Miss Miller!" She buried her face in her handkerchief.

"To Miss Miller?" he asked incredulously. "How comes this about? It puts me quite to sea! I could have sworn—"

"Oh, what is the use of all this!" exclaimed Meg. "We shall not get anywhere at this rate."

She turned to Sir Arthur. "Know then, Major, that it was your esteemed cousin Adrian who abducted me."

He stared at her in wonder, which was quickly replaced by disbelief.

"Miss Miller, I do not know what your game is, but you have overreached yourself," Sir Arthur declared with scorn. "I am surprised at you, Lady Daphne, that you permit—"

But Lady Daphne was not listening. She stormed, "Meg, you are not being just! Why do you not tell the Major that you were masquerading as a shopgirl—and that after he discovered his error, he pledged himself to marry you. It just goes to prove how noble he is!" And she burst into tears.

For a moment the Major did not know what to say. At least it was not as bad as Miss Miller would have it; but, if that was the way of it, he could see that both Miss Miller and the Rouncefords had a mutual problem on their hands. Well, if Adrian was willing to wed the girl, the entire affair could be dismissed as an elopement and would be quickly forgotten.

"I see that I spoke out of turn. My apologies, Miss Miller, but it is not so bad after all. I daresay Adrian will make you a fine husband."

It was Meg's turn to regard him with scorn. "Yes, you are a Rounceford!" she said with a sneer. "I do not marvel that neither you nor your cousins are yet married." She turned to her weeping companion. "I have not changed my mind, Daphne; you are welcome to Adrian. But, dearest friend, consider it carefully. I cannot think of a worse fate than to be married to an unfeeling Rounceford." And she turned away to the window to hide the tears of frustration that filled her eyes.

Sir Arthur blew out his breath. "Whew! Then it is *not* settled! Miss Miller, I beg you to reconsider. It is an excellent way to clear up a situation that will only grow more unpleasant as time passes."

Meg did not consider his suggestion worthy of an answer and merely looked her disgust.

Major Winstock shook his head. "Under the circumstances, there is nought to be done at the moment. It becomes most necessary that you avail yourself of Rounceford hospitality, despite your misguided aversion to it. Something more will have to be done. We cannot let this business rest in so sorry a state. Although I have not the faintest idea of how to go about it, fortunately I know of someone who does."

Chapter Ten

Lady Marcia, with a sigh, closed the novel she was reading, holding her place with her forefinger. She looked up as the rap on her sitting room door was repeated.

"Enter!" she called out.

The door opened and in walked Lady Daphne followed by Miss Miller and a gentleman of military bearing.

"Well, it is high time!" she declared. "Where ever did you disappear to? We have been looking for you all morning— Why Arthur!" It was almost a shriek of delight. "My dear boy!"

Sir Arthur came forward with a grin, bent over and kissed the cheek held up for him.

"Milady, you are positively glowing!" he said with a laugh. "The baths have done wonders for you!"

"Go on with you! You have a tongue like your cousin Marchford." She raised an admonishing finger. "But why have you come so soon? You were not expected for another week. I might have missed you, you know."

"No, I do not know. You are here and I am here, so I have not missed you it would appear."

"Yes, but I would not have been here had not my coach broken down at Sevenoaks, forcing me to return. Let that be a lesson to you!

"Let me look at you! My, how many years has it been?" she asked as she gazed lovingly up at him.

"Milady, I am no turned-up prodigal and well you

know it. It was but three months that you saw me last, at your party in town.''

"Glimpsed you, you mean! Flirting and dancing with all the young things, you had no time for a doddering old lady. Well, you shan't get away now! I must hear all the latest gossip and— Oh, yes, you sold out at last, did you not? I want to hear what you intend to do now that you are become a gentleman of leisure.''

"Yes, yes, of course. All in due time. But these ladies —Lady Daphne and Miss Miller—''

"So you have met them already! You do go quickly to work, I must say. Well, ladies, what do you think of my soldierboy—Sir Arthur Winstock, Knight Commander of the Bath—recommended by the Duke himself? By the way, how is dear Lord Arthur? I always had a *tendre* for him.''

"Wellington has been quite occupied on the Continent. I have not seen him for some time. But, milady, I beg you leave off. I came across these young ladies on the London road. It is not unlikely that they were fleeing from something, I am not exactly sure from what. You know Miss Miller? I am sure you must be acquainted with Lady Daphne Colworth.''

"Yes, yes,'' Lady Marcia said with impatience. "They are my guests.'' Which response left the poor Major more confused than ever.

Turning to Meg, she asked, "Whatever is the matter with you, girl? To leave without a word? Now, that is not mannerly!''

"I beg your pardon, Lady Marchford, but I thought it best. I was sure that had it been known we were leaving, one or both of your grandsons`might have insisted on escorting us. Of one, I have had enough; and of the other, I have had too much!''

The Countess laughed. "Have you ever in all your days, Arthur, known a female more contrary? Well, young lady, you have been well served, for you have been escorted back by my grand-nephew—aye, and the best of all the Rounceford lads if you would have my word for it. Well, Arthur, I take it you have heard of the ridiculous coil Adrian has got us in to.''

"Yes, and I think we had best do something about it and quickly. I have word that Sir Samuel Miller has instituted a search for his daughter. It will not do for him to discover her here before we have informed him of her presence amongst us.''

"That is so,'' agreed the Countess. "He ought to be notified immediately. I think Adrian must go.''

Meg was becoming incensed at the highhanded manner in which grandmother and grand-nephew were proceeding. She stepped forward.

"I should much prefer to go myself. The earlier I return to Harlington, the sooner the episode can be got over.''

"What!'' exclaimed the Countess. "And leave Adrian with his good name all to tatters—not to say anything of your own? My dear, are you quite sure you cannot bring yourself to marry the boy? It would make everything so simple.''

"Yes!'' chimed in Sir Arthur, "it would, indeed! Miss Miller, you cannot fail to see how damaging to you and to us must be the result of this prank.''

"Prank!'' Meg was astounded.

"Yes, prank,'' insisted Sir Arthur. "If you had been truly a mere milliner's girl, there would have been no such serious consequences as we are now faced with.'' He shrugged. "It would have been a mere prank—and nothing that has not happened more times than anyone knows. It is only the fact that you were—er—are respectable that the difficulty arises. It need be no more than a marriage of convenience—''

At that point the two other Rounceford gentlemen entered.

Adrian exclaimed, "Daphne! Thank God you are here!'' as he rushed up to her full of concern. "Where did

142

you disappear to? Marcus and I have been seeking high and low for you. Are you all right? Pray, speak to me!"

Daphne apparently responded to his satisfaction, for he was all smiles despite the fact that her reply was inaudible to the rest of the room.

Meg glanced at Major Winstock. She gestured at the happy couple and said, "I think you have it all wrong, sir. It must surely be a marriage of inconvenience. Adrian must detest the idea as much as I do."

"Well, as I live and breathe," exclaimed Lord Marcus, raising his lorgnette and quizzing first Meg and then Sir Arthur. "You have returned to us, Miss Miller. You put me in mind of the proverbial bad penny. And, Arthur! What brings the Iron Duke's little tin soldier out from London?"

"Marcus, as head of the family, you owe Miss Miller the hospitality due to a guest—and, considering the unpleasantness she has thus far experienced at the hands of a Rounceford, some kindness and consideration as well," declared the Major, stepping over to him and looking up into his tall cousin's face with menace. "If you see fit to maintain your usual supercilious attitude when all the rest of us are concerned to protect Miss Miller, you shall have me to answer to."

"That will be quite enough!" intervened Lady Marcia. "What must Miss Miller think of us if you two go to brawling on the instant you meet? Now, Marcus, Arthur is right! You do have the duty to conduct yourself as becomes the head of the House of Rounceford. And as for you, my little fire-eating bantam, I can assure you that Miss Miller has taken your cousin's measure before this and needs no assistance from you!"

Both gentlemen stepped back rather quickly from each other and looked shamefaced. There was no question as to who was, in truth, the head of the family.

"Now then, put your heads together—you are included in this, Adrian! It is Miss Miller who is our immediate

143

concern, not Lady Daphne. I am sure she will spare you while we give thought to what must be done to extricate ourselves from this fix you have got us into.''

Reluctantly Adrian came over and joined his cousins standing before their grandmother. He said, very grimly, ''There is no alternative. I must marry her.''

''You must needs do nothing of the sort!'' exclaimed Meg. ''Such resignation is intolerable!''

''There, you see, Adrian!'' crowed the Countess. ''You may put the thought out of your mind. I collect Miss Miller is adamant on that score and we will get nowhere by pressing her.''

''*We* may get nowhere, but I should think there is *someone* who can shake some sense into her,'' declared Major Winstock.

Lady Marcia gave him her attention. ''And who might that be?'' she asked.

''I have not heard of anyone standing up to Sir Sam to any purpose. I propose to send my man, Peterskin, post-haste to Harlington. He can accomplish much that we have in mind. He can relieve the Millers of their anxiety for their daughter, the search can be called off, and he can bring Sir Samuel back with him so that we may continue this discussion with some restraint upon Miss Miller's disposition to refuse the only conceivable measure that will defend us all from being made the season's laughing-stock.''

''Major Winstock, a moment please.'' Meg came over to stand before him. ''You are so hot to marry me to Adrian. Why needs must it be him? He is already promised to Lady Daphne. Would not you—or Lord Marcus— do as well?''

''You go too fast, Miss Miller!'' protested Lord Marcus.

But Sir Arthur was quite ready for her. ''My dear Miss Miller, that would hardly be just. It was Adrian who got

144

you into this scrape." The Major shrugged. "It is up to him to pay the piper."

Meg looked at him with intense dislike. "That clears the air and shows us where we stand. To punish Adrian, he must marry me! How very flattering, indeed!"

Sir Arthur flushed. "My dear Miss Miller, that is not at all what I meant. I beg your pardon."

He was at a loss to understand why everyone laughed.

"I warned you, Arthur." Lady Marcia shook her finger at him. "One steps carefully about Miss Miller. But never you mind, she has taken on both your cousins at one time and done for 'em. She was bound to put you down sooner or later, too." Then a thought struck her and her eyes narrowed. "Miss Miller, may I ask you *is* there any other Rounceford you would prefer to Adrian?"

Meg went to the door and turned to face the room. There was a smile on her face as she said, "I thought to have made myself clear on that point. I will try again. If all the men upon the face of the earth were Rouncefords, I should die a spinster! Will you come with me, Daphne?"

Daphne moved towards her and they left the room together.

The door closed behind them and Lady Marcia laughed.

Lord Marcus looked at her in surprise. "The humour of the situation escapes me, milady. What devilish scheme had you in mind to ask *her* which of us she might prefer? It was infernally close! Do you realize that if she had an ounce of sense, I should now be under the necessity of refusing her?"

Lady Marcia regarded the Earl with a pitying smile.

"Milord, let me assure you that it is your own good sense that is lacking. You will agree that she has taken us in great dislike and that she has been afforded ample reason."

"I do agree that we—Adrian misjudged the situation,

but he has been willing to make amends—and his offer was most generous.''

''Bah! She would not have him and I agree with her. From such an auspicious beginning, what can she expect? She is no fool. You should know that. I am well aware how proud you are of your ability to turn a phrase to anyone's discomfiture. I have yet to see you give her a setdown that she cannot turn back on you threefold. That should tell you something.

''A moment ago she seemed to give Arthur an opening. he leapt to it and what was the result? A slaughter of Rouncefords! And so gracefully delivered that you are bleeding before you realize you have been stabbed. You will pardon my bloodthirsty allusion, but you will, I am sure, feel the point of it.''

Lord Marcus regarded his grandmother with a thoughtful expression. Then he smiled and said, ''If I take your meaning correctly, Adrian has acted the fool, even beyond the witlessness of the abduction.''

''Think what you like,'' retorted Adrian, ''she does not hold a candle to Daphne and I am glad to be out of it—if I truly am!''

''We shall not know that until we learn Sir Samuel's opinion on the matter,'' Sir Arthur pointed out. ''And I suggest that we arrange to secure it without further delay.''

In that regard, all were in agreement and Peterskin was summoned.

Upon his appearance, Sir Arthur instructed him to repair to Harlington with the greatest speed; he was not to spare the horses nor the expense. He was to inform Sir Samuel that his daughter was safe and well, and that she was the guest of Lady Marchford. It was her ladyship's wish that Sir Samuel would wait upon her at Tunbridge Wells with a view to discussing matters of mutual importance. Lem was particularly enjoined not to return without the Baronet in tow.

"But, Major, sir, my chief at Bow Street, what about him? He'll be in a fair fidget for me to report. Aye, an' there be the reward—a monkey it were!"

"Never you mind about Bow Street! I shall send in your resignation. As for the reward, we can discuss that with Sir Samuel after we have settled some matters of greater concern. Now go!"

"A moment please, Arthur!" called out the Countess. "I am sure Lady Miller will think to have it done, but you must see to it that Miss Miller's tire-woman as well as her wardrobe are also brought along. The poor dear has not got a thing to wear. Adrian never thought to bring at least one change of clothing for her. So very inconsiderate of him, I must say!"

Sir Arthur gave the necessary instructions together with an amount of money that caused Peterskin's eyes to open wide. He recovered himself, saluted and departed. Sir Arthur turned to his grand-aunt.

"Milady, I believe that is all we can do for the nonce. Until Sir Samuel comes, I fear that we shall have to put up with Miss Miller."

"Yes, but do not think it any great thing. If she will but continue to get on with you gentlemen as she has, I, for one, shall be vastly entertained. As I have noted, there is a great deal more than one might suspect in that child. I am in no rush to see the last of her. How long do you think it will be before we may expect Sir Samuel?"

"But for your last-minute instructions, I should have said not more than three days; however, with the woman and the clothes, perhaps Lady Miller, herself—well, they will certainly require a carriage of some sort. If Sir Samuel will permit Peterskin to do the driving, then I should look for them to arrive in five days' time. I cannot think that Sir Samuel can come away on very short notice, so it may well be somewhat later than that before we shall see him here."

Lady Marcia nodded. "Good, that will give me ample

time to become better acquainted with the girl."

Sir Arthur raised his eyebrows.

"You need not look down your nose at me, my boy! That young lady is something unusual. Considering what she has been through, there has been an amazing lack of fuss from her. All of you gentlemen could do worse than to get to know her better yourselves."

Sir Arthur smiled. "Yes, I must agree. She is truly a cool one. But I fear my taste runs to a prettier and sweeter style of female."

Now, Lady Marcia raised her eyebrows. "Oh, do you have someone in mind?"

"Perhaps I do, but let us not rush our fences. I am fresh out of the Blues and there is plenty of time for me to look about."

"But you do have a mind to settle down."

"I daresay."

"I am pleased to hear it. Not only you, but Marcus and Adrian as well. It would appear that all is not lost to me. I had thought never to behold a great-grandchild of mine, but now my prospects are bright indeed. There must be something in the air to make all three of you suddenly decide it is time to take a wife."

"I had known of Adrian's intention, but Marcus, too? That comes as a surprise," Sir Arthur said.

"May I inquire why you find it so?" asked the Earl coolly.

"After all, old man, if I can believe the gossip, many a pretty cap has been set for you. Wagering, at the club, is no longer concerned with which it shall be, but whether it shall be."

"Well, you may inform your confreres that they can return to their original wagers. When they have weighed the field and reckoned their odds, I shall be pleased to wager a bob or two myself."

"I do not find that particularly humorous!"

"You will find it even less so when the marriage mart

gets wind of *your* availability. Wagers on your chances will then be the least of your worries—and I speak from years of experience.''

''I think we have had enough of that tiresome topic,'' said the Countess.

''I agree,'' said Sir Arthur. ''I should prefer to speak of other matters. What are our neighbours like, for instance?''

''I have no intention of remaining with you, milady, long enough for that topic to become of interest to me. By your leave''—and his lordship departed, quickly followed by Adrian.

''By the way, milady, I recently became acquainted with Lady Honoria Dalrymple. Do you, by any chance, know the family?''

Lady Marcia gave Sir Arthur an appraising look before she answered. ''Sir John Dalrymple, a baron, is a valetudinarian and has only recently come into the neighbourhood. I have heard that the Dalrymples are extremely well off. It is reported that he has three thousand a year. I take it Lady Honoria is his daughter?''

''Yes, a charming girl.''

''Do you know her well?''

''Er—no, not really—but I intend to. In fact I am promised to call upon her tomorrow.''

''Well, it would be nice if she and Lady Dalrymple called upon me. You may extend my invitation.''

''Thank you, I will.''

''Now, begone, boy! I am feeling weary and would rest before tea.''

''I thought I heard a carriage in the driveway, my dear,'' remarked Lady Dalrymple as her daughter entered the parlour. Honoria came over to her mother and planted an affectionate kiss upon her cheek before sitting down beside her.

''Yes, Mamma, you did. It was the Colworth carriage.

149

Daphne Colworth—surely you must have heard mention of her. She is affianced to Adrian Rounceford.''

"Why, yes, I believe Mrs. Wimpole spoke of her. I did not know she was here in Tunbridge Wells—and I never expected that she would call on me. Where is she? Please have her shown to the grand parlour.''

"No, Mamma, she is not here. They could not stay. There is trouble at the Rouncefords'.''

"That is Lady Marcia, Countess of Marchford, is it not?''

"Yes, Mamma. Poor Daphne! She has been so put upon by Adrian Rounceford, her betrothed—and all over a female of absolutely no distinction. A Meg Miller! Adrian abducted her!''

"Mercy, what are you saying, child? Abducted her! Why, I never heard the like! Surely, you must mean she ran away with him.''

"Well, so *I* believe. I am sure she is no better than she should be, but she would have it that she was abducted—and Daphne, her school chum, believes it!''

"*Meg* Miller? And yet a school chum of Lady Daphne Colworth? Then she is not—not a—''

"No! It is hard to believe, but she is supposedly a gentlewoman. She claims a Sir Samuel Miller as her father. That, I daresay, is as likely as all the rest.''

Lady Dalrymple screwed up her forehead in thought. "Miller? Miller, you say? Ah, yes, I remember now. They call him The Flour King. Extremely wealthy, but no blood or breeding there. Well, what can one expect of a daughter from such a family? Where are she and Rounceford now?''

"I have no idea where he is, but Sir Arthur Winstock is escorting the Miller woman to some haven nearby where they can take thought how to proceed. You see—''

"And who is Sir Arthur Winstock?'' interrupted Lady Dalrymple.

"But first let me tell you how it all came about, and you

will see!'' gushed Honoria and, without further pre-liminaries, she plunged into the story. As the tale unfolded, Lady Dalrymple began to feel dismay and was growing uneasy. The figure of Winstock took on heroic proportions, nor could she fail to sense that her daughter had acquired a distinct *tendre* for the stranger. She found difficult to understand the Major's intervention in what seemed to her to be a matter for Bow Street, and she was inclined to credit the whole business to the fact that her daughter was a beauty and far from poverty-stricken. Such a pecuniarily sweet bait was a most excellent lure to attract the offices of military gentlemen; and, invariably, they had not a feather to fly with, being as poor in pocket as they were dashing in appearance and behaviour.

To realize that her daughter gave all the appearance of being smitten by such a one was that which gave rise to her dismay. But as the details of the affair became clear, the thought that her daughter might become involved with one of its principals, thereby losing her reputation, gave rise to such a flutter of apprehension in her breast that she had all she could do to refrain from hushing Honoria and dealing her a reprimand on the spot.

As for Honoria, she relished the tale, and in its telling left no doubt that found Meg Miller entirely at fault for leading Adrian Rounceford astray.

But the fact that Adrian Rounceford found it necessary to propose marriage, and at the expense of his own be-trothal to Lady Daphne, spoke volumes to Lady Dalrym-ple. Had Miss Miller run away with Rounceford of her own initiative, she had made her own bed. The fact that the Rouncefords were in such a turmoil over the affair bespoke otherwise and served as confirmation of the fan-tastic tale. By the time her daughter had finished, Lady Dalrymple had quite made up her mind that she would not permit Honoria to become further entangled in the scan-dal. Until it was resolved, there must be no exchanges with the Rouncefords on any score.

As for Major Winstock, whoever he might be, she was especially determined that Honoria should have seen the last of him. It was, therefore, a tremendous shock for her to learn that not only was the Major coming to call upon them on the morrow, but that her darling daughter had invited the said Major to a dance which she, Lady Dalrymple, had not the least intention of sponsoring.

"Honoria, I am ashamed of you! Do you wish to be considered fast? To invite a man to whom you have not been properly introduced to a dance which I have no intention of giving—well!"

"Oh, Mamma, you cannot be so disagreeable," protested Honoria. "We must have a dance. I have invited him. It would be the height of incivility to beg off. What must he think of me?"

"I do not see that his opinion of you is any matter at all. You do not know him—his family, his prospects!"

"Goodness, how you go on!" exclaimed Honoria. "It is not to be a betrothal party; it is only a dance! You cannot deny me! And, anyway, you will see that he is a lovely gentleman and not the least bit exceptionable."

"But whom else are we to ask? We have no acquaintance here."

"I am sure that can be no great objection, Mamma. We can begin at once to make calls and leave our cards. It is not as though Pappa is so very ill any longer. The doctors say he has shown remarkable progress. I am sure, if I asked him, *he* would have no objection—and it is most important to me."

Lady Dalrymple raised her eyebrows. "Is it, indeed! You have been quite satisfied till now to amuse yourself. I had promised you that if your father progresses as well in the future as he has recently, we should spend the season in town. I think it quite likely we shall do just that and I see no need to go to any expense and trouble here in Tunbridge Wells."

"But this is different!" exclaimed Honoria with a show of petulance. "I did not know there were people of my age about—and, no matter, I have invited the Major and cannot go back on it."

"Dear, I am sure if you will explain to him that your father is not up to it, he must understand. He will have every opportunity to renew his acquaintance with you, and make your father's and mine, when we get to London."

"Oh, Mamma, how can you be so cruel?" lamented Honoria, beginning to show signs of tears.

"My dear child, do not take on so! It just is not done! One does not make up a party for a perfect stranger—a man!—at a moment's notice. Oh, what am I saying? Notice or not, it is beyond the pale of respectability."

"Well, Major Winstock did not find it so! He was quite happy to accept, quite happy indeed!" declared Honoria with a blush at the remembered parting.

"That speaks even less well of your Major. He must know better than that! No, the idea of a dance is repugnant!"

"O-ooh, Mamma!" wailed Honoria, and she began to cry.

Lady Dalrymple was immediately in great distress. She tried to comfort her daughter by enumerating all the wonderful things they would do in London, but it did not serve to stem the lamentations of her daughter. At last she said, "Very well, this is what I will do. The Major will call upon us tomorrow and we will receive him. If he is as you say, an unexceptionable young man, I shall give you your party—"

"Oh, Mamma, how very good of you! I love you very much!"

"Yes, dear, I know; but remember this; there will be no party if I find the least questionable thing about this young man or his connections."

"Yes, Mamma. Of course, Mamma." Honoria kissed

153

her mother and went out of the room to change her riding habit.

Meg stood at the window of her chamber and stared down at the grounds surrounding the Rounceford mansion. The land sloped gently away to a small woodland which bordered the lawn. Even if she had not known it was a cold, dank day, the leaden sky and the thin snow that covered the lawn would have left her in no doubt. It was a steely, grey prospect and it matched her mood.

She did not believe for one moment that she was truly a guest of Lady Marcia. It was rather as though she were a hostage to insure the good repute of the Rounceford family. The only one who bore her any affection was Daphne, and Daphne's affection must be suspect as long as it was believed that Adrian must serve as sacrifice to convention by marrying her, Meg.

Despite the depression these thoughts engendered in her, she could not help but smile at Adrian's behaviour to her of late. She knew that he considered her as an onus upon him. He could not look at her without a pained expression of embarrassment. She sensed his discomfort in her presence and, while she believed it well-deserved, she knew it could not further her own ease of mind as long as her presence only served as a reminder to all the Rouncefords of the scandal.

Now, Lord Marcus she positively disliked. Between them there dwelt a mutual antipathy and she, for one, was at no pains to abate it. The best that could be said of Adrian was that he had made an honest mistake and was prepared to make amends at great cost to himself. Lord Marcus, it seemed to her, had gone out of his way to be unpleasant and, considering that she was the party most harmed, he must needs be a malicious man. She had no regrets that she had given him more than one rare setdown.

Her thoughts passed on to Sir Arthur. Here was a young

man she thought attractive, if only he were not a Rounceford. Despite his name, his appearance strongly marked him as a member of the family. In all but stature he could have been brother to Adrian and Marcus. He was above average height; but, in the presence of his tall cousins, he appeared small, a miniature of a male Rounceford. By the same token his features were finer and he moved with an assured grace compared to which his cousins, although athletic in appearance, seemed almost ungainly. Yes, Sir Arthur was a very attractive young man—until one got to know him. At their very first encounter, she had to admit, she was quite taken with him. He had been charming and considerate; and there was nothing flash about him. He had apparently put his career in the Guards to good purpose and was no mere military dilettante, as Peterskin's attitude seemed to bear witness.

Although it was true that Sir Arthur had been all kindness at the outset and that he had instilled in her breast a feeling of security, it had all gone for nought when she learned of his connection to the Rouncefords. His returning her to the very last place she wanted to be, namely the Rounceford mansion, was all that was needed to put her completely out of humour with him. His subsequent seconding of her marriage to Adrian turned her disappointment to angry indignation, and it left her feeling desolate and despondent. It was a particular disappointment to her, for she believed that under other circumstances she could have liked him, and perhaps more.

Meg sighed and withdrew from the window. The fire had died down to a hot glow and some of the chill from the outside was beginning to invade the room. Any moment now she would be summoned to tea. She rang for a maid to assist her.

While she waited for the girl to appear, she bethought herself of the Countess. Lady Marcia did not puzzle Meg. For all of her being eccentric and headstrong, the old lady struck her as one who had all her wits about her but went to some pains to disguise the fact. Of all the Rouncefords, only the Countess had Meg's respect. She hoped that before her father came for her she might come to know Lady Marcia better.

Chapter Eleven

The cottage orné in which the Dalrymple residence was established temporarily would have made a creditable town house in any of the high-fashion streets of London. Here, out from Tunbridge Wells, mantled in creepers and fringed with excessive ironwork, it looked anything but the rural cottage it pretended to be. But it was all the crack for gentle living in the country, and what it lacked in comfort and warmth it made up for in prestige.

Major Winstock was not one to whom high style and good taste were synonymous; and upon this second visit, when his attention was not confined to the lovely eyes and face of Lady Honoria, he truly saw the place. To him it bespoke wealth and little more. No doubt the Dalrymples could find nothing more suited for the limited time they would be there.

A very stiff butler opened the door to him and led him to the large gothic parlour in which, seated in high-backed Tudor chairs, he found the Ladies Dalrymple. The opening rites of a formal morning call gotten over with, he was offered a seat, and a conversation of sorts was begun.

The relationship between mother and daughter was easily marked. They shared the same eyes and clear skin. There was no doubt but that the elder lady had been a great beauty in her time and still enjoyed sufficient good looks to attract male eyes and instill envy in the fairer sex. Fine features and hair a startling white made her look oddly youthful. Indeed, he could not know that her hair was a matter of great pride to her, and a matter of great profit to the leading hairdresser in Tunbridge Wells, to whose skill its arrangement and colouring was entrusted.

The dullness of the conversation was not helped along by the affectedly languid manner of either of the two ladies. Major Winstock, well aware that Lady Honoria could be quite charming, was prepared to lay the blame for her present lack to her mother. Nevertheless, a half hour of such trivia as was being dispensed was more than he could face, and so he decided to accomplish the purpose of the call before he began to yawn out of sheer boredom.

"I have come, dear ladies, to pay my respects. I reside in the neighbourhood, but until recently my duties rarely permitted me to spend any time here. Now that I have sold out it will be different, of course. I understand from Lady Honoria that you do not intend to settle permanently. I sincerely hope that for the little time you will be here, having now gained each other's acquaintance, we shall see a great deal of each other."

"That is very kind of you to say, Major Winstock," replied Lady Dalrymple as she patted at her hair. "May I ask if we are close neighbours?"

"We are. I reside at the Rounceford estate."

Lady Dalrymple was pleasantly surprised. At least the gentleman was blessed with acquaintanceship in the highest stratum of society.

"Are you a guest of the Countess of Marchford?"

Sir Arthur laughed. "I am sure she would so inform you. My grand-aunt's sense of humour borders upon the ridiculous at times. The fact of the matter is that Lady Marcia's house is the only home I have ever known. I expect I shall stay with her, now, until I can come to make up my mind as to what I shall do next."

"I should think, sir, that taking care of your aunt's business affairs would be sufficient occupation. The Countess is not a young woman, as I have heard."

The Major was not so slow as to be unaware of Lady

158

Dalrymple's purpose in this line of chatter, but he was more than willing to satisfy her curiosity. He suspected that she was interested to know of his prospects, now that she was satisfied as to his family.

In that surmise he was quite correct. As just a common major, K.C.B. or no, she could not be too careful. As a Winstock of the Rounceford connection, even the scandal threatening that house could not diminish her approval of this gentleman's possible interest in her daughter.

Sir Arthur was responding to her last remark. "No, she is not, milady, but she would not have it. I should get a sharp rap cross the knuckles were I so foolhardy as to try such an impertinence. Even the Earl, my cousin and head of our tribe, dare not dictate to his grandmother on that score. No, I shall find something else to do. Perhaps I shall farm the Winstock acres in Yorkshire and continue to breed bloodstock there. I am particularly proud of our horses. They are great goers and great of heart."

"Yes indeed, Major, I am sure they are," said Lady Dalrymple, blinking her eyes. Horses were put on earth to take her from one place to another and she did not see how they could ever figure in any rational conversation. "Er—I am not acquainted with the Countess of Marchford, as you know . . ."

"I am sure we can remedy that easily enough," said the Major, leaping into the breach she had purposely prepared for him. "Pray appoint a time and Lady Marcia will be pleased to receive you."

"Why, thank you. We shall look forward to it, shall we not, Honoria?" she asked.

Honoria, copying every nuance of her mother's tones, indicated it would be most gracious of her ladyship to receive them.

"Er—do you have any brothers and sisters, Sir Arthur?" inquired Lady Dalrymple. "It would be unpardonable not to send them invitations to our little function."

"Lord Marcus and Adrian—Mr. Rounceford—my cousins, are both staying with the Countess at present, as well as our guest, Miss Miller."

A complete silence was the only response to his statement.

Major Winstock stared at the ladies blankly for a moment.

"Did I say something to offend?"

"Oh, no, my dear Sir Arthur, not at all. We shall be pleased to send invitations to your cousins, of course."

Sir Arthur raised an eyebrow. "And Miss Miller?"

"Well, really, sir, this Meg Miller—" began Lady Dalrymple.

"Surely, Sir Arthur," chimed in Honoria, "you cannot expect us to invite *her*!"

"May I ask why not?" The Major put his question quite calmly, but his eyes narrowed slightly.

"Honoria has told me of her recent odious behaviour. I do not think her presence at any respectable affair is to be desired, but I am sure there are pleasanter matters to discuss than the goings-on of a Meg Miller."

"Madam, I beg you will pardon me if I differ with you. Perhaps Honoria did not get the details of the matter correctly. Please understand that Miss Miller is the *guest* of milady, the Countess. The business you have reference to was an unfortunate one and while I do not wish to discuss it, I see that I must—to this extent, in any case.

"Miss Miller is a highly respectable young lady. I have met with her, as has Lady Honoria, and she is an attractive person—"

"Not in the first stare of beauty," put in Honoria. On the instant, she regretted having opened her mouth, for the look that Sir Arthur turned upon her was disapproving.

He tilted his head towards her. "No, milady, she cannot hold a candle to you, but she is not without charm, you must admit." He turned back to Lady Dalrymple. "My dear madam, it is not for me to dictate whom you shall and whom you shall not invite. I must say, however, that Miss Miller, as a guest of the family, has first call upon us. We could not leave her to her own devices for the sake of our own entertainment. That would not be civil in the least.''

Lady Dalrymple immediately retreated from her position. "Dear Major Winstock, how bad of me to have misunderstood so. Honoria, you naughty child, you did not make it at all clear to me about Miss Miller. Of course we shall be delighted to have her attend with your cousins. Do you think her ladyship might come as well? For I should dearly love to have her."

She frowned at Honoria, who took the hint.

Honoria placed her hand on Sir Arthur's arm and said plaintively, "Sir Arthur, it truly was my fault, but you can hardly blame me." She smiled winningly. "Lady Daphne informed me of the circumstances with Miss Miller present. It was in the coach, you know. Indeed, Miss Miller had no objection to my hearing of it. Really, she took it all so calmly that I was sure she had instigated it. She even laughed about it. Most unmaidenly, I do assure you. Why, if anything so dreadful had happened to me—I think I should have been prostrated for weeks."

There was a half-smile on Sir Arthur's face as he said, "Aye, bonny Meg, a wee trooper of the front rank!"

"What a very odd thing to say about a young lady!" declared Lady Dalrymple. Honoria looked completely at sea.

The Rounceford clan and their two young-lady guests were assembled in a small parlour on a particularly inclement afternoon. The dark-grey clouds, with nary a break in them, kept promising snow, and the air outside was cold, laced with biting gusts of wind. It was the sort of day when one was thankful to be indoors before a blazing hearth fire.

Meg, as was her wont, sat by a window gazing out upon the dull vista. One hand played with a curl, twisting it around a little finger and then untwisting it. Despite the reposeful appearance of her figure, she could hardly sit still in contemplation of her forthcoming deliverance from her present embarrassment.

Lady Daphne sat upon a stool at the feet of her ladyship, holding up a skein of yarn for the Countess, who was engaged in knitting a heavy muffler.

The three gentlemen were standing by the hearth, where a blazing fire leapt and snapped, as they sipped mulled ale. Every now and again, one or another would cast an eye at the old lady and turn away with a pained expression.

It was the muffler. They each of them feared to be the recipient of yet another of Lady Marcia's pedestrian productions. They had already been presented with more mufflers than they cared to recall. Truly, they did not wish to deny their illustrious ancestor her pleasure, but why could she not have been a fashionable body and embroidered rather than knit? It would have been her female friends who would have to bear with her creations then, and not her long-suffering male descendants. The devil's own wrap could not have been more stifling than a Lady Marcia muffler.

The conversation amongst the gentlemen was not particularly brilliant. Adrian's thoughts were engaged with the coming of Sir Samuel and his own undoubted feeling that the Baronet would demand his being wed to Meg at once. Now that the trouble had been thoroughly brewed, Adrian was no longer in doubt as to what he really wanted. He glanced at Lady Daphne, who smiled back at him, and his heart turned over.

Lord Marcus' thoughts were also engaged, and the occasional glance he threw towards the little figure at the window was an indication of their direction. He was confounded by Meg. He knew himself to be very capable of pleasing the ladies, a figure of high fashion and possessed of a sparkling wit. Females from all ranks had ever only the most charming manners for him; that is, until Meg.

He could not bring himself to believe that he had had no good effect upon her, yet the evidence was all too plain. His few attempts at mending matters between them had been rebuffed; and when, in turn, he had given her a setdown that would have caused any other female to flee in blushing confusion, she had not only turned the tables on him, but did so with so scathing a rejoinder that he felt foolish at having failed, and graceless for having tried.

And so he stood with one hand on the mantlepiece and but one ear attuned to the remarks concerning whether the ground was already too hard for a last hunt of the season, while he tried to determine why his interest in Miss Miller should continue. Could it be that she represented a challenge of a sort he had not met with before? Or could it be that there was that about her which attracted him despite her blatant hostility towards him? He thought of the way her face lit up and her eyes sparkled when she smiled. The way she carried herself—and her person, small though it be, was well-nigh perfect. And he sensed a proud spirit, one not easily cowed, and speculated as to how she might be to someone she had a true affection for. He found himself admitting that Adrian's taste was not to be faulted in this instance. Meg Miller was one with whom intimate acquaintance might prove quite diverting. But, dammit all! There was no time. Her governor would arrive soon and between them there was now so much unfriendly ground to get over. As that thought struck him, he was surprized at the magnitude of the disappointment he felt.

The conversation had now shifted to a discussion of the merits of a cavalry charger as a hunter and Sir Arthur was holding forth. But part of his mind, too, was engaged far afield from his discourse.

He was actually in a quandary over his remark, that Lady Dalrymple had found so odd, anent Miss Miller. It was not that what he had said was uncalled for. No! Its subject certainly merited the accolade, although it was as certain that neither Lady Dalrymple nor her daughter appreciated it. What he had found to be so inexplicable at the time was the great feeling of pride that swept through him as he had made the remark.

What the devil was it to him that little Meg Miller had such spunk? Yet, there it was again, that great feeling of pride for the mettle she had shown. The strain upon his sensibilities was in no way lessened by having to observe his particular vision of loveliness in so uncharitable a mood. Although Lady Honoria's excuse for her behaviour was plausible, it had not pleased him to see the alacrity with which she had fastened the blame upon Meg. It was unseemly in her.

He cast a glance at Meg's figure, silhouetted in the light from the window. It was borne in upon him, too, that Meg, in her own way, was a very attractive young woman. Suddenly, in his mind's eye, Lady Honoria's features were slightly less heavenly than they were a moment ago.

"You were saying?" asked Adrian, as Sir Arthur unaccountably paused in his equine peroration.

"Ah—oh, yes!" exclaimed the Major, startled, and he resumed the discussion.

Lady Marcia was on edge and well aware of the reason for it. Sir Samuel's advent was on her mind almost as much as it was on Meg's. She had never met the man but her ears had been filled with numerous accounts of the Baronet's business acumen, his feats of tremendous physical prowess, and, what was most surprizing and least understandable, his gentility of manner. Discounting it all by half, he still must be a person to be reckoned with. She was, herself, a member of an aristocratic family tracing its ancestry to Hastings and before. During her lifetime, she had had little to say to and less to do with the new gentry that had sprung up. When such contacts proved unavoidable, it had never been any task to put the upstarts in their place and keep them there.

But Sir Samuel, she feared, must prove to be in a class by himself. No, not by himself, for Meg must certainly share it with him. She glanced over at Meg, and thought that, indeed, it must go hard with anyone to have to face the imposing combination of Sir Samuel and his dauntless daughter, together. It was a rare thing in her to be worried about having to deal with people, but the Millers were bound to prove exceptionally difficult to handle seeing as how it was the Rouncefords who were at fault to begin with. She had dismissed as paltry the excuse that Meg had not appeared to be a gentlewoman. Nothing could justify a forcible abduction in this day and age.

She had got to face an irate father and a contrary, if appealing, daughter with no way of disguising the vulnerability of her house. In her lifetime, no hint of scandal had ever attached itself to their name and she was determined that, cost what it would, the name of Rounceford should continue unblemished. Her thoughts regarding that price were become an ever-increasing source of anxiety to her, and the tension it gave rise to was becoming unbearable. She sensed the turbulent emotions of all the room's occupants and became even more irritable.

"Don't tug so!" she cried out at Lady Daphne, shattering that young lady's reveries of the moment. Her abrupt complaint pierced through the murmur of male voices, cutting it off short. The smash of a tumbler and a harsh "Drat!" from Marcus served as an exclamation point to the interruption.

After the briefest pause, everyone but Meg joined in a hubbub of chatter and movement. But even Meg was startled out of her brown study. She turned, with lacklustre gaze, to see what the commotion was about.

Lady Marcia made voluble apology to Daphne and the world at large, but it was lost in the uproar of so many

165

trying to speak at the same time. Then, as suddenly as it had started, it stopped—and allowed the Countess to be clearly heard.

"Oh, I am at sixes and sevens with everything! I do wish that girl's father would get here!"

Meg immediately arose. She had hoped that at least in the Countess she had found a friend.

"Milady, you cannot wish it more than I!" she declared coldly, and started for the door.

"No, no, Meg! No, no, my dear! Stop her! Stop her, someone!" cried Lady Marcia in great consternation.

Meg found herself abruptly held to the spot by the strong hand of Lord Marcus on her shoulder. He turned her about very gently but firmly and held her prisoner in his arm.

"Meg, my dear little friend, you mistake my meaning. I do want your father here, but it is only to settle the business once and for all. I am not at all anxious to see you gone from here. No, not at all, my dear! Please believe me when I say that you are welcome to stay with me for as long as you like. I have enjoyed having you with us so very much and will be desolated at your departure."

Meg was plainly startled. It was not what she expected to hear at all. She looked hard at the Countess.

Lord Marcus' arm was still about her shoulders. It was no longer serving as a bar to her moving and his purpose in letting it remain there was not evident. He looked down at her.

"My dear Meg—I hope you will permit that liberty—as family head, I desire to second without qualification my grandmother's invitation to you. Your presence amongst us has been—er—a bit of a tonic, if I may say so."

Meg looked up into his face, a biting retort on the tip of her tongue. But she never gave voice to it. His brilliant smile quite dazzled her so that she could only smile good-naturedly back at him.

Lord Marcus blinked in pleasant surprise. He had never

seen that merry, elfish expression on her face before and its effect upon him was something he had not been prepared for. It made him start.

"You will excuse my surprize, but I have never been so beamed upon in my life. You are the strangest mixture of honey and vinegar I have ever encountered."

Meg laughed. "Your lordship's compliments are equally strange. I daresay you will never turn my head with them."

Lord Marcus' smile diminished. "No," he agreed, "nor I doubt if anyone else's ever will."

"If we have peace once again, young lady, I would appreciate being so informed," demanded Lady Marcia with a show of feigned impatience.

Meg stepped over to the Countess and planted a kiss on her cheek. Lady Marcia took Meg's hand.

"Thank you, my dear. I have so enjoyed the chats we have had together these past few days. You *must* come again. You are a most unusual girl. It fills me with awe that a little thing like you should have ventured forth into the streets to labour amongst base commoners. Really! Looking at you, I still cannot make up my mind to believe it. Well, let it be a lesson to you! Now you know what happens to young ladies who spurn the protection of their families! I quite agree with Daphne. Adrian can hardly be blamed for his interest in such a taking thing as you are." She sighed. "It is too bad that he went about it in such a clumsy fashion. Had he succeeded, I daresay it would have been the making of him."

Meg gave a little chuckle, but Lady Daphne, all indignation, arose to protest.

"Milady, what are you saying!" she gasped.

"Oh, Daphne, contain yourself," admonished Meg. "Don't you know when you are being had?"

"Oh," replied Daphne in a small voice as she resumed her seat.

"I say!" exclaimed Sir Arthur, "I had quite forgot!

167

Lady Dalrymple is giving a dance within the fortnight and we all are to be invited. I expect that she and her daughter will be calling upon you, milady.''

"Drat the woman!" exploded the Countess. "What a time to choose! And, furthermore, I know nothing of her. It is not to be thought of, with Sir Samuel about to descend upon us at any moment and Meg our guest. I do not see how we can accept. I am sure I shall have the headache when she calls.''

Sir Arthur was quite upset. "But there can be no objection! Meg is invited too," he protested.

Lord Marcus spoke up. "Good! Then I claim Meg for the first dance.''

Everyone turned to look at him.

"A gesture to smooth over ruffled waters," he announced with a grin.

"Well, you are out there!" declared Sir Arthur. "I believe that your rank will require you to partner Lady Honoria, the daughter of the house, for the first dance.''

"I have not the pleasure of her acquaintance. What is she like?''

"I shall introduce you. She is a beauty, but far too innocent for your taste or I should not have consented to your being there!''

Lord Marcus laughed. "So that is how the wind blows! I begin to understand. How well do you know the young lady?''

"I have called upon her but once thus far, but I have every intention of pursuing my interest in her.''

"In that case, I see that we must accept," declared Lady Marcia, "if only for Arthur's sake.''

"Thank you, milady. Then it is settled, Marcus. You will lead off with Lady Honoria, and I with Meg.''

"I think not," responded the Earl coolly and emphatically. "We shall accept, but for a more important reason than Arthur's interest. It is of the greatest moment that I, as head of the House of Rounceford, signify our approval—er—that is not exactly what I mean—rather, that Meg is amongst us as an honoured, nay, a cherished guest.''

Sir Arthur frowned. ''I intend no disrespect to Meg, but you must see that you cannot do this without slighting the Dalrymples. I assure you, Meg, that were the circumstances other than they are, I should not have the least objection.''

''You are too kind, Sir Arthur. But the matter is easily settled, for I need no one's seal of approval. I shan't go!'' she declared.

''But you must!'' chorused Lord Marcus and Sir Arthur together.

''To what purpose? Sir Arthur is correct if you, my lord, are the ranking gentleman. There can be no alternative. So, while I appreciate your intent to restore to me my good name, it may not be done if it is to be at the cost of the Dalrymples' feelings. In any case, I like not the heavy sense of duty and obligation that colours both your bids to be my partner at the dance.''

''Dammit, girl!'' exploded Lord Marcus. ''You persist in misunderstanding me. I assure you it is not out of a heavy sense of obligation, as you put it.''

''Oh, then you do not feel obliged to me?''

''Of course I do! We all do! The Rounceford family must do everything in its power to bring this business to rights before it matures into a vicious scandal. But that is not to say that my wish to lead you onto the dance floor is solely due to such consideration.''

Meg, a half-smile on her lips, looked at his lordship with a quizzical expression as he bowed gracefully. Her smile grew brighter and she curtsied in response.

''You flatter me, milord,'' she murmured.

''I think not,'' he replied.

''Oh, I say!'' exclaimed Sir Arthur with annoyance. ''Marcus, this is foolishness beyond compare! I would not have Meg miss this dance, by any means, and I agree that

169

it would be most desirable for you to lead off with her—
but since it cannot be, I shall do the honours. I can assure
you, Meg, that it is not a duty I shall find at all onerous.''

"But a duty nevertheless, I think," said Meg drily.

"Oh, but—" Sir Arthur began to protest when his other
cousin cut in.

Adrian appeared to be seething with conflicting emotions as he strode over to them, leaving Daphne abruptly.
She had a queer expression on her face as her eyes watched
him cross the room.

"Here, now!" he cried. "It is *I* who have to make
amends! Let there be no more discussion; it is I who shall
be Miss Miller's escort and partner. It can hardly be
otherwise."

"Oh, my dear Mr. Rounceford!" Meg exclaimed.
"Such gallant self-sacrifice must surely find its own
reward. As for me, I shall have none of it."

"And quite right you are!" said Sir Arthur. "Adrian
has done enough already. Indeed, I should say more than
enough!"

Meg turned to him. "Sir Arthur, do not think that I find
your attitude of mind any more congenial than your
cousin's. I had rather be thought a woman of ill-repute
than one who requires the assiduous protection of gallant
gentlemen only because she might be thought to be one.
What do you think? That I am some maiden at Arthur's
court in Camelot come seeking a boon? Gentlemen,
knights-errant all, I pray you go questing in any direction
but mine to perform your feats of gallantry."

Adrian exclaimed, "What the devil is the girl speaking
of?"

Sir Arthur muttered, "She must be mad."

Lord Marcus raised his lorgnette and studied the young
lady deliberately.

Thump! went her ladyship's stick upon the floor.

"I have heard enough of this nonsense! It is all very
amusing, but we are getting nowhere. The child shall go to

the dance and she shall have Marcus to open the dance with her!''

Immediately there was a loud murmur of objections. Lady Marcia raised her hand and there was silence.

"There will be no slight to the Dalrymples. It is the easiest thing. All that need be done is to insure against Marcus being the ranking peer at the affair. I am sure that Augustus will oblige me with his presence.''

Sir Arthur exclaimed, "Not Sussex, surely!"

"And why not the Duke?" demanded Lady Marcia.

"For one thing, he is as close to being a man of letters as one of our Hanoverian Princes can be. I am sure he will not come, and, if he does, must surely detract from the pleasure of the occasion," declared Sir Arthur.

"His Royal Highness is, for his rank, an unassuming gentleman, not at all high-nosed. I warrant he may not join in a romp, but his conversation is nice to degree and he will cast no damper upon the gathering.''

"That is all very well, but I hardly think that Lady Dalrymple can accommodate him. Their cottage is not up to the needs of royalty.''

"Silly boy! Augustus will stay here with us. I am sure we Rouncefords are, and always have been, up to seeing to the comfort of princes; kings, too, if the truth be told. His Highness will not tarry for any time; it will be a short and informal visit.''

"How can you be so sure?" asked Adrian.

Lady Marcia smiled wisely and said, "That is my affair. Now then, the business is settled, I think.''

Great as was the affection of Daphne for Meg, she could not abide the interest all were taking in her friend, especially that of her own Adrian.

She finally declared, "It can hardly be of any consequence. Sir Samuel Miller will have come and gone by then, taking Meg away with him.''

Lady Marcia nodded. "That is a possibility, but I hope that he can be prevailed upon to stay. It would be the very thing for him to appear in our company as well. What say you, Meg?''

"It is, indeed, my intention to leave with my father.''

"My dear, you have every reason to be piqued with us even yet, but I think you are too intelligent to give way to your resentment to your own cost. I shall expect you to go to the dance with Lord Marcus attending you—''

"I cannot promise that my father will approve, nor wish to extend his stay, milady,'' Meg pointed out.

The Countess raised her hand. "Never you mind, my girl. I have no doubt that if you wish it—and explain the necessity for it—he will not gainsay you.'' She gave Meg a shrewd smile. "You do know how needful it is, for all our sakes. I shall leave it to you to explain it to Sir Samuel and I shall be sadly disappointed if he does not accede to your wish in the matter.''

Meg sighed and gave a little shrug. She knew well enough that if her mother were to be present, Sir Samuel could be won over, but she was not sure at all that his daughter could accomplish it by herself.

Chapter Twelve

There was a new feeling throughout the household on the day following. The sun made its appearance at last and set the bleak world a-thawing even as the tension, that had overstretched the nerves of everyone, gave way to a feeling that things were no longer as bad as they had seemed.

Now that it had been settled that Meg was to make an appearance at the party where Lord Marcus would devote himself to her, the gentlemen and ladies not only breathed more easily, but could even afford a greater degree of cordiality amongst themselves than had been, heretofore, in evidence.

In the back of their minds, the imminent arrival of Sir Samuel, and all it portended, left a residue of unease, but each tried, and with success, to believe that no better measures could be taken and that Sir Samuel must approve.

The new day and the new feeling were heralded by Sir Arthur searching out Meg. He found her in the company of Lady Marcia and Lady Daphne, all chatting away quite merrily.

"Your pardon, miladies, if I interrupt, but I would have a word with Meg," Sir Arthur said after the usual greetings.

"I give you leave, Arthur," responded the Countess, "but do not keep her away too long. We have much to speak of and too little time to do so."

Sir Arthur held out his arm to Meg, who approached and laid her hand upon it. Bidding Lady Marcia and Daphne adieu, they passed from the room.

They walked through the corridors, side by side, without saying a word, Sir Arthur guiding Meg along. When they came to the conservatory just off the main parlour, Sir Arthur opened the glassed door with an "If you please" and allowed Meg to pass in before him.

It was spring in this room. In the midst of winter, the glass-panelled walls looked out upon a sunny panorama of melting snow, while within, they were surrounded by the floral humidity of burgeoning plant growth. It acted upon them in a way to make them feel lighthearted—as though it were May, when the earth is putting forth its sweetest odours and finest colours of the year.

From Meg it brought forth a deep longing for the true spring season, when all these tribulations might be behind her and she could regain the peace of spirit she so much desired.

After a moment of silence during which they both savoured the delightful aromas, Sir Arthur spoke.

"My dear Meg, I have asked you here that I may tender you a heartfelt apology. I do so as much for all of us Rouncefords as I do, particularly for myself. Your treatment by Adrian—totally unpleasant, I know—I need not dwell upon. But my recent lack of sympathy and understanding was, beyond measure, odious. I beg you will forgive me."

Meg nodded, but she refrained from making any comment. One could not render the business in any favourable light with words, nor could one lessen the seriousness of the offence to her by hypocritical mouthings. In any case, she was not in a mood for more than courteous acceptance of peace offerings.

Sir Arthur continued. "Good! Please understand that I should have been delighted to have the first dance, but

174

under the circumstances it was necessary to defer to Marcus, you will admit?'' He paused.

She nodded.

''I can assure you that, and only that consideration, prevailed with me to step aside, but the second dance on your program—for that, I shall defer to no one. I pray that you will so favour me.''

Meg had not expected the bid and was untouched by it. Sir Arthur had done all he need do to establish a basis for civility between them without it.

She shrugged and her hand strayed up to toy with a glossy black ringlet. ''If you wish it, Sir Arthur,'' she responded coolly, ''but surely you have already done your duty to me and need not be further troubled. I am sure that his lordship's attentions to me at the Dalrymples' will be all that is necessary to allay the mischief. I shall be a sufficient trial to him, I daresay; it would be too bad of me to spoil your evening as well.''

Sir Arthur grinned. ''I did not do that well at all, did I?''

A tiny smile appeared on Meg's lips. ''I do not understand you,'' she said.

''I meant the apology sincerely, but my wish to stand up with you was no part of it. As you say, Marcus has the duty to do so and he will carry it off in the most unexceptionable manner, so that there is no need for my services on that score. So you see, then, why I say that my wish for the dance is apart from anything else. I had hoped that you would have me as a partner—let me say that it would be a pleasure and a privilege if you will accept. You see,'' he went on with some difficulty, ''I—I admire you tremendously.''

His earnest manner did touch her. She could appreciate the cost of such an effort to so proud and dashing a man as Sir Arthur was.

She smiled up at him. ''I should be honoured, Sir Arthur.''

He let out a breath of relief and bowed to her. "I shall be looking forward to it, Meg. I am so very pleased that we have got over the ground without too bad a spill."

"I am, too; but is not that Lady Marcia's cane I hear? I had best return to her before the floor is damaged beyond repair."

Upon Meg's return, Lady Marcia made no attempt to disguise her curiosity and began to interrogate her before she had even found her seat. Her ladyship wished to know—no, she demanded to know—what business Sir Arthur had had with her.

In anyone else, Meg would have regarded such prying as sheer impertinence, but she suspected that Lady Marcia was more interested in Meg's affairs for Meg's own sake than from mere idle curiosity, and so Meg had no reservations about informing Lady Marcia that her grand-nephew had requested a dance of her.

"And did you grant it?" the Countess asked eagerly.

Meg blushed slightly and admitted she had. She smiled as she did so, quite aware of the sharp scrutiny by the older woman. Lady Marcia appeared quite satisfied with her response and, without further comment, resumed her cross-examination of Meg with regard to the latter's adventures in the shop of Madame Celestine.

Lady Marcia, like so many of her gentlewoman contemporaries, had never considered a couturiere's shop as anything but a supply of fashionable, female habiliments served up without effort at her slightest wish. It was all very pleasant, and shopping for clothes was an important diversion in her life. Of course, when the bills for such an amusement were presented, despite her great wealth the pleasures often turned sour and, as though to exact a toll for this, the bills, more often than not, were well-aged before they were honoured.

It was indeed a revelation for both the Countess and Daphne to be taken behind the scenes by the word-pictures

Meg drew for them. Meg, with her wit and her habit of bringing to their notice, in a good-natured way, the humourous side, always kept them entertained. They were as much absorbed in her adventures as they were enchanted with their narrator, the Countess especially.

As the days had passed, Lady Marcia had put the time to good advantage. She had extended herself to make Meg believe that not only was she truly welcome but that she, the Countess, was genuinely interested in her. The result was all that she could have wished, and she was able to see, then, the sort of person Meg was in truth.

As Lady Daphne and Meg sat before her, she could not help comparing them. Daphne, as pretty as a penny and sweetly charming, could hold her own in most feminine company, but here, beside dark-haired Meg with her expressive eyes, laughing one moment, innocently impish the next, it was seeing vibrant colour rendering soft pastel insipid.

For a hundredth time Lady Marcia sighed regretfully to herself and thought, what a fool was Adrian. While one part of her mind continued to enjoy the recounting of Meg's reminiscences, the rest of her attention was devoted to an examination of Sir Arthur's motives. If they were what she hoped, then this darling girl might yet be bound to the Rounceford name in a permanent way.

Another interruption of her entertainment was brought about by the intrusion of Lord Marcus. It would appear that he, too, wished to have a word with Meg.

Meg smiled and looked askance at the Countess. She arose, begged Lady Marcia's leave, and was escorted out of the room on Lord Marcus' arm.

She was led to the library where a cheery blaze on the hearth lent a cozy note to the otherwise somber room. Lord Marcus led Meg over to the fireside divan. While she settled herself upon it, he drew up an ottoman. Carefully arranging his coattails, he sat himself down. Although his seat was much lower than Meg's, he experienced no difficulty in gazing levelly into her face, despite her habitually erect manner of sitting.

"Are you comfortable?" he asked with a smile.

"Yes, thank you, milord," she answered, smiling back at him.

"May I pour you some sherry?" He reached for a crystal decanter.

"Thank you. I am quite dry. I seem to have been talking all morning."

"May I ask to whom?"

"To her ladyship. She would have me tell all about Madame Celestine's."

"Oh, yes, the shop," he remarked with a grimace. "I should not think it a pleasant topic."

"I can assure you, Lady Marcia is positively fascinated with it. I daresay it would be quite a bore for you."

"I admit that matters of a millinery nature hold little attraction for me."

"Well, then, now that I am comfortable and we have settled it that my adventures as a shopkeeper's assistant are not the reason for my being here, shall you tell me what you wish to say or shall I guess? I am sure it is not sweet nothings you wished to whisper in my shell-like ear."

He grinned saucily. "One never knows; it may come to that yet."

Meg chuckled. "That, milord, is a whopper if I ever heard one. Now that we have come to know each other so much better, I *do* know my place, you know."

"Ah, so that is the sticking point. I was afraid it might be. Will you accept my most abject apology, once again, for having behaved so completely the graceless boor? I know it is a great deal to ask, but think; I was sure at the time that you were—er—you were—"

"I had me hooks into 'im, yer ludship, an' 'e wore agoin' ter pay through the nose!"

It was not the most accurate simulation, if the truth be told, but Lord Marcus thought it delightful and laughed as

178

though it was quite the cleverest thing he had heard. The pert gestures, the saucy grin, and the sparkling eyes that accompanied it may have had much to do with his lordship's high opinion of the performance.

"Come now, Meg, be serious!"

"Oh, but I am! You were quite right in your opinion. I offered to accept a carte blanche from your cousin."

"You do not mean that!" he said with impatience.

"But I do! If you doubt it, you have only to ask him."

Lord Marcus rose abruptly and began to stride about the room. His agitation was great as he paced back and forth casting a look of stern reproach at Meg at each circuit of the library.

Suddenly he stopped. With the frown somewhat lessened, he turned and directed a penetrating look at her. Slowly a smile dawned on his face.

"You little devil!" he exclaimed. "You were taking him to the fair! What a booby you must have made of him! Oh, if I could have been there to see it done! Adrian and a carte blanche for the likes of you! Ha! Ha!" Lord Marcus' laughter was quite hearty.

Meg gazed upon him and smiled, but her eyes were not laughing.

"Milord, what must I think? I deliberately gammoned Adrian, and with some success; but I did not do so with you, yet I am sure I could not have made you think worse of me if I had set out to do so."

"Of course, my dear, that is exactly so. If you are trying to give me one of your famous setdowns, I tell you, you shan't succeed; not this time. What you are saying, and I quite agree with you, is that if I laugh at Adrian I must laugh at myself as well. Your manner of holding a mirror to me is deucedly unpleasant. I look forward to when you tire of the sport."

"Oh, dear, you are being too agreeable. I do not deserve it."

"I am sure you don't," agreed Lord Marcus. "But I am
179

on my best behaviour. I have made up my mind that I shall not be put out of temper no matter how much you try me—and I am sure you will try me far before you have done.''

"You daunt me, milord," Meg said with a chuckle. "But seriously, I am in debt to you for putting yourself out for me at the forthcoming dance. Please be assured that the burden of entertaining me there will not last beyond the first set.''

Lord Marcus smiled down at her. "You may find this hard to believe, Meg, but I have very broad shoulders and you may rest easy. The burden you mention will not trouble me greatly.

"If I should show signs of fatigue after the third or fourth dance, it will be time enough to discuss what is to be done to ease the load.''

Meg's eyes opened wide. "Milord! One dance was all that was proposed! Two dances is to single me out, but three dances and my father must begin to question your intentions.''

"Ah yes, your father! I think I shall be interested to meet the gentleman. I hope he is better behaved than his daughter. I would not care to be *set down* by him!''

Meg laughed heartily. "Adrian told me about Sir Sammy's introduction at the club. I seem to have inherited his spirit, if not his strength.''

"Do you think he would invite me to Harlington?''

"But, milord, there is nothing for you at Harlington; we should be hard put to entertain you. There is no season and there is no hunting, and the fishing is for schoolboys using a bent pin. You would be bored before bedtime.''

"Let me be the judge of that. I cannot believe that the Miller family can be anything but interesting. I have heard much of your father, and I know you. If your mother is half as charming as her daughter, I shall not be bored.''

"Yes indeed, if you find my father and myself charming, you must meet milady mother. She, you will fall in love with. I have not half her measure of charm and she is very beautiful as well.''

"Well then, I must to Harlington, and since I shall fall in love with her on sight, I daresay I shall have Sir Samuel to contend with.'' He knit his brows. "Now there is a formidable opponent! I say, do you think that if worse comes to worst, instead of vying with your father, I should be deemed a coward if I were to content myself with a lesser prize?''

"What nonsense is this? What lesser prize at Harlington?'' asked Meg with an uncertain smile.

"If I may not have your lovely mother, I am sure her daughter will be sufficient consolation.'' He took up her hand, laid a kiss upon it, and left the room.

Meg remained staring after him in great surprise.

On the second day after Miss Miller's disappearance, Sir George Hobcourt decided that the iron was hot enough to strike. He therefore presented himself at his mother's residence more than pleased with his accomplishment.

"Oh, George, where have you been? I am quite distracted! Have you heard the terrible news?''

"What may that be, pray?'' asked George, fluffing out his frilled cuffs.

"Miss Miller has been abducted!''

Sir George let his quizzing glass fall to the length of its gold chain. "You don't say!'' he exclaimed. "When did it happen? What is being done?''

"But two days ago. Bow Street says that they have traced them south and I am expecting to hear that they have her safe at any moment. Oh, why did I ever allow it?''

"Come, come, milady. I am sure it is not as serious as all that. Abduction? I hardly think so. Probably ran off with some fellow who took her fancy. I do not see the necessity for Bow Street.''

Lady Amelia regarded her son with disgust. "Have you

181

lost all of your wits? But of course they are needed and I do not wish to enter into a debate with you. There is no time. We cannot trust them to act quickly enough. You must go and find her, George!''

''Me! I should think not! Good lord! I should chase over the countryside after a baggage who cares not a wit what people may think? Not on my life, b'gad!''

Storm clouds gathered on Lady Amelia's face. ''George! Whatever has gotten into you? I insist that you go after her at once! What better way than this to advance yourself in her good graces? And if anything has befallen her, she will be only too grateful to you to even hesitate to accept your offer.''

George looked shocked. ''Have you taken leave of your senses? Marry her after this! Why, I should be the laughing stock of the world! Marry my friend's sparrow? I say no!''

''What are you saying? What friend? What friend could do this awful thing to you?'' Lady Amelia's face was livid and her eyes glowed.

Sir George was stricken speechless. He had slipped and slipped badly. Under his breath he cursed himself for a fool.

''Do not stand there like an idiot! I demand an answer! What sort of friend would cast dishonour upon us? Well, speak!''

Sir George, angry at himself, found his voice. ''What dishonour? A female of no account runs off with someone. We can not be held accountable for that. How you talk!''

''I tell you all the facts point to an abduction—and we *are* accountable for her. She was our guest. She was under the protection of the Hobcourt name. Are you not Sir George Hobcourt, last of the Hobcourts? Was she not, therefore, under your protection? I ask you again: who is this odious friend?''

''Bah! I say good riddance! You make too much of it.

Who, after all, is Meg Miller? Little better than a 'cit' who does not know her place. I say again good riddance to her. This will teach her to respect her betters!''

"That is what you say, is it? Very well, then. I shall inform Sir Samuel of all that I know. I am sure he will wish to pursue the matter further with you."

Sir George gulped. "Sir Samuel?" he asked weakly.

Lady Amelia did not relish seeing her offspring cringe, but she relished even less the consequences of this shameful deed. She did not wish to think of what would be said when it became known that Miss Miller, the daughter of her dearest friend, came to grief while residing under her roof.

"What friend, George? You will answer me now or you will answer to Sir Samuel before you are much older."

Sir George had the strongest feeling that after Sir Samuel had gotten the answers from him, he still would never be much older. Faced with that fearful prospect, Sir George did not see that he had much choice. He consoled himself with the belief that his mother would shield him from the direst consequences, as it would be to both their advantages for her to do so. In any case, he could only have played out his string until Adrian was caught up with. It had been a major oversight on his part to forget that, although Sir Samuel was a base-born commoner, he commanded such power and prestige as many a duke might envy. Nor could he doubt that he was in peril of being challenged to a duel by Adrian when all accounts were rendered. It did not lessen his panic to realize that it was his own stupid self-assurance that had brought him to this pass.

For all his fear, as he proceeded to inform his mother of all the details of the affair, he still could not help feeling proud of the manner in which Adrian had been taken in, but if Lady Amelia was impressed, it was by how complete a scoundrel she had raised to manhood.

Her voice was loaded with contempt as she said, "So

183

that was the way of it? Well, my son, know this: if it ever comes out how you were involved in this, we are ruined. We shall be ostracized and you will never marry to advantage. There is only one way out of this business for us. You must marry the Miller girl without delay! It is fortunate that you know where they went. Get going, at once!

"Adrian Rounceford! I find it hard to believe. To permit himself to be inveigled so! Well, that is one good thing. Meg has a head on her shoulders and it is quite possible that she can foil such a blockhead. Nevertheless she will need help. It is a pity that she must be wasted on you but it cannot be helped. I doubt if you can appreciate how lucky you are to get a girl like that. She is so much more than you deserve.

"But before you go, hear me and hear me well. If, after all this, you fail to win her, do not come back to me! I shall not know you!"

Chapter Thirteen

When Meg arose on the following day, she found herself loath to go down for breakfast. If she could have slept, she would not have gotten out of bed at all. As it was she dismissed the maid and conducted her own toilet, dawdling over everything while she gave herself to think over the events of the past few days, not excepting the interesting exchanges that had taken place between her and each of the two cousins yesterday.

It was hard to believe that all these episodes and encounters had occurred only because she had taken it into her head to work in a dress shop. On the face of it, a forcible abduction must be a heinous crime, yet she had not suffered any harm. In fact, the inconvenience of the affair was, to a great degree, compensated for by her having been brought into contact with an entirely new group of people.

She found it ludicrous that she could find the Rouncefords an interesting and charming family circle, even including Adrian. Each one as high in the instep as could be, but once the opening hostilities had been gotten over, there was a genuine warmth. She had tried hard to discount it by telling herself that their concern for her was founded upon their concern for their own good name, but it had not convinced her. Almost overnight she had become an intrinsic part of the Rounceford domicile and could not help feeling quite at home. In truth, the emotional exchanges that she had had sooner or later with each of them was no more than might be encountered in any domestic scene. Considering the circumstances that had brought her to them and the very little time that they had known her, converse between the Rouncefords and herself was become remarkably free.

The Countess was an entirely lovable lady, once one understood the pose of cantankerous senility she attempted to pass off on one. There was no question in Meg's mind that Lady Marcia's approval was a keystone in her own acceptance.

Sir Arthur, for all his dashing exterior, was not at all typical of the noblesse who devoted themselves to the military. She had never been able to reconcile Wellington's defeat of Napoleon with her picture of the British officer. As great a soldier as the Iron Duke was, he could never have carried it off all by himself, yet the military dandies she had heard tell of could never have been of much account. Sir Arthur solved the puzzle for her. An officer cadre comprised of men like him must have gone far to help Wellington bring down the Frenchman.

For all that Sir Arthur's manner was direct, she would have liked him better if he was less forthright and given to some lightness of manner. She smiled as she recalled his confusion as he put in his bid for a place on her program.

Of course, it was amazing to think that, after his heartless suggestion of a marriage of convenience as a way out of her trouble, he could be so civil to her. At least there was no sham about the young man. For all his seeming lack of tact he was not unlikeable—and he was exceedingly graceful. She was bound to find dancing with him quite pleasurable, she thought.

And then, of course, there was his lordship. How could she have taken him in such dislike? Perhaps it was his overweening pride, which he made no attempt to disguise. And yet the man was so vulnerable to her slightest remark. That he had wit, she was sure; but how it came about that she had more than once penetrated his polished exterior and put him to rout surprised her. In fact she was a little ashamed for having indulged herself so at his expense, but—she chuckled at the thought—he insisted upon making himself a target, and that was hard to resist.

His parting remark, as he had left her, still was a puzzle. What he had intended by it, she was not sure. One could be tempted to regard it as a proposal of sorts, a preliminary to a more direct offer; but they hardly knew each other. If he were a fortune hunter, of course, her prospects were more than ample to warrant such an overture; but in the course of her conversations with the Countess, more than once she had been assured by her ladyship that the Earl of Marchford could look as high as he cared to for a wife. If only he would look, Lady Marcia had remarked.

Then, what else could he have had in his mind? An indecent offer? She hardly thought so; not after all the furore that Adrian's endeavour along that line had invoked. If it was neither one nor the other, then she must conclude that it was merely an empty gallantry—and the thought angered her, for she had been sufficiently taken in by it to have lost most of a good night's sleep. Truly, she should have known better. The man was an audacious flirt. She contented herself by stigmatizing him as a loose fish, and dismissed him from her thoughts.

And then there was Adrian. As sincere as Arthur, but just not up to snuff despite the excellent impression he made at first sight. And he was so stuffy! She had not heard that he had given over the idea of marrying her—and his devotion to Daphne could not be more obvious. What a little hell Daphne must be making of it!

It was becoming a bore and Meg made up her mind to see to it the question was settled once and for all. She was not about to become a burden of punishment to any man— not even her father would be able to change her mind about that! And the sooner everyone realized it, the better.

She pictured each of the Rounceford men in turn. All in all, it was unusual that in one family there should be three such handsome cousins and not one of them less than charming. Each by himself was enough to attract a lady's eye, but, when viewed in company of one another, their faults rather than their virtues came to the fore—or did it only seem so to her prejudiced eye?

Meg sighed and finished dressing. The coming dance, at least, was a consolation to look forward to. If she danced with no one else, her two Rounceford partners would be enough to make the occasion memorable.

Meg could no longer stay in her room. It was getting on towards noon and she had already received an inquiry from the Countess as to her health coupled with a summons to present herself downstairs without delay.

For no particular reason she descended by the great staircase which brought her down by the entrance hall, and so was on hand to witness the arrival and the strange welcome accorded to Sir George Hobcourt.

At the sight of him being helped out of his greatcoat by a servant, Meg paused in her descent. She was just in time to see Adrian come out of the library and stride over to him.

"Ah, old friend, we are well met, for I have something for you!"

With that, Adrian swung a mighty, right-handed blow to Sir George's jaw, knocking him to the ground.

George lay stunned for a moment; then, as his misty mind began to clear, he slowly sat up and supported himself by leaning back on his hands.

He shook his head a few times before he looked up at Adrian, who was standing over him with his fists clenched.

"I say, what was that for?" demanded George, glaring up at his friend.

"You know damn well what that was for, you hound! If you will oblige me by getting up, it will be my pleasure to knock you down again! Now, get up at once!"

"Damned if I will! What's the sense to 't? Believe me,

old chum, you are off your rocker, and I'll not get up until someone takes you in hand!''

He began to massage his aching jaw and look around, when he caught sight of Meg on the staircase.

"Oh, there you are, Meg! I thought I should find you here after I went first to Adrian's''—he caught himself up and abruptly changed the subject—"I say, will you call someone to take this madman off me before he kills me? He is quite out of his mind, you know. Knocked me down he did. Terrible way to greet a chum.''

Adrian looked up, too. "Yes, Meg, this is the villain behind it all: my friend, George Hobcourt. But, of course, you must be acquainted with him.''

Meg was plainly startled. "I do not understand you, Adrian. Yes, I know Sir George and he knows me, but if you think that is reason enough to knock him down, then I must agree with him and call you mad.''

"Indeed I am angry enough to be mad! It was this—this foul friend who pointed you out to me.''

"What is this I hear, Adrian?'' exclaimed Meg horrified. "You did know my true identity when you abducted me? You must be baser than I had believed!''

"No, no, Meg, you have it all wrong! He it was who pointed you out to me as being a shopgirl with romantic inclinations.''

"If that were my only qualification to attract your interest, I am not at all flattered.''

"What the devil, girl! Of course, that was not why I approached you!''

"May I inquire as to what else you found to interest yourself in me?'' Meg asked in all innocence.

Adrian began to boil. He stood there, his eyes growing larger and his face getting redder as he attempted to keep a hold on his temper. It was to no avail.

"Blast!'' he shouted. "Don't you understand? If Hobcourt had not lied to me about you, I should never have carried you off!''

"Oh, I see," said Meg, nodding her head sagely. "Then it was because you thought that I enjoyed being snatched away that you so obliged me—or was it George you were obliging? I am not sure I have the straight of it yet."

"That will be enough of that, young lady!" admonished the Countess as she came marching in. She shook her finger at Meg as she came down from her perch on the staircase. "Naughty girl, you should be ashamed of yourself to be teasing poor Adrian so!"

"Oh, I am, milady, I am," declared Meg, bowing her head, but not before the merry twinkle in her eyes was noted by all.

A voice murmured at her side. "The Rouncefords' assassin strikes again! And so neatly the victim is never aware that he has been had."

Meg looked up into Lord Marcus' grinning face and blushed.

"I assure you, milord, I should never have done so had I known there was an audience," she murmured in response.

"Yes, I think I believe you. But what is all this about? That *is* George Hobcourt on the floor, is it not? And, from the way he is feeling his jaw, I take it that Adrian has more than chucked him under the chin."

Lady Marcia brought her stick crashing down on the floor.

"This is no place to be discussing what appears to be matters that require looking into. You, Adrian—and you, Arthur—where is that boy?—"

At that moment Lady Daphne entered the vestibule. Upon seeing Sir George recumbent on the floor, with Adrian standing over him, she gave a little scream, threw up her hands, and rushed into Adrian's arms, crying, "Oh, Adrian, speak to me! You are not hurt! Tell me you are not hurt!"

Meg chuckled.

The Countess exclaimed, "Pfagh!"

Sir Arthur, who came wandering in, said, after one look at the tableau, "I say, Adrian, what have we here? A drama? Conquering hero receiving his just reward, eh? Well, just don't stand there! If you do not know how to conclude the scene, I shall be most happy to show you how it is done."

The two lovers sprang apart, Adrian looking foolish and Daphne, a deep crimson suffusing her features.

"There you are, Arthur! Where have you been?" cried Lady Marcia. "I want you and Adrian—and, of course George, there—Adrian! I do wish you will let him up! I wish you all to retire with me to a more appropriate chamber where we can discuss what has befallen."

Meg heard Marcus breathe a sigh of relief and mutter, "Thank heaven, she has forgotten for once that I am family head."

"And, of course, you also, Marcus," added the Countess.

"Too soon, I spoke too soon," Marcus groaned with resignation.

Sir Arthur hauled George to his feet, and the little party moved into the east parlour, leaving the two girls to themselves in the great entrance hall.

"Pray tell me, Meg, why is Sir George come to call? And why had Adrian and he come to blows?"

"As to the first, I am sure I do not know. As to the second, you had best seek an answer from Adrian. I do not wish to discuss it."

Meg made a face and changed the subject. "Well, we are quite left to amuse ourselves. It is too nasty to venture out of doors and there is not much to read. While they are having what gives all the signs of being a lengthy conference, we may as well— But someone comes!" she declared as the sound of a large vehicle was heard coming up the drive.

It came to a halt and Meg, without waiting for the knock, threw the door open.

There on the doorstep stood Lady Elizabeth, with Sir Samuel's great arm about her.

"Mamma!" cried Meg, and she threw herself into the warm embrace of her mother.

Meg did not ring for the servants; instead she assisted herself, helping her parents to doff their wraps and cloaks. As she did so she managed to make Lady Daphne known to them and, in answer to her father's inquiry regarding the Countess of Marchford, she explained that something had come up to occupy the attention of the Rounceford family and she would prefer not to disturb them at the moment.

Lady Daphne gracefully excused herself and left the Millers to enjoy their reunion undisturbed.

"Now tell me, Meg, what is amiss? You look to be in good health and spirits," said Sir Samuel, taking his daughter by the shoulders and scrutinizing her face.

"There is naught to worry about, Pappa. I have received no harm. How much have you heard?"

As it turned out, Sir Samuel and Lady Elizabeth had heard a great deal. As he explained to her, once he had understood that that Peterskin fellow knew something, Sir Samuel had nailed him to the spot until every scrap of information had been elicited. Meg's mother and he had come as quickly as they could, Sir Samuel refusing Peterskin's offer to drive them. They might have arrived even sooner, but, despite Lady Bess' remonstrances, they had made frequent stops to rest, for it had been a crushing drive for her.

"Well, now that we have the villainy confirmed in all its ugliness, I do not see any reason to stand on ceremony. I am sure that I can live without the honour of being presented to Lady Marchford. Under the circumstances, I should not hold myself responsible for what might pass between us. Go get your things, girl, and we shall be off."

"Oh, no, Father, you must not do that! The Rouncefords have been most kind, and are at this moment trying to make heads and tails of this embarrassment."

Meg's protest did not wash with her father.

"They are trying, you say? I should like to know whatever for! It is as plain to me as the nose on your face that this Adrian fellow of theirs is the cause of it all. He shall be made to pay and, believe you me, it shall not go easy with him.

"In the meantime, it is best we bundle you off to the Continent until this blows over. Leave it all to me; I shall know how to deal with the Rouncefords as they deserve. They will learn what a hard thing it is to trifle with the Miller name. Now get your things; we leave immediately."

"Oh, Momma, cannot you do anything with him?" pleaded Meg, turning to Lady Elizabeth.

"Why should I, dearest? What is wrong with your father's plan?"

Meg hesitated. She was thoroughly aware of the fact that her father was very angry and therefore what she was about to propose, namely, continuing her stay with the Countess, must sound particularly brainless under the circumstances. Yet she truly believed that it was the best thing to do. With the forlorn hope that her mother would see it her way and rally to her support, she took a deep breath and plunged in.

"Poppa, it is all too true that I have undergone the rudest treatment at the hands of one of the Rouncefords, but I have come to think that I was not completely blameless in the matter. For all of that, I have suffered no great harm and am in a way to reaching some accord with them.

"You see, if it had not been that he thought I was one of Madame Celestine's—"

"Yes!" interrupted her father. "That, young lady, is something we are going to have words about, many of them, I assure you. How your mother could have been so

193

cow-brained as to permit you to degrade yourself—"

"Degrade myself?" Meg came very erect as her indignation showed itself in her every aspect. "I cannot believe that Sir Samuel Miller, who made his fortune grinding corn with his own two hands, dare think that his daughter could demean herself by doing much the same thing!"

"It is *not* the same thing! I was brought up to it and I had to earn my living in that fashion because it was all I knew how to do. You were a deal more fortunate. I was able to provide for you well enough to bring you up a lady. Aye, a fine lady—fit to be daughter to the finest of ladies, your mother! Why, you are well provided for beyond many a nobler woman's dreams! You may have had as fine a husband as you can wish; but do you appreciate this? No, you do not! You with your harum-scarum fancies—and that your mother should abet you in them! . . ."

Meg would not have her mother bear any part of the blame.

"Leave Momma out of this, I pray. It was never her idea!"

"That is neither here nor there! The fact of the matter is—well, what have you left now? When it comes out that you have served in a menial—"

"I was not a menial!" Meg protested.

"Silence!" thundered her father. "That was scandal enough, yet we could have circumvented it. But no longer! You and this Rounceford fellow have done for you now. You are ruined and must thank your lucky stars for any husband we can find for you. Now, let there be no more discussion. I would have you away from here before we are put to the distasteful necessity of meeting with the Rouncefords. Get your things at once, do you hear!"

The peremptoriness of her father's command was both strange and horrid to her ears. Meg could not believe that this, her father, could have become so heavyhanded with her, his favourite daughter. Tears welled forth and coursed down her cheeks. She turned in appeal to her mother.

"Momma, please help me! I tell you it is not as black as Poppa paints it. The Rouncefords—"

"No, Meg, it will not do," said her mother, shaking her head. "Your father is right. It was too bad of me to allow you to venture forth against my best judgement. It is a dreadful case we find ourselves in and we must leave. But, dear heart, do not cry. At home we will talk of it—in a way that we cannot do here. I am sure we will find a way to carry it off without the loss of too many feathers. Go, dear child, and get your things. It would try me to the end of my being to have to be civil to the Rouncefords at this time."

In sheer desperation Meg declared, "No, Mamma, I will not!"

Lady Elizabeth looked at her daughter with a mixture of pride and sadness. For Meg to withstand her only demonstrated how truly distraught her daughter was. But they were all distraught and they would reap no profit by extending the discussion in this place and at this time. Other than Meg's being upset, she could see no valid reason for her disobedience and so she quietly, but firmly, informed her daughter that she should protest no longer and do as her father bid her.

Meg paused a moment and then, without another word, turned and left the hall.

She returned in a very short time, carrying her cloak.

"This is all I have," she remarked sadly.

Sir Samuel laid a comforting hand upon her shoulder. Lady Elizabeth laid a kiss upon her brow.

When they had donned their wraps, Sir Samuel, Lady Elizabeth, and Meg gathered outside only to find that their carriage had already been taken to the stableyard behind the house. Sir Samuel was about to repair to the yard to seek his conveyance, when they saw a horseman come dashing up the drive. He was heading for the stable when he spied the little group on the doorsteps. In a flurry of mud he wheeled his horse sharply around, trotted over to them, and dismounted.

"That wore a spankin' pace ye set me, guv'nor!" cried Peterskin with a grin spreading over his mud-covered visage. "I'd ha' been here before ye, but I don't know this country so well as I thought. Well, why do you wait upon the doorstep? The people are at home, awaitin' fer ye!"

He went to open the door which, not a moment ago, Sir Samuel had shut.

"That will not be necessary. We have got what we came for, and if you will be kind enough to see that our carriage is brought out, we will be on our way."

Lemmy looked surprised.

"But surely ye cannot have seen the Rouncefords a'ready! I was certain sure there'd be such a deal of explaining to be done that 'twould be days before ye'd be setting out again."

"Never you mind that, Peterskin. Do as I say—and you may inform your people that we have been and gone. The less said the better, I think."

"Well, I don't think Sir Arthur will take it kindly of ye, yer honour."

"Sir Arthur may take it any way he likes—and that goes as well for the rest of them. Now, get moving, man!"

Lemmy saluted and left. He found the horses already unharnessed from the coach, so it was some minutes before he was able to have the rig ready. He drove it out to the waiting Millers and assisted the ladies to step up into it.

As Sir Samuel took up the reins, Lemmy called up to him, "Sir, the beasts be blowed! Ye'll not be able to push them."

"I am aware of that. Now, is everything safe and secure?"

"Aye, right 'n' tight; but, guv'nor . . ." Lemmy began to shift his feet.

"Yes, what is it?"

" 'Tis about the reward I'd be askin'."

"Oh, yes, I had quite forgot. Here." Sir Samuel took out a roll of bills that made Lemmy stare. He counted off five notes, folded them, and handed them down to Lemmy.

"I thank ye, sir! Lemmy Peterskin's at yer service whenever ye've a need fer 'im!"

Sir Samuel cracked his whip and the coach rolled off down the drive.

Chapter Fourteen

"Dash it all! Here, I have been telling you over and over again, it was just a bit of fun!" George Hobcourt complained as he paced about the room, appealing in turn to each iron-grim Rounceford face. "Who could believe that Adrian would swallow it, feathers and all?"

"Hobcourt, you had better shut up!" Adrian flared at him, gritting his teeth. "A bit of fun, was it? I shall give you fun in a moment but you will not laugh!"

There was a rap on the door and the butler entered. He approached Sir Arthur.

"Sir Arthur, your man, Peterskin, is without and—"

"Send him in, man! Do not stand there! Send him in at once!" cried Sir Arthur. The butler left and the Major turned to the room.

"Well, now, Sir Samuel is about to descend upon us. We do not have much time. If he proves to be in a doggish humour, I say give him Hobcourt for a bone to gnaw on."

"Hear! Hear!" cried Adrian.

"I say!" Sir George's face was flushed with apprehension. "Not the thing to do, you know! Not at all sporting of you!"

Sir Arthur wheeled upon him. "Then you take it right, sir! It was not meant to be, and I should be vastly diverted to witness the interview that Sir Samuel would conduct with you."

"And so should I!" chimed in Lord Marcus. "But I

think it a better course to be prepared to calm the man. George and his little tale must only put him into a greater rage. No, we must do what we can to get over the initial hostilities as quickly as possible.''

He paused for a moment as he gave it some thought, then his face brightened. ''I have it! Meg! We must have Meg present. I cannot imagine her father—or any man, for that matter—flying off the handle but she must quickly bring him to his senses.''

Lemmy Peterskin entered.

''Ah, Corporal-Major, how soon may we expect Sir Samuel?'' asked Sir Arthur.

Lemmy opened his eyes wide. ''Beggin' yer pardon, sir, but he has went!''

There were explosions of surprise and disbelief throughout the room. Sir Arthur's voice overtopped them all.

''What the devil are you saying, Corporal? Where is Sir Samuel?''

''Sir, he be well on his way back to Harlington; he, his lady, and Miss Miller.''

Immediately Peterskin was made to tell how he had met the Millers on the doorstep and seen them off. When he had finished, Sir Arthur, in a toneless voice, dismissed him.

''That was most discourteous of Sir Samuel,'' remarked the Countess. She shrugged her shoulders. ''Now, there is nothing left to say, is there? He has taken Meg—and, I suppose, the problem as well. It is a shame, for I was sure we had hit on a way to solve it. Arthur, I do not think that I shall be in spirits to attend the Dalrymple affair. You will make my apologies to them.'' She looked around her at the young men. ''I think, too, that I have had enough of all of you. I am off to Bath in the morning. Well, what are you looking so glum about?'' she snapped. ''Count yourself lucky, Adrian; another father might have insisted on marriage.''

"I was prepared for that," responded Adrian quietly.

"Oh, are you disappointed, then?"

Adrian turned away without speaking, but Lord Marcus stepped in to defend his cousin.

"Hardly that, milady. Poor Adrian has been steeling himself for the encounter. Now that it appears there will be none, he finds himself at a loss. I daresay he will recover once he realizes he has escaped a horrible fate."

Sir Arthur countered with a small frown, "Adrian, surely you do not see it that way! Marcus exaggerates to the point of insult. I can think of far worse fates than to be wed to the little Miller girl." He nodded as he became more certain. "Yes, she's a fetching little thing, and one thing is sure—for all her lack of birth, she is finely bred and not at all behindhand in the wit department." He leered at Marcus. "How say you to *that*, milord Earl?"

Lord Marcus bowed to his cousin. "I bleed from the thousand wounds she inflicted upon me in her short time with us. Your salt I do not need; they are painful enough without it." He stood erect and, reaching for his snuffbox, helped himself to a pinch. "Shall we leave it that, at some cost to my self-esteem, I have taken the measure of my adversary and admit she is a worthy foeman? Our next encounter, let me assure you, will find me at less of a disadvantage."

"Oh, then you plan to meet with her again?" queried the Countess.

The Earl shrugged. "No, milady, I have no such plan. Sooner or later, I daresay, we shall meet again. Even the inhabitants of Harlington must, on occasion, find themselves in London. In fact, before my unbearable presence forces your ladyship's retirement to Bath, I shall away to pursue the business that brought me to these shores in the first place."

"Harlington is but a stone's throw from London, I believe," declared the Countess.

Her exquisite grandson gave her a queer look before he shook his head and laughed.

"Well, *I* am off to Harlington!" interposed George Hobcourt.

The four Rouncefords turned as one upon him. "*You?*" they chorused.

"And why not me?" demanded Sir George. "It seems to me someone must marry the girl. It is obvious that Adrian will not—"

"Dammit!" cried Adrian. "I call upon you all to witness that I have always stood ready to—"

"Well, are you off to Harlington, then?" asked George with a sneer.

"Yes, by heaven!"

"You are a nitwit, Adrian!" exclaimed the Countess. "Meg would not have you though you were served up with an apple in your mouth. She made that clear enough!"

Sir Arthur stepped towards Sir George, with one hand at his hip where he formerly carried his saber, and pointed at him with his other hand.

"Before I see this scapegrace force his attentions upon Miss Miller, honourable or otherwise, I shall—"

"You are an ass, cousin!" remarked the Earl.

Sir Arthur whirled upon him, his eyes blazing.

"Marcus, how dare you?" he shouted.

The Earl stepped closer to his smaller cousin and, grinning down into his face, said, "From all I have heard of Sir Samuel, now that Meg is back under his protection, I cannot see that your hand and sword can add one mite to the security she must now enjoy. If you feel so strongly about the girl, you might do well to go to Harlington yourself."

"And so I shall!"

"When?" demanded the Countess.

"Directly! Peterskin! Where is that fellow? Pull me the bellrope, will you, Marcus?"

Marcus accommodated his cousin and countered, "Will there be no one of us to attend Lady Dalrymple's function?"

Sir Arthur stood transfixed. He passed a hand over his brow. "Confound it all! I cannot beg off. I—I shall have to postpone Harlington. But never doubt it; I shall leave for Harlington the day after."

There was a rap on the door and the butler appeared.

"Yes, Jamieson, what is it?" asked the Countess.

"Er—someone rang, your ladyship?"

"Oh—oh, yes, Jamieson," said Sir Arthur. "Never mind, I shall not need you."

"I think we all stand in need of some refreshment," declared Lord Marcus.

"Very good, milord." Jamieson bowed and departed.

"Marcus, I have been thinking," began the Countess pensively. "I cannot guess the sort of household that Meg would keep, but of one thing I have no doubt."

"And that is?" asked Lord Marcus, knitting his eyebrows.

"It would never be dull."

"Quite so, milady." He laughed. "That it could never be!"

"Meg, my dear, come and sit beside me," said Lady Elizabeth, beckoning to her daughter. They were in the music room where Meg had been idling away at the pianoforte, playing little melodies in a minor key that promised to set milady's teeth on edge. Aside from the doleful thrummings that her daughter's compositions abounded in, Lady Elizabeth's mind was at sixes and sevens over what must be done to salvage her daughter's good name. Thus far in the lengthy and vehement discussions she had held with her husband—in Meg's presence and otherwise—she found that she could not suggest anything better than his original proposal, namely that Meg be sent to the Continent in the company of some worthy female for at least six months, certainly no less.

"We have talked of you and roundabout you, my dear, but we have not spoken *to* you and, truly, it were wiser that I, at least, do so. I did not need those woeful sounds from the instrument to tell me that you are not happy."

Meg smiled. "Was it so mournful? Yes, Mamma, I am unhappy. I had so hoped that my experiences in London would be interesting—well, you must admit they were," she said with a little gurgle of laughter. "But after all that excitement—however disgraceful—I cannot help being even more bored with things here than ever before. Especially since you carried me off before the Rouncefords could finish it properly."

Lady Elizabeth looked up from her needlework, a quizzical expression on her face. "I do not understand you. Surely they had done their worst!"

"Oh, yes, that is true enough; but, you see, Mamma, there was to be a dance at the Dalrymples', a respectable family close by, and the Earl of Marchford was to stand up with me for the first dance and Sir Arthur—that is Major Winstock—for the second."

Lady Elizabeth was surprised. "I understand even less than before! Why, indeed, should the Rouncefords distinguish you so after the disgraceful behaviour of that odious individual? I should think that they would have been happy to see the last of you. With people's tongues what they are, you must indeed be a source of gossip, something I am sure they have every wish to avoid."

"But that is exactly what they had it in mind to accomplish. If I were seen in the company of dear Lady Marcia and standing up with Lord Marcus and Sir Arthur, why people would be hard put to smell scandal in that. In fact," she chuckled, "they would be more inclined to smell orange blossoms, I think."

Lady Elizabeth looked puzzled. "Orange blossoms? Your allusion escapes me."

"I beg your pardon, but have you not heard? In London

203

it is lately all the crack to be married with orange blossoms in the French style.''

"Is that a fact? What a lovely idea—but I begin to see what you mean. And, yes, it could not have failed. Why did you not speak of this sooner? I begin to think that your father and I should have had cooler heads.''

"Yes, Mamma, but my father was not in any mood to be reasoned with. I noted that you did not try. Certainly, *I* dared not after his unusually oppressive manner to me. But it is water under the bridge now, and the dance will have to go on without me.'' Meg let out a deep sigh.

"Surely, I cannot have been mistaken. I had thought that your depressed demeanour was the not unlooked for result of your sufferings at their hands, and yet this dance you speak of—can it be the true source of your disappointment?''

Even as she spoke, Meg's face lit up into a smile. Meg laughed outright as she exclaimed, ''My sufferings? Hardly that! Truly, Mamma, it was the most comical thing! Come, let me tell you exactly what took place. Adrian Rounceford must surely be the last of the romanticks, the very last . . .''

Meg spared no detail of the escapade in her telling and, before she was finished, Lady Elizabeth had tears in her eyes from her laughing so heartily.

"Oh dear!'' she gasped. ''The way you tell it, dear child, is enough to make one split one's stays. Oh, that such a ludicrous business should be so damaging to one's reputation!''

"But it need not have been so if only I could have remained with the Countess.''

"Yes, I agree, but do I detect in you a note of some other regret?''

"Oh, it is just that I was looking forward to the dance with some anticipation. The Rounceford gentlemen, not excluding Adrian, are, beyond compare, graceful and far from the least handsome of men. And, once everything was out in the open, I was deferred to as someone to be shielded. It was the most flattering experience. I think I should have found dancing with them some consolation.''

Lady Elizabeth, a wise smile on her face, dropped her work, leaned back in her chair, and looked carefully at her daughter. She had never in her life heard Meg say anything so complimentary about any member of the opposite sex.

Her smile did not disappear as she retrieved her sewing and bent to it again.

"I daresay," she said.

Meg was back at the pianoforte, the melodies that came tinkling forth notably cheerier than before, when Sir Samuel entered, his face ruddy as ever. He was smiling.

" 'Tis a beautiful day, m' love! Perhaps you would care to join me in a drive? I am free for a time. The two of you have been closeted in this house these two days with nary a breath of air.''

Lady Elizabeth offered her cheek and received a loud salute upon it. "Perhaps, my dear, later in the day. I feel quite cozy at the moment and Meg and I have some things we wish to talk on.''

"As to that, Bess, I can guess what it is. But I think such talk can come to an end now, for I have arranged a way to quiet all clacking tongues and see Meg settled," Sir Samuel announced with great pride.

Lady Elizabeth looked her inquiry at her husband and Meg, ceasing her toying at the keys, wheeled around on the bench to face her father.

"I tell you, Bess, when it comes to the little vexations of life, there is nothing like a good woman to settle 'em, but it takes a man's thinking to lay the great trials one encounters.''

"Yes, love, I am sure you are right, but we would like

to learn what it is you have managed for Meg."

"Colin MacTavish!" announced Sir Samuel. "He is still willing to take Meg to wife!"

Sir Samuel paused and silence filled the room. There were no sighs of relief, no cries of praise. His face fell as he looked first at the pained expression on his wife's face and then witnessed the dismay on Meg's.

"What's this!" he cried, his ruddy face crimsoning deeper in annoyance. "Perhaps ye find young Colin not quite up to your fancies. Well, let me tell you this: MacTavish may not be quite your idea of what a husband should be, but for you, Miss Meg, ye'll not find better under the circumstances. Here's a man willing to o'erlook the disgrace that's been brought upon us and take ye to wife. More than that, he's honest and as fine a man of business as ye could wish. Aye, he has none of the graces ye might set great store upon, but he'll prove a mite steadier than all the man-milliners flittin' about town these days!"

In a quiet voice, masking the agitation in her breast, Meg asked, "What have you agreed to pay him for this great act of charity?"

"Pay?" sputtered Sir Samuel. "I mentioned no payments. That is a devilish way to put it!"

"Pappa, I have always known that when I came to marry you would endow me handsomely, no matter whom I chose; but Mr. MacTavish was bound to drive a hard bargain. What would he have of you?"

Sir Samuel answered uneasily, "I have always thought he would make an excellent partner. What more trustworthy partner could a man have than a son-in-law?"

"I am sure Mr. MacTavish would be no less trustworthy were he not married to your daughter," retorted Meg. "As for me, I cannot think of him as young Colin on any count. Even if he were five years younger, for truly young he never was. I know him well enough to be sure that we could never deal well together—and I do not love him nor could I ever!''

"Think well what you are about, young lady!" stormed Sir Samuel. "The alternative may be far less pleasant. If you will not have MacTavish, then it is to the Continent you go, well chaperoned I assure you—and I will see to it! Oh, you will go—be certain of that! Even if I have to wrap you in brown paper and ship you like a parcel of goods.''

A smile broke forth on Meg's face. She said, "I should much prefer a warm broadcloth wrap, Pappa, It would be so much more practical.''

Sir Samuel fought hard to maintain his indignation, but under the merrily dancing eyes of the daughter he loved so dearly, he lost ground rapidly and a deep chuckle escaped him.

"You both have had your say. Now I shall have mine," Lady Elizabeth interposed. "I see no need to rush matters. Whatever needs must be done will be done; but it is clear no one of us is capable of thinking clearly on it. There is time enough for Meg to go abroad when all else has failed. We must each give sober consideration to every possibility—and, Meg, I pray you will try to treat the matter with more gravity than you have yet shown.''

"But, Mamma, I cannot conceivably—"

"Meg! That will be enough. I am not agreeing nor disagreeing with what your father has proposed. As I have said, there is yet time to discuss your future dispassionately. It is too grave a matter to be badgered about, as you and your father seem disposed to do.''

"Yes, Mamma.''

"Sammy, I know you wish to do what you think best for the child, but I am concerned that she should be happy as well as safe and I think it is not so simple a task as may at first appear.''

"Yes, m' love," acknowledged Sir Samuel with a sigh.

Chapter Fifteen

It was a week since Miss Meg Miller had quit the Rounceford domicile so abruptly, when, under clear but cold skies, two horsemen approached the outskirts of London from the southeast.

"This has been a dull ride, Marcus," complained Sir Arthur. "When I invited you along, it was for pleasant company and *that* you have not been. Why, you have hardly said a word!"

"I was sure you had not noticed it. In any case, the air has been so filled up with praise of Wellington and his exploits, I could not have got a word in had I wished, cousin."

"Well, someone must speak if there is to be a conversation."

"For these past ten miles, all I could have ventured were groans. It is too long since I have sat a horse at such length—and I am feeling it, I swear! I am the complete fool for having let you talk me into this. It is no way to travel! When I think that I have a perfectly good curricle waiting back at Tunbridge Wells, I curse myself for being ten times an idiot."

"Bah! There is nothing better than a fine steed! If the Creator meant for us to drive, he would have endowed us with wheels."

"Cousin, if you mean what you say, then you bore me. Such tommyrot has not been heard in the land since—I do not know when. What can one expect from the cavalry? In any case, enjoy your horses and leave me to enjoy my wheels!''

Lord Marcus continued. ''I would hesitate to call this a conversation. Here, let me try. Why are you so bent for London? Now that I come to think of it, were you not to attend the Dalrymple party?''

''I told you it was abandoned. They gave it up,'' said Sir Arthur in a tone of annoyance.

''Ah, yes, so you did. They must be queer fish. Oh, well, I am sure it would have been quite tedious.'' The Earl yawned at the thought. He turned in his saddle to look sharply at his companion. ''But what of the young lady? I recollect there was a young beauty, Lady Honoria by name.''

Sir Arthur grimaced in disgust. ''Aye, a veritable dream to look at, but more than that—beware! Her beauty is truly beyond belief, as pretty as a day in spring, all grace and loveliness.''

''Well, why do you stop? At last you have hit upon a topic of interest. Pray continue, cousin. You did say beware?''

Sir Arthur shrugged. ''Beneath that delightful exterior dwells a shrew—she is a veritable mantrap. I called upon her and her mother to present the Countess' apologies at not being able to attend.'' He shook his fist at the recollection. ''One would have thought I had turned traitor to my country, the outcry it brought forth. Immediately the old dame was at great lamentations over what she insisted on was a snub of the worst kind. I was nonplussed to understand it all. I had hoped that Honoria, upon observing the distressing and ungracious manner of her mother, would have profited from so bad an example. But no! Upon learning that you might not attend either, what must she do but bewail all the trouble they had been put to only to have it all come to naught. I assured her that Daphne, Adrian, and I would attend. She then proceeded to do her mother one better. She gave me a queer look, burst into tears, and quit the room. I looked to Lady Dalrymple in the faint hope that she might provide me with some explanation. That lady, in a voice of doom, informed me that there would be no dance. She was not about to join with 'that Miller woman' and become a butt for Rounceford amusement.

"I tell you, Marcus, not even the Frenchies angered me so! It was all I could do to remain civil and dismiss myself. Had either of them been a man . . . Well, I must agree with you; it would have been a most tedious affair."

Lord Marcus made a face. "As it was originally planned, I think not."

"I do not see your meaning."

"It is of no importance. Are you then rushing off to London to bathe your wounded feelings in riotous living? I had thought you were on the lookout for a wife."

"I am not so easily crushed, cousin. It is still my intention to wed. I came on purpose to Tunbridge Wells to consult with my grand-aunt as to the eligible females in her acquaintance, but now I find it is not necessary. Adrian, the fool, has done me the greatest favour. It was the greatest stroke of fortune that he—unwittingly, I know—arranged for me to meet Meg Miller."

Lord Marcus turned sharply in the saddle.

"Then London is not your destination?"

"No, I shall leave you there, for I am on my way to Harlington as, no doubt, you have already guessed."

"Are you so deeply enamoured of Meg?"

"How can you be so foolish? You know how little acquainted we are! But I cannot stand aside and see Hobcourt get her. And he may be there already, so I must not delay."

"You do not really believe she will accept him?"

"But I do! In her desperate straits, that is exactly what she might do—especially if her family force her hand— not knowing that I am prepared to offer for her."

"Indeed, how very generous of you!"

"I know you are wishing to make game of me, but you shall not succeed. This is a matter of great importance to me."

"I should think to Meg Miller, too!"

"But, of course! My offering for her must be so much more than she could have hoped—and as I am a deal more presentable than Hobcourt, she cannot help but be grateful. Yes, it bids fair to work out well for everyone."

Lord Marcus chuckled aloud, making no attempt to hide his mirth.

"Marcus, I am quite serious! Why do you laugh?"

"The picture I have conjured up of you paying court to Miss Miller on such terms quite unmans me. She will slice you to ribbons in less time than it takes to tell."

"You are out there! I can see that you are not as observant as you might think. Had you not noticed that she does not deal with me as harshly as she does with you?

"And there is something else. Your appreciation of the charms of the sex has, no doubt, been jaded by too many Parisian ladybirds, and you have failed to see that Meg Miller is not unattractive. I daresay it would take little enough for me to develop a genuine *tendre* for the lass and it would not be at all surprising to me if her interest in me was more than anyone might suspect."

Lord Marcus' mirth continued unabated.

"You laugh!" remarked Sir Arthur in a superior tone. "You think that she may give me a setdown? You need not. Indeed, you are in for a surprise if you think so. I am not without talent in that department and shall get along famously. And have no fear, cousin; for as my wife, she will be properly behaved and mild-mannered. She will soon know that I will not tolerate her looking down her nose at my relations.

"She has taken Adrian in great dislike, you will agree. It is not to be wondered at. But I have never seen *you* to arouse such enmity in a female, before. I assure you I shall bring her around. It would not be seemly for my wife to be

211

continually at odds with you—or Adrian, for that matter.''

"Let me warn you, Petruccio, her name is Meg, not Kate!''

Sir Arthur looked at Lord Marcus blankly. "Milord, I fear for your sanity!''

"Are you not familiar with Shakespeare?''

"I should say not!'' Sir Arthur disclaimed vehemently.

Lord Marcus shrugged. "It is no matter.''

They continued their ride in silence for a while. Lord Marcus appeared pensive and would look at Sir Arthur as though seeking an answer to something that was bothering him.

At last he spoke. "Arthur, you say you do not love Meg. I cannot believe it is only your kindness of soul that moves you to fend Hobcourt from her. Tell me, what is behind this trip to Harlington?''

"As I have said, whether you agree or no, Meg Miller is an attractive young woman. She is also quite wealthy—in any case, I daresay her husband will share handsomely in Sir Samuel's estate. Better that fortunate man be me than Hobcourt.''

"So that is why you sold out! You could no longer afford your commission in the Blues.''

"The devil you say! I may not hold a candle to you, my boy, but I can damn well afford a colonelcy if I so desired! You forget all the Winstock holdings were settled on me.''

Lord Marcus yawned. "This particular topic has been drained of its interest and I am beginning to feel peckish. Some roast of beef, a tender fowl and, perhaps, a taste of Yorkshire pudding washed down with mine host's finest would not go amiss with me. What say you?''

"There is an inn a little farther on; we would do well to break our journey there. After, I will take the road to Harlington.''

"Very good—and after, I shall join you.''

"Whatever for? You cannot mean to accompany me all the way to Harlington! I can just see it—the Earl of

Marchford taking his ease at Harlington, of all places, and in a cit's overblown cottage, no doubt. I tell you, you will be bored clear through to your liver and lights!''

''No, I shall not be bored at all. I expect you and Hobcourt to provide me with all the entertainment I could ask.''

''How so?'' asked Sir Arthur, beginning to frown.

''Why, it will be the spectacle of the century! The domination of Meg Miller by the brave soldier, Major Sir Arthur Winstock, K.C.B., late of the Blues, assisted by Sir George Hobcourt—hmm, there is just nothing impressive one can say about him! It will be worth a sojourn in Harlington; and, although one is usually obliged to cheer for the underdog—or dogs, as in this case—it is Meg that I am for and will put my money on!''

Sir Arthur gave his cousin a withering look. ''We shall see who will laugh in the end! I can assure you there will be no entertainment. I am no green hand. You forget, I am a cavalryman!''

''I do try, but you never will permit it. You remind me of that not less than a dozen times a day. But what has that to do with the winning of Meg Miller?''

''Cousin, the first thing a cavalryman learns is how to handle a horse. It is a deal more intricate than riding to hounds.''

''I will grant you that, I am sure; but I see even less connection—''

''The second thing a cavalryman learns is that a woman is no more difficult and can be brought to heel in much the same fashion.''

''Any woman?''

''Any woman—and I speak from experience!''

''Cousin Winstock, now you can never dissuade me from accompanying you! I would not miss your bringing little Meg to heel for all the wealth in England.''

Sir Arthur tossed his head. ''Come, if you will; I care not.'' After a moment's silence he commented, ''It will be strange, however, your putting in an appearance there. It is not as though you were paying a call in passing. Harlington is too far off the highroad for that excuse to pass."

"Never fear. The Millers will not think it strange. I promised Meg that I should call upon Lady Miller. I cannot think of a more opportune time to do so."

Sir Samuel Miller examined the tally sheet of the past month's production from his mills for the second time. It was all very clearly laid out in Colin MacTavish's tight but neat hand and he was sure that his review of the figures would uncover no errors. But this was a monthly ritual he had carried on for years and he had every intention that this month would be no exception. Unfortunately neither his eyes nor his mind would accommodate his will. While his mind refused to disentangle itself from the concerns of his eldest daughter, his eyes kept wandering off the sheet in his hand to stare vacantly into space.

Bess had informed him of how his refusal to listen to his daughter had brought the Rounceford scheme to save Meg to naught. She had not put the entire blame upon him, but reserved a goodly share for herself, for, as she explained to him with a small smile, she had listened to Meg when she should not have and did not listen to her when she should have.

Nevertheless, Sir Samuel took all the blame upon himself, remembering quite clearly that he had been in no good humour to listen to anybody that day they had rescued Meg from the hands of the Rouncefords. No, dammit, not rescued—he must get to change his opinion of them, but it would not be easy. He had come to appreciate the dilemma they had had to face. They were a fine family of fine people from all he had ever heard of them and he could not hold them accountable for the misdeeds of the family fool, to hear Meg tell it. After all, had they not attempted to provide Meg with their approbation in such fashion as would squelch all rumours? He writhed inwardly at the thought that he, as much as anyone, had insured that the stain upon Meg was now become well nigh indelible.

He could no longer insist upon MacTavish as a husband for her with a clear conscience. Although he believed young Colin to be the only possible candidate left to preserve Meg's acceptance by society, in the face of his daughter's adamant refusal to consider MacTavish, it was suddenly all beyond him and he found himself too confused to think clearly on the matter.

Without Bess' support, his tentative agreement with MacTavish was worth nothing and he was now certain that she had no liking for him as a son-in-law. It began to look as though Meg's trip to the Continent was become a certainty.

God help them all if he were to find himself saddled with a French spendthrift dandy! He never doubted his daughter's good sense to avoid fortune hunters; but, as in the case of this Adrian Rounceford, it was all too easy for a female to be compromised by an unscrupulous male—history was replete with horrible examples of the failure of the best of chaperons to preserve their charges.

Sir Samuel shook his head and smiled. He could never trust Meg to the care of anyone but himself. With her strange ideas, she was bound to give a predacious male the impression she was fast, and there was no changing her. And she was a headstrong devil of a girl, which added to the problem. He doubted if once on the Continent even Lady Bess could keep Meg safe.

Well, it would go hard with him to do it, but Colin MacTavish had always claimed to be able to run the business with help from no one. Good! He would now have his chance, for Sir Samuel would make certain beyond doubt that Meg's stay upon the Continent would be an unexceptional one. The Millers would make the grand tour—and that way it would not appear as though Meg was being sent off into exile to expiate her sins.

If MacTavish did well, his reward would be a partnership—no, by heaven! he would give him shares. The first thing he would do on his return would be to secure a royal charter and the Miller enterprise would become a Corporation of Proprietors. Then he could sell shares in the firm to interested outsiders. After all, he had no sons to whom the business might pass. In this way, the fruits of his labours could be readily apportioned amongst his widow and his daughters whenever it became necessary to do so.

"Hah!" he exclaimed with satisfaction, slapping down upon his writing table the papers he held. He was about to reach for some others when he was interrupted by his footman.

"Yes?" he said, looking up at the tall, wigged and powdered servitor advancing upon him bearing a calling card on a silver salver.

"It is a Sir George Hobcourt, sir. Are you in?"

"What the devil can that puppy want of me?" growled Sir Samuel. Thinking that perhaps he bore a message from his mother to Lady Elizabeth, he asked, "Are you sure it was not Lady Elizabeth he asked for?"

"Quite sure, sir. He said it was a matter most urgent."

"Well, since he has come so far from his London haunts, I suppose I must see him. Very well, I will see him here."

A few minutes later, Sir George made his entrance. Sir Samuel motioned him to a seat and called for some brandy.

"Good day to you, George. How does your mother?" If Sir George had any hope that his rank would help forward his task, Sir Samuel's informal manner of addressing him told him differently.

"Well, enough, Sir Samuel. I hope I find the Miller family in good health."

"So they be; but I am a busy man, so let us get down to why you have come to call upon me. But stay! I have a bone to pick with Lady Hobcourt, and since she is not here, you will do. She has tendered me apologies enough since Meg's return, but not one word as to how my Meg should have been so little protected as to fall prey to the first villain to encounter her.''

Sir George blinked. Never in the past had he looked upon Sir Samuel as a possible enemy, one who might wish to do him an injury. Now, sitting before him, he was suddenly aware of what those tremendous shoulders, those thick powerful arms, those huge hands, could accomplish in that direction. He pictured one of the hands balled into a great fist. He winced as he imagined it crashing into his jaw.

It came upon him that never in his life had he felt so fragile. Not for anything would he dare to inform this glittery-eyed father of the part he had played in Meg's abduction. He was consoled by the fact that the business he was come upon must soothe the man's anger and render pointless any desire for revenge—even if his behind-the-scenes villainy should ever be brought to Sir Samuel's attention.

''Er—sir, you might say that is what I have come about. You cannot know how devastated Lady Amelia and I were upon learning of Miss Miller's misfortune. Now, it has been in my mind for some time to pay court to Miss Miller. As a demonstration of my continuing devotion, and to make reparation for any failure on the part of the Hobcourt family, I wish your permission to approach Miss Miller and ask for her hand in marriage.''

Sir Samuel sat back so suddenly that his chair creaked beneath him. He looked at Sir George and made no attempt to hide his surprise.

This he had not counted on. Meg's hand to be sought for by a gentleman of good family and of wealth was so complete an answer to his daughter's problem that he could not help grinning with the relief he felt.

Of course, as a man, Sir George did not total up well. It was common knowledge that he was a loose fish, a rip, and not to be relied upon at all—but then, Meg was Meg and she might be the making of him. Provided she would have him, that is.

Sir George relaxed in his seat. The look upon Sir Samuel's face was not such as to discourage him, and he was pleased that the hardest part was gotten over with so easily.

"When may I call upon the ladies, sir?"

"Ah—I think you had best put it off for a day. I am sure you will be received on Thursday." Sir Samuel had no false notions as to Meg's action on having this prize sprung upon her and he wanted time to prepare her. "Will that be convenient?"

"Eminently so. I shall look forward to it with great pleasure."

Sir George arose, took his leave, and was conducted out by the footman who had brought him in.

As Sir Samuel watched his caller depart, he noted the exaggerated tilt of the young man's head, the exaggerated chest, the exaggerated walk, the exaggerated adornments, and he could not help thinking that the Continent for Meg must be preferable to this gilded puppy no matter what the cost.

The Earl and the Major pulled up in front of the only inn that Harlington boasted. The inn they had stopped at late yesterday afternoon had proved unexpectedly commodious. After having disposed of adequate quantities of good food and drink, Lord Marcus, despite the humbleness of the hostel, decided against continuing with their journey that day. For one, he was not up to threading his way through London traffic; for another, due to the unaccustomed hardship of the saddle, he was aching all over and believed that a good night's rest would do much to restore him.

As it proved, the beds were well aired and the rooms

spotless, so that, retiring early, they arose early and found their travels through London and over the short byroad to Harlington no strain at all.

Upon entering the inn at Harlington, they were immediately set upon by mine host who was plainly thrilled by this fresh invasion of the gentry. It had been a matter of amazement when, yesterday, he had been called upon to provide for one splendid gentleman. The appearance of an additional pair, though neither was as splendid as the first, filled his heart with great joy, and visions of gold pieces pouring into his till chinked and clinked in his head.

He rushed over to greet the new arrivals, but before he could make his welcome evident, a voice from near the hearth cut him short.

"Greetings, Milord Marcus! Sir Arthur! Will you join me?"

The two travellers looked away from the innkeeper and spied Sir George Hobcourt seated at a small table. They strode over to him and exchanged greetings. Once again Sir George invited them to join him.

Lord Marcus shook his head. "No, I thank you. I believe I shall take this opportunity to stretch my legs. A stroll through the town will be just the thing. I have never been here before and, I daresay, I never shall again. Harlington does not appear to be very large and I do not think I shall miss it. But, now that I am here I might as well add to my knowledge of insignificant places."

Sir George laughed. "You will not be above twenty minutes making a circuit of the place. I will have something set by for you against your return."

Lord Marcus nodded an acknowledgement and left Sir Arthur preparing to assist Sir George in demolishing a late breakfast.

Sir Arthur remarked, as he took a place at the table, "I

219

think a light repast would not be amiss. We started out from the south of London, near Lambeth, and quite early.''

He began to eat.

Sir George pushed his own plate away and studied his companion.

"So you have come as you said you would," he remarked. "I am surprised. Marcus had baited you and I was sure you would have thought better of it. You can not make me believe that he was serious."

Sir Arthur replied, "True enough, old man, until I got to thinking it over. The more I thought about it, the better it seemed, until now I find it a capital idea and am come to pursue it further."

Sir George laughed. "Then I fear you had this journey to no purpose." He began to preen himself.

"How so?" demanded Sir Arthur.

"For the reason that you are too late! But yesterday I was closeted with Sir Samuel Miller and it is as good as settled, I tell you. He looks upon my suit with favour. In fact he was all smiles, in the highest spirits, when I left."

Sir Arthur's face fell. "You have agreed on a settlement?"

"Er—no, we did not see the necessity. There can be no difficulty in that department that our respective lawyers cannot work out."

"And Meg? I cannot believe she has actually accepted you."

Sir George shrugged. "A mere formality, I assure you. I call upon the ladies tomorrow. It will be all tied up neatly by teatime."

"I see!" A calculating look came into Sir Arthur's eyes. "Tell me, what do any of the Millers know of your part in Meg's betrayal?"

Immediately Sir George looked worried. "I really do not know."

"Obviously you said nothing of it to Sir Samuel or you

220

would not be so happily seated here with not a mark or bruise upon you."

"Look you, Arthur, I am no sapskull. Good heavens! Have you seen the man? And if I had, it would have accomplished nothing but to make for bad feeling all around. If I did wrong, I am marrying her and no more need be said."

Sir Arthur merely stared at his friend and grinned. It was such a grin as to make Sir George's blood run cold.

His eyes opened wide and he gasped, "I say! You are not going to tell him?"

Sir Arthur began to laugh as he pushed back his chair. He rose from the table and walked away, calling loudly for the innkeeper to attend him.

Sir George remained at the table, sitting quite still, his eyes following Sir Arthur out of the room. His face was a picture of apprehension.

Lord Marcus stepped from the inn doorway out onto the road. The air was more bracing than he had remembered it. He attributed it to his present inactivity and the effect of the inn's cozy warmth. Wrapping his cloak about him securely, he marched off briskly and it was not long before he was once again comfortable.

A dozen minutes or so of vigorous tramping brought him beyond the bounds of the town. He smiled. George had been quite right. Harlington's entire extent was a very short walk, indeed.

He had no desire to explore the countryside and so he turned about and began to make his way back. He took his time about it, peering into the tiny shops that were dispersed here and there along the thoroughfare that comprised the only street.

For all its lack of size, there were a fair number of people going in and out of the shops. Lord Marcus wondered if so much of it was for shopping as to exchange gossip. He believed the accuracy of his surmise confirmed, when upon further observation, he determined that the crush of shoppers were almost without exception members of the gentler sex.

Although, of course, he had no acquaintance with them, he felt it incumbent upon himself to tip his hat quite frequently, especially as so many of the passersby were so pretty.

His salutes were acknowledged each time without fail. The ladies of Harlington could not mistake the fact that he was a gentleman, and a stranger to their town, but such a polished gentleman, such a charming stranger, they could not find it in their hearts to ignore his courtesy towards them.

All in all, it quite set the Earl up in his own estimation and he began to feel that his short stay in Harlington might yet prove entertaining.

He was not more than a few minutes' walk from the inn when a well-appointed light carriage, with one footman up, drove by briskly and came to a stop a little way down the street. Two ladies, both diminutive in stature, were helped to alight and they started for the door of the shop before which they had stopped.

Lord Marcus' heart gave a slight start as he recognized Meg. There was no question in his mind but that her companion must be Lady Elizabeth, the similarity in their figures and in the way they carried themselves being quite marked.

His first impulse was to call out to them, but a second, more serious consideration restrained him. What his welcome from Meg might be, here where she was at home, and secure, he could not foretell; but the chance of Lady Elizabeth giving him a cut was too probable to be ignored.

He waited until they had entered the shop before he strolled up to their carriage where he took station and awaited their return.

It was not more than twenty minutes before they came

out. He straightened up and, having caught their eye, ceremoniously bowed to them.

"Milord Marcus!" exclaimed Meg in surprise.

"Meg, we are well met." He turned to her companion with a winning smile upon his face.

Meg turned to her mother. "Milady, may I present his lordship, Marcus, Earl of Marchford." Then she turned back to him and with a smile of great pride announced, "My mother, Lady Elizabeth Miller."

Close to, Lord Marcus had to agree with Meg's opinion. Lady Elizabeth was indeed a beautiful little woman. He could see where her daughter had come by her lustrous raven tresses and her sparkling dark eyes. Despite a matronly air about her, Lady Elizabeth put her daughter in the shade for personal beauty.

He was aware that two pairs of eyes were scrutinizing him and he made every effort to maintain his poise. But it was not all that easy, for there was a question in one pair and a distinct challenge in the other.

"I happened to be passing by and I thought to call upon you if convenient."

"That is a fib!" exclaimed Meg with a laugh. "One just cannot be passing by Harlington. It is too out of the way by far."

"Meg! Behave yourself! What a thing to say!" protested Lady Elizabeth, very much embarrassed by her daughter.

Lord Marcus grinned, held up his hand, and said, "I beg you, Lady Miller, do not be embarrassed. I have long known that I am fair game to your daughter—and, as it happens, she is right. I should have known better than to try. You see, my cousin, Sir Arthur Winstock has—er—business in the neighbourhood and I elected to accompany him; but it is true that I had hoped to make your acquaintance. Your daughter's description of you was indeed justified and, seeing you, I can say my journey has been worthwhile."

With a half-smile on her face, Lady Elizabeth responded, "Your lordship is kind, and I begin to think, from what Meg has told me, that we *are* well met."

But Lord Marcus had not finished. He turned to Meg and said, "And you, Meg, are every bit as lovely."

Meg cocked an eye at him in a way he well remembered. "You do it too brown and are now become an empty flatterer."

His smile undimmed, Lord Marcus retorted, "I was sure you would be able to put a proper value upon the compliment."

Meg flashed him an angry look, but it was quickly replaced by a smile that matched his own. "Not bad at all, milord. Was it not Shakespeare who said, 'the smallest worm will turn being trodden on for all the good it will do him'?"

He started to chuckle. "That last I am sure he did not say—nor intend!"

"Oh, Meg, how very unkind of you!" exclaimed Lady Elizabeth. "Milord, you should not encourage her. I fear she is incorrigible."

"Milady, I fear I am too. It is not often I am o'ertopped and I have yet to give your daughter a setdown she has not turned against me. I blush to admit it, but I have met my match."

Lady Elizabeth gave him a queer look while Meg chuckled.

Meg remarked, "Take care, milord, or my mother will believe that you have it in mind to make me an offer."

"As to that there will be offers enough without one from me," he declared. "Which reminds me, my cousin and I should like to call upon you on the morrow. Will you be at home?"

Lady Elizabeth was quite flabbergasted. She managed to say that they would be at home and Lord Marcus then took leave of them. He left two ladies staring at him in great surprise.

"It is high time you returned, Marcus," was Sir Arthur's greeting to his lordship as he entered the tap-room. "Whatever could you have discovered to have kept you so long? We had best go right out to the Millers' and leave our cards; it is already too late to make a call today."

"No need of that. I have had the good fortune to meet Meg and her mother on my way through town. It is all arranged. We call upon them in the morning."

"The devil you do!" exclaimed Sir George. "Are you deliberately trying to queer my lay? Here's Arthur threatening to expose the whole bloody mess, and here's you stepping on my heels to go calling on the Millers."

Lord Marcus raised an eyebrow in inquiry at his cousin. Sir Arthur returned him a sour smile and shook his head.

"He feels so guilty about his underhanded ploy that he suspects everyone is as base as he. I merely mentioned the business to him—and look at him! He is quaking in terror. His suit is lost before even it begins, I think. I have no need to disparage his character to achieve my purpose with Meg Miller."

"Yes, I do not doubt that the idea of George receiving signs of affection from Meg is plainly incredible, but do not be so sure that your place by her side will be so easily won. By the way, do you know I suspect she is a blue-stocking into the bargain?"

The faces of Sir Arthur and Sir George mirrored each other's dismay.

"You cannot be serious!" cried the former.

"Never on your life!" cried the latter.

Lord Marcus shrugged. "Believe what you will, but the little minx quoted Shakespeare to my discomfit."

"She did not give you another setdown?" inquired Sir Arthur with some signs of glee.

Lord Marcus laughed. "Aye, she did it again. I tell you either I am woefully out of practice or— Well, we shall see how softly she handles the pair of you!"

Sir Arthur exclaimed, "Fie upon you! You make her sound a shrew!"

"Well, she is that!" agreed Sir George. "I can tell you I should not be here except she cannot afford to pour out her venom upon such an eligible suitor. B'gad, whenever she visited the old lady I was hard to find. Hmph! It will be different when she is my wife. That tongue of hers will sweeten and quickly!"

Both Rouncefords stared at Sir George aghast.

"By heaven!" exclaimed Sir Arthur, "if I had thought that slug had any chance at all with her, I should not hesitate to gut him!"

Lord Marcus wheeled on his cousin. "I do not hear from him mouthings which differ in any degree from those very sentiments expressed by you on our ride out. If I did not think that Meg could handle the two of you together and with dispatch, I—"

"Do you say she will not have either of us?" demanded Sir Arthur of his cousin.

"You know her! Do you think that you can fool her for one moment? A fine set of husbands you would make! George, you give all the appearance of a man set upon revenge. And you, Arthur, if you are in love at all, it is with her purse!"

"You, Marcus, are a deal too nice!" retorted the Major. "She must marry to save her name. Certainly I shall observe all those proprieties that females set such store upon; but as you say, she will not be fooled—and I have no intention to do so. The situation is thus and so. My name and my protection in exchange for her fortune is not a bad bargain in the best of times. She cannot help but accept."

"I can offer as much!" declared Sir George.

"If I were Meg, I should say a plague on both of you!"

"All this talk settles nothing!" declared Sir George petulantly. "Tomorrow will tell the tale!"

"I very much doubt it! Unless I mistake it greatly, yon

little lady will tender her hand only to her own advantage,'' said Lord Marcus. He paused and, for a moment, a faraway look came into his eyes. ''I wonder what he *will* be like?''

''Who?'' chorused his companions.

''The man she finally accepts!''

They both gave him looks of distaste and proceeded to bury their faces in the mugs the innkeeper brought in.

Chapter Sixteen

"My dear, Meg and I will retire now to the drawing room. Do you remain at table for your port or must you continue your labours in the library?"

"Neither, my pet," responded Sir Samuel, arising from the dining table. "If you will permit it, I should like to join you. Perhaps we might share a cordial while I impart to you some good news."

"Except that you have news, we should never permit it, should we, Meg?" said Lady Elizabeth with a laugh, as her husband drew back her chair so that she might rise. Taking his arm with a loving pat, she let him conduct her from the room, Meg following behind.

The two ladies were comfortably seated. Sir Samuel stood before the hearth and, like a politico about to face disaffected constituents, he prepared himself to put as good a face on what he had to say as he could.

"Ladies, our problem is solved. Our dear Meg is about to be provided for. Yesterday, I had a visitor—a young man—an eligible young man." He paused to see how his audience was receiving his communication. Indeed, they both were all attention, sitting upright in their chairs, expectantly.

"Yes, an eligible young man and interested in you, Meg. He wishes to make you an offer! What say you to that?"

Meg shook her head admonishingly. "As yet, Pappa,

you have not identified this young man. Until you do, I have naught to say.''

''Yes, Samuel, do get on with it. Who is this eligible young man?''

''He is of fine family and reasonably well up in the world—and we are all of us acquainted with him!''

Lady Elizabeth was now become very impatient. ''You still have not put a name to him. It will surprise me no end if this paragon has none.''

''I shall keep you in suspense no longer. He is Sir George Hobcourt!'' announced Sir Samuel with bated breath.

''The suspense was to be preferred,'' commented Meg caustically.

''How very interesting,'' remarked Lady Elizabeth with a complete lack of enthusiasm.

''I cannot believe it!'' Meg piped up.

''You are not doubting my word, girl?'' demanded Sir Samuel indignantly.

''Not your word, Pappa, but his! It is a mighty strange thing, for the last time we had any conversation together, Sir George was most unfriendly.''

''Well, you must admit, dearest,'' interposed her mother, ''that your conversations with some people can hardly ever be termed friendly. I truly pitied Lord March-ford this noon. He was most magnanimous to refrain from giving you the snub you so richly deserved.''

''Marchford here?'' exclaimed Sir Samuel in great surprise.

''Yes, it would appear his cousin, Major Winstock, has some business to attend to somewhere in the vicinity and the Earl is with him.'' Lady Elizabeth turned to her daughter. ''That is what he told to us, is it not?''

Sir Samuel asked, ''What business could a Rounceford have in this byway? I doubt that it can be to any good purpose.''

''It is a puzzle,'' declared Lady Elizabeth, ''especially

as his lordship appeared somewhat diffident concerning it. In any case, he and his cousin plan to call upon us as they are in the neighbourhood. Will you be in to them?"

Sir Samuel pondered for a moment. Finally he shrugged. "I do not see why I should, but I suppose I must— Oh, blast! But young Hobcourt is calling then, too!"

Meg laughed aloud and clapped her hands. "Oh, wonderful! Between the Earl and Sir Arthur, Sir George is bound to be confounded. I shall look forward to a very amusing time, I am sure."

Sir Samuel drew in a deep breath. "I take it then that Hobcourt, too, is not up to your fancy!"

Meg smiled up at her father. "Dearest Pappa, I should so love to see Paris. Shall we be able to spend much time there?"

Lady Elizabeth brought her handkerchief up quickly to her face to hide her smile.

Thursday morning, as Meg began to prepare herself to receive the visitors, she could not help feeling pleased. To have had to entertain George Hobcourt, by himself, would have been an ordeal she could not have borne. It was the luckiest thing that Lord Marcus and Sir Arthur were to be present, too. For one thing, George would have to maintain a check upon his behaviour towards her. He would not dare be his usual odious self in such company, nor would he dare to make a scene when she rejected his proposal as she had every intention of doing. It was a bother, she had to admit, that she did not understand at all why Sir George should be, suddenly, so desirous of offering marriage to her, especially now. Well, that was no matter. There was nothing he could do or say to raise him in her good opinion.

When it came to select from her ample wardrobe appropriate garb for the occasion, she spent a great deal of time looking over her collection of morning dresses. She wanted to appear at her best. As she explained it to herself, when one must undergo a trial, it helps immensely to know that one's appearance is faultless. She could not help thinking how very much at a loss she felt at the Countess' in Tunbridge Wells. Everyone there, and especially the Rounceford gentlemen, always appeared to the best advantage in their fine clothing. Having nothing to change to and still having only her shop costume, she had felt like some poor relation and it had no little effect on her manner to them.

This time she intended to pass muster with the best of them and the thought came unbidden to her mind that, certainly, Lord Marcus was the best of them.

It gave her quite a turn; so much so that she had to suspend for a moment what she was doing to think out the why and wherefore of this strange conclusion. Strange indeed, for Lord Marcus was not a whit more handsome than Adrian and, to the *ton* in general, Sir George would be accounted in greater style. It truly startled her to find herself so strangely biased in his lordship's favor. It was more than startling, she realized; it was upsetting to her. Firmly she put the thought out of her mind and resumed the business of selecting the most stunning creation in her wardrobe.

Her choice finally came to rest on a morning dress in the Greek fashion, very high in the waist with narrow yet voluminous skirts falling in straight, soft folds. Her long, close-fitted sleeves were puffed at the shoulders and the gown terminated at her neck in a tiny ruffled collar. The ensemble was of a dull coral and devoid of ruffles other than at the neck and wrists. The effect was extremely graceful, adding height to her figure and setting off her ebon hair and brilliant dark eyes.

Her face was framed with shiny ringlets, some of which hung down over her forehead, disguising its broadness and emphasizing the piquant quality of her features.

When all was finished, she paraded herself before her

mirror, cocking her head, curtsying to her image and smiling. The smile was one of great satisfaction. She was sure she had never appeared to better advantage.

She dismissed her dresser and left the room, the smile still on her lips.

As her daughter came into the parlour to join her, Lady Elizabeth sat back in her chair as though to get a better view of the young lady.

"Meg, how adorable!" she exclaimed. "Why, you have quite taken my breath away. Charming, quite charming!"

"Thank you, Mother dear," said Meg, sweeping into a deep curtsy. She then stepped over to a small chair and sat down, carefully arranging the folds of her gown.

Lady Elizabeth smiled. "I declare, but I have seldom seen you in such style! Have you changed your mind about Sir Hobcourt?"

Meg grinned back at her mother as she shook her head. "Hardly that! I have merely dressed for the occasion, nothing more."

"So you say, but I think you intend to lead the poor fellow down the garden path before you send him packing. I pray you will not. Lady Amelia still calls me friend."

"Of course, I shall not—but I have no intention of appearing in the mopes, either!"

Her mother started to resume the embroidering she had been working at when her daughter had entered, but a thought struck her and she let it lay.

"There are two other gentlemen callers this day. It could not be that you have gone to such pains for either of them, I am sure?"

"Mamma, when I was at the Countess', you know very well I had not a single change of clothing with me. Borrowing bits and pieces from Daphne did me no good at all, for she is so very blond. Now that they are come to visit me in my own home, why should I not clothe myself properly? They can hardly have any idea at all of what I look like for all the days I was forced to spend with them.''

"Yes, dear, I am sure it must have been most exasperating, especially if Mr. Adrian Rounceford is as well set up as this cousin we met. My, they are very striking men! No, I cannot blame you for wishing to appear at your best.''

"Mamma! That is not at all what I said!'' protested Meg, smiling and frowning at the same time.

"Yes, child, but it is what you meant, I am sure—I wonder, now. They are all of them cousins and all quite handsome. One is forced to conclude that all Rounceford male offspring are bound to grow up into handsome men. How very nice it must be to know your sons must turn out so well.''

Meg's eyes opened their widest. "What are you saying, madam?''

"Oh, dear, I do not know what has come over me, running on in such a distressing fashion. I fear your mother is entering upon her dotage, my dear.''

"That is a whopper! The very idea of you in your dotage! But what must you take me for if you believe that I have taken special pains because the Earl is coming—''

"Oh, it is the Earl, then?''

"And his cousin, Sir Arthur! Mamma, this is too bad of you! I have never given a thought to either of them, especially after what I suffered at their hands.''

"I cannot doubt it, my dear. I am sure they both put their cousin Adrian up to it. And, yes, your sufferings were of the greatest, for have you not told me so yourself?''

"Indeed, I never did! Mamma, you are making game of me! One could think that you are trying to put thoughts into my head.''

"And one could be right! Adrian's behaviour was at the

outset reprehensible, but beyond that, nothing you have said makes the gentlemen out to be less than upstanding. They, all of them, Adrian included, were extending themselves to see you protected from the consequences of the deed. Am I mistaken?''

"No, Mamma," admitted Meg in a small voice.

"Then I shall say no more, my dear. You are a grown woman and must needs know your own mind. If you do not know what you want, no one else will."

"But I do not! Oh, suddenly it is all so confusing!"

"Well, then, there is hope yet for us all!" declared Lady Elizabeth. As she picked up her embroidery, the sparkle in her eyes was very reminiscent of her daughter's.

"I hear a carriage!" cried Meg, looking up from the book she had been pretending to read for the last quarter hour. She got up quickly and went to the window.

An exclamation of "Oh, no!" followed by a choked gurgle caused Lady Elizabeth to cast an inquiring look at her daughter.

"Oh, you will not believe this—but they are all getting out of the same carriage. There is Sir George and Sir Arthur and Marcus. My, how splendid they all look." She turned from the window. "You see how right I was to select my attire with care? But what a weak fish Sir George must be to require support in his hour of trial!" she laughed. "He had been wiser to select less striking companions, for they do put him in the shade. They are coming in!" she exclaimed as with a chuckle she came back to her seat.

"Now, remember, Meg, I will not have you shame me. If you cannot say what is proper, I would have you say nothing at all. It is a bad business for George Hobcourt; do not make it worse!" admonished Lady Elizabeth.

As the gentlemen were expected, they were brought

directly to the ladies by a frozen-faced butler who gave no sign of the turbulence within his breast the visit of so many distinguished young gentlemen gave rise to. As soon as he delivered the callers, he rushed away belowstairs to inform Cook of the unheard-of presence of not one, not two, but three flash coves "as ever I set eyes on!"

The butler and the cook had been in the Miller service since long before Mr. Sam Miller had become Sir Samuel and never had they seen the like. Three young gentlemen and one an *earl*!—to come calling at one time—surely, it could not be on Miss Meg's account. Why, she was the plain one and even her two very pretty sisters were never so distinguished—no, not even when they were being sought in marriage!

"I tell you, Cook, somethin's afoot!" proclaimed the butler with a knowing nod.

"Well, if there be such," retorted the cook, "you can lay a tanner on it Miss Meg's at the bottom of it! Be they handsome, the gentlemun?"

Between describing the visitors and arguing as to what the visit augured, the two senior servants, attended by an entranced audience of lesser domestics, carried on an extended debate which verged upon the acrimonious and settled nothing.

Lady Elizabeth invited the gentlemen to be seated. Sir George sat down immediately, but the Earl declined as did Sir Arthur, following his lead so it seemed. Sir George, not sure but thinking he might have committed a solecism, became confused and made to rise. Halfway out of his seat he recovered his wits and sat down again, feeling quite the fool.

Meg shot a glance at Lord Marcus, who regarded her with a look of blandest innocence.

She began the conversation by launching an inquiry regarding their drive out; the condition of the road, the weather, did they have difficulty finding their way? Sir George opened his mouth to respond, but Sir Arthur was the quicker, and he and Meg were soon deeply engaged in a very trite exchange of the most inconsequential trivialities. A small frown appeared on Lady Elizabeth's smooth brow, but she refrained from commenting as the ill-timed conversation gave signs of petering out. She had not counted on her irrepressible daughter, however.

Meg made a *moue* in Lord Marcus' direction. He responded by lifting an eyebrow slightly as though to ask a question. She returned him a little frown as though to demand. He grinned as though he understood, and launched himself into the dying conversation, thereby endowing it with renewed life. He received a smile of thanks.

The exchange was not lost upon Lady Elizabeth who, in a choking voice, declared, "We are honoured by your presence, gentlemen; but I am sure that one of you has matters of more moment to occupy him than the vagaries of the weather or the latest frolics of the Four-in-Hand Club. Meg, why do you not take Sir George to the library? No, your father is there. Well, I am sure the music room will do. Er—you might play that plaintive little thing of Herr van Beethoven—you know the one I mean?"

"His Moonlight Sonata?" suggested Meg.

"Yes, dear. It will set the mood," Lady Elizabeth said sweetly.

There was a muffled shout of laughter from the window and all eyes turned upon Lord Marcus.

"I beg all your pardons. I seem to have developed a cough of a sudden," he apologized.

Sir George began to twist his head this way and that as he tried to determine what was transpiring. He had the distinct feeling that he was being made a mock of, but how and by whom he had not the faintest idea. Drawing himself up into as dignified a pose as he could achieve, he

236

glared at Lord Marcus once, before he bowed to Meg and declared, "I should be delighted."

She took his arm and they departed from the room.

"Surely it is a foregone conclusion," remarked Lord Marcus.

"Yes, I am quite sure it is," said Lady Elizabeth in unthinking response to the thought that was uppermost in her mind. She gave a start as she became aware of what she had said and looked sharply at the Earl.

"Be assured, milady, you have not let the cat out of the bag," he said soothingly. "We are fully aware of the purpose behind George's visit. Knowing that, and seeing Meg's approach to the business, it takes no great mind to conclude she will not have him."

Lady Elizabeth smiled her acknowledgement. "Yes, I daresay, but I wish it were otherwise. That will be her second chance, since her misadventure, that she is casting away.

"Oh, I suppose I should not speak of this, but it is enough to break my heart. You see, Meg has been much sought after. For the longest time we had the highest hopes that she would find someone to please her and settle down. Now, it is too late and, still, despite all that has occurred, she will not choose. She can hardly expect another such opportunity. If at least she would not reject them all so very definitely!"

"That is distressing, madam. If she had accepted him, Adrian would not have made a bad husband."

"Oh, dear, I had forgotten him! That makes three of them, then. You must admit, milord, few females could expect so many offers after such a scandal."

"Well, you had best make it four, milady," spoke up Sir Arthur. "I was quite sure that George had no chance or I should have spoken sooner."

Lady Elizabeth turned to him in surprise.

"You have no objection, madam?"

"Why—why, no! But is not this rather sudden?"

"That it is, but the secret of a successful campaign is always to take advantage of the turn of events. Timing, ma'am, timing is of the essence!"

Lady Elizabeth blinked. "Er—yes, I suppose so," she said rather weakly.

At that moment a carriage was heard to dash madly away.

Lady Elizabeth sighed.

Sir Arthur stepped forward and with a smile of satisfaction, he clicked his heels and bowed to Lady Elizabeth.

"By your leave, milady!" He gave her a sharp salute, turned, and marched out of the room.

She looked helplessly at Lord Marcus and slowly shook her head.

He shrugged. "He is no match for her."

"That is only too true, but perhaps the very unexpectedness of him offering will at the very least give her pause to think. If only she will choose—and a man she will be happy with—her husband need never worry for lack of anything." She caught herself up short. "Please, I beg of you not to mistake my meaning. We do not hope to buy her a husband—"

Lord Marcus laughed. "Your pardon, milady, you may think my hilarity out of place, but it strikes me that no one can choose for Meg—indeed, even dare to choose for her. I shudder to think what she would say to that! And so I do, too, for my brave cousin who, unfortunately, is quite witless enough to believe that Meg is in a box to which only he has the key."

"Then there is not the shadow of a hope."

"I fear not."

"Well, then, there is no point in putting it off any longer. I expect we shall be going off to Paris before the year is much advanced."

"Paris, you say?"

"Yes. Sir Samuel and I think it best. We will go on tour for some six months, perhaps longer. Meg has expressed a particular wish to see Paris."

"Under the circumstances it is well-advised. The business could have been gotten over so much more easily had the dance—but that is past mending. I wish you all a pleasant enough time over there. Perhaps on your return you will inform Lady Marchford, my grandmother. She is quite anxious to have Meg stay with her for a long visit—and she is completely out of humour with Sir Samuel for depriving her of Meg's delightful company. She argues thusly that Sir Samuel is too selfish since he has had Meg all her life and she has had her but a few days."

Their pleasant laughter together was brought abruptly to an end when Sir Arthur, flushed of face and breathing heavily, burst into the room.

"Madame, my compliments!" he said hoarsely. "I am suddenly called away and must leave immediately." He bowed and turned to the door.

"I think you forget something, cousin," remarked Marcus drily.

Sir Arthur wheeled upon him, completely beside himself. "Do I, sir?" he snarled.

Very calmly Lord Marcus pointed out to him that they were bereft of their conveyance since Sir George had taken it. Although it was rather thoughtless of him to leave them stranded, it was his vehicle and so they could not complain too loudly.

Lady Elizabeth said, "You shall not be put to any inconvenience. I will have our carriage brought out. My sincerest apologies, Sir Arthur, for—"

A movement of colour at the threshold made them all turn to look. There was Meg.

She stood rigidly erect, her face white, her lips trembling. She stared long and hard across the room at Lord Marcus.

His lordship could not account for her troubled counte-

239

nance. Oddly enough, he found it disturbing and a feeling of apprehension began to mount in his breast. He raised an eyebrow as much out of surprise as inquiry and was astounded to see tears well up in her eyes before she abruptly turned away and disappeared.

Chapter Seventeen

The two cousins sat side by side in the luxurious but overlarge Miller vehicle as it made its way ponderously towards Harlington town. Neither appeared to be interested in conversing and they sat, almost immobile, each wrapped in his own thoughts.

The Earl was undergoing a strange sensation, and he could not fathom it. It was not strange in the sense that it was totally unfamiliar. He had felt it before, a very long time before. Yes, the last time he had felt like this was the day he had been promised his first pony, or the day his schooling had come to an end, suppressed excitement with a strong dash of great anticipation. Somehow, and he could not say how, it was connected with his last sight of Meg. His mind's eye was occupied with the picture of a tiny, pale face, tear-bedewed. Its expression was one of accusation and that of course was preposterous, he thought, for he could not see that there was anything to fault in his behaviour to her. But something had upset her and he would have liked to know what and why.

He was considering the distasteful expedient of bluntly asking his cousin what had taken place between Meg and himself when Sir Arthur suddenly exploded with a filthy expletive concerning the female of the species.

Lord Marcus snapped at him, "Cousin, if you have reference to Miss Meg Miller, I suggest you say no more in my presence." There was a distinct threat in his voice.

Sir Arthur turned to him in surprise. "Have I said somethine to offend?"

"You most certainly did!"

"Then I beg your pardon. I fear I have been thinking out loud."

"If that is the case, then I must conclude you are in a foul humour, still. I take it that you did not get on as swimmingly as you expected with Meg?"

"Ha! I'd as like to have drowned!"

"Well, you cannot say I didn't warn you. I daresay there was, perhaps, something unequine about her response to your expert management?"

Sir Arthur looked at his cousin with a pained expression. "You need not rub it in. She trounced me quite thoroughly; yet I still have not the faintest idea why she should have done so. I say, with Hobcourt, she is a shrew and I am well out of it!" he declared with undisguised animosity. "In fact, I can say further that we did what we could and she would have none of it. The Rouncefords need no longer concern themselves with her. She is beyond being helped by us!"

"No matter what she has put you through, I fear that our beloved ancestor will not agree with you."

Sir Arthur sighed. "You know she is a takin' little thing—and, today, to see her so, dressed up to the nines! Aye, she can be a very striking-looking female. Do you know, I am sure that I could have developed a genuine *tendre* for her? But such temper! Just who the devil does she think she is?"

"You may as well tell me about it. I cannot imagine why an offer from you should so raise her back up. Hobcourt, I can understand. His reputation goes before him, but I am sure you could not have been offensive to her."

"Well, I cannot imagine it either! It began quite cordially. After saying the usual things, I made my offer. Of course, she was surprised. It was understandable. She could hardly have looked for anything so advantageous, considering her circumstances.''

"Of course, you told her that?"

"And why not? We both knew the tally. I saw no need to pussyfoot about.''

"Go on."

"I am sure she saw eye to eye with me on that score, for she gave me to understand that it was a high compliment I offered her. She then went on to say that she regretted that she could not accept. Well, I expected no more. It was all too sudden and, being a female, she must have time to think—or make some pretence in that direction. It is, you will admit, a well-known and accepted strategem of the sex.

"I was inclined to leave matters stand—to say I would ask for her answer another time, but I thought it were well if, before I left, I supplied her with some cogent arguments to support my case.''

"Oh, I say, Arthur! Do you handle your horses so, too—with cogent arguments?''

"Marcus, you took me too literally. Of course, a woman and a horse are not the same thing!''

"Perhaps you would have done better if you had managed her as you might a horse.''

Sir Arthur was miffed. "I have nothing more to say! I have never believed Adrian to be the brainy one of our house, but at least he is not afflicted with your ungodly love of inanity!''

"No need to get all up in the boughs, old man. I do beg your pardon, most humbly. I promise I shall not open my mouth again until you have finished. Please continue; I am truly interested.''

Giving him a look of hurt disapproval, Sir Arthur resumed his story.

"I pointed out to her the necessity of her availing herself of the protection of marriage as soon as possible. Since she would not have Adrian—and I could not blame her—and you, the Earl of Marchford, would never condescend to a miller's daughter, it was incumbent upon her to accept me. Perfectly reasonable, don't you think? Yet, from then on it was hell to pay! Everything went to pieces. No, she did not yell and shriek, but what was worse, in a voice so low as to be a whisper, she described the Rounceford family in such terms as it made my blood run cold. Such intense hatred for us I have never heard, nor do I ever wish to hear such again. Honoria at her worst would never voice such distaste of us!''

Even as he listened to this remarkable statement Lord Marcus' mood changed. Suddenly he felt totally relaxed; the feeling of apprehension dissolved completely in a wave of exhilaration. So powerful an emotion was it that he thought he should burst and, prevent it though he would for his cousin's sake, it escaped him in an outburst of exultant laughter.

''Dammit, Marcus! You try me beyond all endurance!'' exclaimed Sir Arthur.

''Do not mind me, cousin! I am not laughing at you. I am laughing at myself. What a bloody fool I have been.'' He got up from his seat and put his head out the window. ''Hi, coachman, I know you can get more speed out of those ugly brutes! See to it!''

At once the coach began to roll and pitch as it gained speed over the rutted road. It left Sir Arthur fuming, while Lord Marcus chuckled with glee at every bounce and jolt.

It was very little time before they drew up before the inn. Lord Marcus was the first one to leap out and run into the inn.

A welcome sight greeted his lordship. Lemmy Peterskin, his arms hooked over the bar, was drinking from a large tankard which he held to his face with both hands.

''Peterskin, you have come! Where is Carlton?''

Broadly grinning, Lem turned and said, '' 'Tis my guess yer valet be a-ticklin' the biddies i' the kitchen, yer lordship.''

"Command him to attend me in my room at once! And if you came in my curricle as I requested, I'll have no further need of your horse!"

With that, his lordship strode quickly over to the staircase and raced up it, taking two and three stairs at a time.

"Well, where are they?" asked Sir Samuel as he stepped into the room. Lady Elizabeth was seated at a small table partaking of a light repast consisting mainly of tiny sandwiches. "It is well past the hour for making calls. I say, what do you have there? They look very tempting to a starving husband. May I join you, my dear?"

"Of course, Sammy, but pray ring for Everhard. I am sure there are not enough of these tidbits to more than whet your appetite."

Sir Samuel did as he was bid and drew up a chair. Seating himself beside his wife, he began to pop tea sandwiches into his mouth at an alarming rate.

Everhard, the butler, appeared and received instruction to see to it that Sir Samuel was provided with more suitable food. He departed.

Taking a breather, Sir Samuel remarked, "I take it, since you have not answered my question, that the gentlemen have not called. I am not surprised. Did they have the goodness to send some excuse?"

"Oh, but they have been and gone these past hours!"

"And I was not told?"

Lady Elizabeth glanced at her husband and sighed. "There was no call for it, my dear. And if I had told you of it, you would have only been angered."

"Hmphh! I did not think that caper merchant would come up to scratch."

"Young Hobcourt did make his offer, but we both knew what would happen there. It came as a great surprise to me, however, that Sir Arthur Winstock followed him closely with an offer of his own!"

"I hesitate to learn the result. I already know or you

would not sound so despondent."

"He received the same reply. I can only judge that the terms in which they were refused must have been something a deal less than pleasant, for the first dashed madly away and without a word. The second was so furious he could hardly speak to say his farewell. It was all he could do to maintain a civil tone to me while our coach was brought round to carry them back to town."

Sir Samuel looked confused. "Our coach?" he asked.

At that, Lady Elizabeth could not repress a laugh. "Yes, they had all come together in Hobcourt's carriage, and when he left so precipitously it was, of course, in his own carriage. It is bad enough that I can expect Lady Amelia to be distant to me the next time we meet, but I have the strongest feeling that Sir George and the Rouncefords will be on less than the best of terms with each other, too."

Sir Samuel grinned. "She does have a way with her, you must admit." He brought his hands down with a mighty slap upon his thighs and leaned back in his chair. "Well, m' love, I think we must expect to have her on our hands forever," he said with resignation.

"Will that really be so bad?" she asked.

"No, of course not. It is her own happiness I am thinking on. Well, perhaps a change of climate will bring about a change of heart, eh? Where is she now?"

"That is a surprising thing! She is up in her room and, if she is not crying her heart out at this moment, I do not know my own daughter."

"That's a woman for you! Well, she brought it on herself—but I do not wish for her to be so distressed. We must get her away from all this! I will make arrangements for our journey abroad at once."

"Yes, please do so. I think I know wherein her trouble lies and it will do her no good to carry on about it. It cannot be helped."

"Pray tell me what you know of it."

"This morning Meg came down looking lovelier than I have ever seen her look before. Her eyes were dancing; there was colour in her cheeks; she was positively gay. And her toilet was exquisite. Knowing how she felt about Hobcourt, my heart was rejoiced, for I was sure that Major Winstock must have been the one for whom she had made such an effort. I did not say anything.

"When the gentlemen called, it did not take me long to be disabused of that notion. I could see that there was nothing between them. Naturally I was greatly surprised when the Major, right upon the heels of Sir George, made his offer. She did not return to the parlour, but merely looked in. It was only his lordship she looked to. Then it was my heart sank. It could not have been plainer than if she had said it. The Earl of Marchford was her choice!"

"Good heavens, Bess! I always thought her a sensible girl! Look m' dear, for my part, she is worthy of a duke, but"—he paused, with lips pressed together and his face screwed up in thought—"mayhap I can find an earl for her. There must be some few in need of money. If not an earl, surely a marquis—"

"Oh, no, Sammy, that will never do!" cried Lady Elizabeth. "It is not the same thing at all. Put it out of your mind!"

At that moment the butler entered, followed by a footman bearing a tray heavily laden with steaming platters of food.

"Cook has done you proud as usual, I see," remarked Lady Elizabeth with a smile. "Whilst you eat, let us speak of other matters. The trip, now . . ."

The curricle of the Earl of Marchford came dashing up to the Miller door. Leaping out, Lord Marcus handed the reins to Carlton and instructed him to walk the horses until told otherwise. Carlton was not happy to be assigned the

247

duty of a groom, but it was not the first occasion and, while his face expressed his disgruntlement, he complied without comment.

His lordship raced up the stairs and knocked on the door. A footman opened to him and stepped back one step in sheer wonderment. What was this! The Earl of Marchford calling a second time on the same day, and at this unfashionable hour!

"Your lordship, I fear that Sir Samuel and his lady are not disposed to—"

"What of Miss Miller?"

"Oh, there, too, your lordship. Miss Meg is not down—"

"Never mind that! You tell her that I wish to speak with her!"

"But, your lordship!" gasped the footman.

"Go to! I'll brook no denial!"

"This is most irregular, your lordship!"

"I'm sure it is. Now tell her I would have a word with her at once—and be persuasive, man!" He gave him a broad smile as he handed the servant a heavy gold coin.

"Yes, m' lord! At once, m' lord!"

His lordship paced back and forth in the small parlour to which he had been conducted. There was a smile on his face as he beat his fist into the palm of his hand at every other step.

The door opened behind him and a small voice asked, "Milord, you wished to speak with me?"

Before turning to face her, he wiped the smile from his face and adopted a serious mien.

"Yes, Meg. I beg your pardon for having disturbed you at this odd hour, but I have a particular request to make of you."

"Before you begin, milord, it is better if I speak first. I know I shall not have another opportunity."

He looked at her in surprise, but said nothing while he waited for her to continue.

"My behaviour to Sir Arthur was inexcusable and, in fact, I may not offer an excuse for it; yet, I am aware that I caused him great distress and would beg you to express to him my sincere apologies."

Lord Marcus found this not to his liking. Had she thought better of Arthur's offer and was she now trying to mend her fences? The very thought shook him—but for a moment only, for she was continuing.

"Be that as it may, my answer to Sir Arthur is unchanged and I regret that you have had this second trip for nothing."

He waited to be sure she was finished. She stood before him with her head down, her hands clasped before her. He noted that her slim fingers were not at rest; they kept working and twisting against each other.

"You may be at ease on that score, my dear. Sir Arthur would not have you now on a silver platter with diamonds on the side."

She raised her head to look at him.

"Then that is not why you came? But I cannot think of any other reason for you to call at this odd hour."

"Yes, I have already been told as much by your footman. But then, neither you nor he is at all well informed as to the reasons I do anything. Do you find that strange?"

"No—no," she faltered. She smiled a little as she said, "But I was so sure that Sir Arthur was your reason for coming. Are you quite sure?"

"Quite."

"Then why have you come?"

"It seems to me I was about to explain it to you, when you insisted upon having your say first. Now if you have done I shall be pleased to do so."

"Yes, of course," said Meg, slightly flustered. "I—I

beg your pardon. Won't you be seated," she said as she sat down.

"Thank you." He selected a chair and brought it close to hers before sitting down.

"I intend to visit Paris shortly, and I understood from Lady Elizabeth that your parents and you have that intention, also. Is that correct?"

"It is, milord."

"I would be honoured if you would permit me to accompany you."

Meg's first reaction to this odd request was a feeling of warmth and pleasure at the prospect of seeing Paris in his company; her second, and more considered opinion, was that it would be in the nature of an ordeal for her to have to associate with him for so long a period. Being together with him, she was sure, would be extremely pleasant. But when the time came for parting—that, she preferred not to have to undergo.

But one does not refuse outright an earl—especially a respected and wealthy Rounceford earl. Her mind raced to find some way to put him off, or at least postpone the refusal she must give him.

"Surely, it is not I you should be making application to. I will send to my father to receive you," she said as she made a motion towards the bellrope.

His hand on her arm made her pause. "There is no need. I shall ask him presently; but not before I know *you* will not be inconvenienced by my presence."

Meg shrugged. "It is of no matter at all to me. I am surprised, however. Have you not just returned from Paris?"

"Just so; but since I learned of your impending visit I have experienced an overwhelming desire to return there."

It was more than Meg could stand. It was becoming increasingly more difficult for her to maintain any semblance of poise before him, and the conversation struck

250

her as inane. Because she could not fathom his purpose behind this unheard-of request of his, the bitterness she was feeling came to the surface.

"Especially in such low company as a miller and his family!" she declared. The resentment in her voice was so pronounced that his lordship had to rise from his chair and step over to the window to hide his smile.

It took but a moment for him to regain control of his features and he was back before her, saying, in an offhand manner, "As a matter of fact, yes! I have never experienced what pleasures may be found in company with a miller and his family."

"Let me assure you, milord, such pleasures as there may be are hardly suited to one of your rank. You will have a most tedious time of it."

"I should prefer to judge for myself."

"Then you will insist on accompanying us?"

"You do not regard the prospect with any enthusiasm?"

"We are not accustomed to associating with nobility of high rank." Meg had become very stiff in her manner.

"Do I detect a note of pride? My dear Miss Miller, let me assure you that an earl is every bit the equal of a miller—yes, and of a miller's daughter as well!"

Meg was completely unprepared for that. She stammered, "I—I beg your pardon, milord. It was not what I meant—"

"It is very bad of you, Meg, to put such unreasonable obstacles in my path. I have trouble enough trying to gather the courage to ask you to marry me without such questionable tactics. You have no idea of how I tremble at the thought of the crushing setdown you will deal me should I be so bold."

Meg gasped. Her mind could not grasp what she had just heard. But her heart was more easily convinced and it began to pound with joy. She could make no move, she could say no word, she could only stare at him. As though

251

in a trance, very slowly she rose from her seat and uncon-
sciously put up a hand.

Taking that little hand in both of his, Lord Marcus
stepped close to her.

"Meg, dearest Meg, I beg you to pardon my clumsi-
ness. I have had no practise in this and if I deserve a sharp
trimming for doing it so badly, get it over quickly and say
you will have me."

"Mi-milord . . ." It was the easiest thing to find her
way into his arms. . . .

For some minutes they were too occupied to indulge in
any meaningful conversation.

Then Lord Marcus whispered into the ear of his love, "I
would not have you misunderstand my motives. I have
done many things in Paris, but never have I spent a
honeymoon there with a miller's daughter. I look forward
to it with great anticipation."

Meg, her head comfortably nestled upon his lordship's
chest, gurgled, "Alas, milord, I regret that you must be
disappointed then, for you will spend your honeymoon
with a countess, a miller's daughter no longer."

Lord Marcus was about to retort that a countess would
be no new thing to him when he thought better of it and
said instead, "Well, I have never dallied with a Countess
of Marchford in Paris, either!"

At that, Meg pushed herself back from him so that she
could look up into his face. She cocked her head and with a
measuring eye, she asked, "And what other countesses
have you dallied with?"

The Earl of Marchford decided then and there that if he
could not match wits with his love, at least he knew of a
way to shut her up. He proceeded to do so with pleasure
and Meg did not mind at all.